THE FRONTMAN

LAWRENCE PARLIER

Black Rose Writing | Texas

ISBN: 978-1-68433-494-0
PUBLISHED BY BLACK ROSE WRITING
www.blackrosewriting.com

Printed in the United States of America
Suggested Retail Price (SRP) $19.95

The Frontman is printed in Calluna

*As a planet-friendly publisher, Black Rose Writing does its best to eliminate unnecessary waste to reduce paper usage and energy costs, while never compromising the reading experience. As a result, the final word count vs. page count may not meet common expectations.

Dedicated to the memory of my father.

Charles Leo Parlier

(1931-2016)

THE
FRONTMAN

Breaking news out of London, KAXZ news has learned that multi-platinum recording artist Kerry Vance was found dead this morning in his London hotel room.

Vance had just played to a sold-out crowd in London's Palladium the previous evening to kick off the European leg of his Blood and Honor world tour.

Vance got his big break in the music business when he was picked to replace original Zephyr vocalist Jarvis Gray during the band's first world tour back in 1975. Vance went on to a legendary solo career that earned him several Grammy nominations and an American Music Award for his song Solstice Moon. Details are sketchy at this hour as to the cause of Vance's death, but as information becomes available, we'll be sure to pass it along.

Q101 will be playing songs from Vance's decades-spanning career at the top of every hour today.

Again, multi-platinum singer-songwriter Kerry Vance was found dead in his London hotel room this morning. He was 62.

CHAPTER 1

Orange juice fell in a collapsing arch to splatter across the spotless expanse of a cool white tile floor. Its carton splashed down into the mess, falling unminded from Sarah Koop's shaking hand as news of Kerry Vance's death came across the radio.

Sarah gasped, raw emotion escaping as if she'd been struck by an invisible hand. Kerry Vance, her father, was dead.

"Mom, are you okay?"

Sarah stood in shock staring out of the kitchen window as one of Kerry's newer songs was played in his memory. Her heart rose into her throat. The opportunity to know her father was gone. Her own pride had robbed her of the chance.

"Earth to Mother. Seriously, are you alright? You spilled orange juice all over the floor."

"Huh?" Sarah looked down at the puddle. "Ah, damn it." She grabbed paper towels from the counter and bent down to the mess. "Tracy, will you go get the mop and bucket for me?"

Sarah ignored the look of indignation on her daughter's face as she dropped her spoon into her cereal bowl and slid out of her chair. The news had hit her so violently she realized she had missed the details of the announcement. As soon as Tracy was off to school Sarah would hit the internet and see what she could find.

Sarah gazed at her daughter as she handed over the mop and bucket. Tracy's deep blue eyes and auburn hair had always been a mystery to her.

She bore no resemblance to her side of the family, nor her father's. Sarah liked to believe that she'd taken after Kerry's family somehow, but she'd always been too afraid to broach the subject with her mother. Her mother would not discuss Kerry Vance under any circumstance. Sarah spent a good part of her life wondering if her mother's refusal had been borne of hatred or heartache. Now that Kerry was gone Sarah resolved to know the truth of it.

"Why are you staring at me?" Tracy asked. "You're freaking me out. What's the deal with you this morning?"

"Didn't you hear the radio? One of my favorite singers died."

Tracy frowned as Sarah took the bucket and dropped it into the sink. "Yeah? So? It's no reason to go off of the deep end, Mom, geez. It's not like you knew the guy."

Sarah dropped her eyes. She turned to watch the water fill the bucket. It was true. Sarah only knew him as well as any of his other fans. She had spent a lifetime fooling herself into believing that was all she needed to know. Now, it wasn't enough.

Sarah had never told anyone that Kerry Vance was her father. And not just out of fear of her mother's wrath. Most of the people in her hometown knew. And, for the most part, abided by her mother's wishes and never brought it up. As she'd grown up and gone away to college, she realized there wasn't anything to be gained from mentioning it. She really didn't know him. She wasn't even sure that he knew about her. Sarah liked to believe he didn't. It was easier that way. The thought of him abandoning her was hard to take.

"Yeah, well, Tracy, as you get older you'll find yourself mourning the things that were always steady in your life as they pass. Musicians and actors you grew up with, teachers, even old buildings, homes and cars. They just become a part of your world and you don't even realize how much they mean to you until they're gone."

Tracy crinkled up her freckled nose. "Teachers? Really? I doubt I'm going to waste much time missing any of them."

Sarah laughed, shaking her head. That girl's attitude had to have come from Kerry Vance. And she wasn't even a teenager, yet. Sarah still had that to look forward to.

"If you say so, kiddo, but let's give it about twenty more years and then we'll compare notes."

Tracy rolled her eyes and went back to the table to finish her breakfast. Sarah remembered all too well what it was like at that age, 12 going on 21. She was just a few months older than Tracy when Anna spilled the beans about her parentage.

It was the day her whole life changed. And now, without warning, it had changed again. There would be no more second-guessing. There was no going back. The opportunity to know her father had passed. All she could do now was find a way to honor his legacy... .and find peace with her decision.

CHAPTER 2

Avery Clark's hangover manifested in a nerve-wracking jolt as consciousness struck once again. He was reasonably sure he was still safe at home but, as his brain throbbed wildly inside his skull, he felt far too lousy to open an eye and take a look around. He had fallen in and out of sleep, or stupor, or whatever nullifying void the Universe reserved for madmen and drunks, for hours. His wish for oblivion once again shattered as he passed back into reality and pain. Not that he was fatalistic or suicidal. He wasn't one of those tedious artists that extorted sympathy yearning for Death's embrace. He was just a very weary man trying to dodge the heartache of an exceptionally trying year. But for all of his concerted efforts at a well-appointed inebriation, it wasn't working. His Zoe was gone and now Kerry Vance was too.

It was too much to bear.

As he lay there in tears probing the edges of his grief, he heard the dull squeak his apartment door issued upon opening. He couldn't tell if someone was coming in or leaving, but he wasn't about to sit up and look. If somebody was breaking in with the idea of stealing his stuff then, *so be it.* He didn't care. He was just grateful to be home.

Then, as the blurry details of the evening's events slowly rose into memory, somebody let the full shock of unadulterated sunlight blast into his apartment. It was a damned dirty rotten thing to do.

"Aww, what the fuck," Avery's startled whine broke the silence. He sat up on the couch, smacking himself in the head as he tried to shield his eyes. "Goddamn it, Jimmy, is that you? My head is already pounding. Why are you here so early?"

"It's not early. It's 4 o'clock in the afternoon." Jimmy frowned as Avery yanked the blanket up over his head. "Why are you sleeping on the couch?"

Avery squirmed around beneath the blanket, struggling to find a comfortable position. "Ah, man, the mattress is all fucking wet. I must have spilled beer on it when I went to lie down."

Jimmy didn't reply. He could only shake his head as he looked around at the devastation inside Avery's apartment. The kitchen table was covered in ashes and marijuana crumbs while soggy cigarette butts fell from overturned beer bottles left to spill on the floor. The chairs had all been tossed around the room with one of them landing on the kitchen counter to smash a stack of dishes.

Beneath the table, a broken bottle of Johnnie Walker Red rested between a lone gym shoe and an overturned ashtray. Clothes were strung from the front door to the bedroom door where Avery's computer monitor had shattered against the wall. Across the room, Avery sat with his head in his hands rubbing his temples. In the glare of the afternoon sun, he looked a lot older than his forty-five years. The gray in his curly brown hair seemed more prominent. But it was the deep-seated weariness set in Avery's ice-blue eyes that worried Jimmy.

He looked defeated.

"Christ, Avery, look at this place," Jimmy said. "What the hell did you do last night?"

Avery leaned forward, wrapping the blanket around him. "Fuck, I don't know. I was pretty well blitzed when I got here." He glanced around the room. Surprise registered on his face as he surveyed the damage. He shook his head slowly, disgusted, before dropping back against the couch. "Roll those damned blinds back a little, would you? You're killing me."

Jimmy acquiesced, opening a couple of the windows first to combat the stale odor of pot, alcohol, and cigarettes permeating the space.

Avery sat up straighter in the muted glow and let the blanket fall to his lap. He ran his fingers through his unruly mess of hair and yawned. "I need a beer."

Jimmy scowled, dropping down onto the couch beside him. Avery had always been a drinker, but since Zoe's death, it had snowballed. Now, with Kerry gone, he feared Avery had gone off of the rails. "You sure that's what you need right now?"

Avery shot him a snarling glance as he snatched a pack of cigarettes from the coffee table, "Positive." He lit the last cigarette then flung the empty pack across the room. "I need to get my shit together so I can go find out what in the hell happened to Kerry, man. The stuff I've been hearing doesn't add up."

Jimmy rolled his eyes. To him, Kerry Vance was just another burn-out, a rock-n-roller who spent as much time smoking crank as he did performing. It was no big surprise he'd checked out early. But he and Avery had been close friends for years. They genuinely cared for one another.

Avery was devastated.

Jimmy couldn't help feeling jealous. He and Avery had been friends since childhood. But now they didn't run in the same circles. None of Avery's partying companions wanted a cop hanging around.

"I'm just trying to look out for you," Jimmy said. "I know it's been a rough couple of days. I think you need to slow down a little."

"Jimmy, man, don't start with me," Avery said. "I've got enough to deal with. I know you and Kerry never really hit it off but I'm telling you something's wrong."

"Christ, Avery, you can't be surprised by this. The man was toxic. He's lucky he even made it into his sixties."

Avery slammed his fist down on the coffee table with enough force to knock over another empty bottle lingering at its edge. "Goddamn it, Jimmy, you don't understand. They're saying Kerry died of a heroin overdose. He never did heroin. He hated the shit. Kerry was a speed freak; cocaine, crank, bennies when he could find them. The motherfucker wanted to *go*. Now if his heart had exploded from doing too much speed I'd accept it and move on. But this isn't right. I have to get to the bottom of it."

Jimmy stared at Avery irked at his demeanor. "And just how exactly are you going to do that?"

Avery shook his head, rubbing his newly sore hand. "Well, I know I'm not going to get any answers out of that wife of his. I bet she's already calculating his assets. What I need to do is get ahold of some of his roadies and get their take on it."

"And then what?" Jimmy asked. "Look, the Brits are still working their inquiry. If there was any foul play involved they'll find it. Just let them do their job."

Avery stared Jimmy in the eye. "The Brits don't give a fuck. An overdose is an overdose. They don't care if it's heroin or aspirin. It's just another dead musician to them. I read Carol was already trying to get them to release his body so she can bring him home. It makes me wonder if that crazy bitch wasn't in on it."

Jimmy sat back on the couch rubbing his eyes. Avery was grasping at straws. "Maybe you're right. You know them better than most people. But, even so, nobody ever knows anyone completely. If Scotland Yard suspects foul play, they'll dig into it. I've worked with them before. They're not remiss when carrying out an investigation. Just wait until they publish their findings before you do anything rash, okay?"

Jimmy watched Avery's head drop. He had been through too much already. Losing Kerry now so close to the anniversary of Zoe's death was a blow he wasn't sure Avery could bounce back from. The substance abuse was only going to make things worse.

Jimmy didn't want to lose him, too.

He laid a hand on Avery's shoulder. "You need to think about your career. If you go running around making waves, it could cost you. You know how hard you've had to work to get back on top. Don't do anything that will set you back."

Avery pushed Jimmy's hand away. He rose off the couch and headed for the bedroom door. His gait was more than a little unsteady as the room shifted around him. "I don't give a damn about my career. It's not important to me anymore. All I want is the truth about what happened to Kerry and by God, Jimmy, I aim to get it."

CHAPTER 3

Kerry Vance's raspy tenor cut through the humid air inside the tiny dance club office. The ferocity in his voice sounded like an exterminating angel hell-bent on destruction. The song, a hard-driving, bawdy, celebration of life on the road rang hollow against the weight of his untimely death. Calliope Asteri leaned over the desk, turning the radio up as tears mingled with the glaze of sweat on her cheeks. The lyrics may have been shallow but the power of his voice touched her. Calliope closed her eyes and let it wash over her. Even though she hadn't seen Kerry in years, the depth of her grief overwhelmed. The memories of their time together came back to her in slow mad rushes... and along with it, her guilt.

Her time with Kerry had been a turning point. Even though it hadn't lasted long, it was special. She'd always kept his memory tucked away. The news of his death was quite a blow. When the package from Kerry was delivered a few days after his death, Calliope's surprise bordered on shock. After the way things ended between them, she'd have never guessed it.

Calliope was mystified as she carted the plain brown box into the house. After setting it on the kitchen table, she cried for half an hour before she gathered the courage to open it. At the top of the box was an envelope with her name scrawled in red ballpoint pen. Calliope's tears blurred the lines on the page as Kerry's words filled her.

It started with an apology she didn't deserve. As she read on Calliope realized that Kerry had reached out to her to make a final request.

And...it was insane.

She read the letter a second time to make sure she understood it. The fact that Kerry had found himself in such dire circumstances was heartbreaking. Tears poured down her face anew as she thought of him in his last days. Calliope set the letter aside and emptied the remains of the box. There, inside a bubble wrapped cube, she found bound stacks of hundred-dollar bills, at least a hundred thousand dollars-worth, along with detailed instructions for how the money was to be used. It was then that the full implication of Kerry's request struck. Calliope paced around her kitchen weighing her options. She'd be taking one hell of a risk trying to pull this off. But she also knew that she was one of the few people on the planet capable of doing so.

Kerry understood this or he'd have never asked. Ultimately, Calliope realized she couldn't let him down. She owed him too much. As crazy as it was, she had to see it through. So, without a second thought, Calliope packed a bag, locked her house down and set out to meet Kerry's body when it arrived in New York. But, before she left, she had to convince her sister, Cori, to cover for her while she saw Kerry's plan through.

"Aww, c'mon, Calliope, turn that shit down, would you? I've got work to do."

Calliope jumped, startled, as her sister strode into the office. "Geez, Cori, you scared me."

"Are you still crying? You really need to pull it together."

Calliope wiped at her eyes as she eased back down into the chair. Cori was a hard case. Calliope didn't think anything affected her anymore. She was all about business and had very little patience for matters of the heart.

"I just can't believe he's really gone."

Cori's expression eased as she sat down across from Calliope. It wasn't like Calliope to get this upset over anything. Cori and her sisters had seen too much tragedy over the years. She'd have thought they were immune to it by now. "I'm sorry Calliope. I didn't mean to be rude. I know he meant a lot to you."

Calliope sighed, wiping her eyes. "He was a good man. That's why I have to go."

"Are you sure that's a good idea? You're taking a hell of a risk. Someone might still recognize you."

Calliope cast her gaze downward. She couldn't tell Cori what Kerry had asked of her. There was too much riding on it. But she also knew her sister's paranoia wasn't completely without merit. "I seriously doubt it. That was almost sixty years ago. I doubt anyone involved in that little fiasco is still alive. I just need to be there, Cori. I can't let him go without saying good-bye."

Cori saw the grief in her sister's eyes. She was jealous that Calliope still felt things so strongly. "All right, and if anyone asks I'll say you're holed up with one of your loser boyfriends. That'll cover you for a few days."

Calliope smiled. Of all her sisters, Cori acted the most like their mother. At rare times, like this, she was grateful for it. "Thanks, Cori."

"What do you want me to tell Harry if he comes around?"

Calliope frowned. "You can tell him to fuck off. And then tell him to stay out of my business."

Cori smirked, "Yeah, because that'll work. Just stay out of trouble, Calliope, please?"

Calliope winked before turning toward the door, "I'm not promising anything."

CHAPTER 4

The vigil outside of Kerry Vance's memorial service was a much bigger deal than Jimmy would have ever imagined. There were at least two thousand people gathered outside of Jansen Hall and spilling out into the park.

He'd expected a small crowd of snot-nosed punks amped up on Red Bull and reefer. The diversity of ages and races present came as a shock. Jimmy had always considered Kerry Vance a marginal act. But as he looked out at the sea of faces awash in the glow of candles dispersed across the park, he realized he was wrong.

"Jesus, would you look at that crowd," Avery said, his hoarse voice slurring. "I'm telling you, Jimmy, that man was something special."

Jimmy shrugged, confounded, as they climbed the steps. Avery maneuvered them with a belligerent vigor as the whiskey took hold. He was livid that Avery elected to bring along a bottle of liquor but decided not to make an issue of it. The past few days had been tense between them. The only reason Jimmy had agreed to come along at all was to make sure that Avery didn't cause any trouble.

As they stepped inside the cavernous room Jimmy was struck by all of the famous faces gathered inside. A flash of sudden self-consciousness overtook him as he took a look around. "Oh my God, is that Mick Jagger?"

Avery glanced at him, scowling. "Yes, and that's Slash over there and that's Rob Halford; big fucking deal. They're all here to mourn a friend just like we are, so don't act all weird, OK?"

Jimmy nodded. He didn't have a clue who Avery had just mentioned, but he tried his best not to stare like a fool as they passed Ann Wilson.

He watched silently as Avery hugged his way through the mourners. He had a natural ease with people that Jimmy envied and definitely didn't share. Perspiration erupted on his brow as Avery introduced him to a statuesque brunette who was, more than likely, a super-model. Jimmy shook hands politely then stood around grinning like a doofus as the two recounted the story of a wild weekend spent with Kerry in Miami. As the story droned on Jimmy caught sight of a willowy dishwater blonde arguing at the anteroom door with a dour, older redhead. The older woman's cruel expression took Jimmy by surprise as she poked her finger repeatedly in the younger woman's shoulder.

No one close paid any attention to the exchange until the younger woman threw up her hands and screamed "Fine, I'll do it!" before running for the door, tears pouring down her face.

Something about her struck Jimmy square in the gut. "Hey, who's that?"

Avery turned to see the younger woman push her way outside. "Beats me, man, I didn't get a good look at her. Why?"

Jimmy shook his head, furrowing his brow as he stared at the door. "She was just arguing with that old bitch over there."

Avery arched his eyebrows, amused by Jimmy's choice of words. "Which bitch?"

Jimmy raised his chin toward a woman at the front of the room. Avery followed his gaze then nodded. "Well, I'd say you've got her pegged right, old buddy. That's Carol Merrick, Kerry's widow."

Jimmy grimaced, turning back around. "Well, she was being damned mean to that little girl there. I felt bad for her."

Avery smiled at the brunette and winked. "She's a piece of work, that's for damn sure. I was debating whether to say something to her or not. But if she's all pissed off, I think I'll just leave her alone. She's not a big fan of me anyway."

"You're probably better off," Jimmy said. "She has a security detail with her. She might have you tossed."

Avery looked over Jimmy's shoulder at the three steroid cases in black tie loitering around her. "Why in the hell would she need security at a memorial service?"

Jimmy shrugged. "Maybe she's worried about a deranged fan or a stalker."

Avery laughed, "Or anyone else that's ever been on the receiving end of that mouth of hers."

Avery left the brunette with a kiss on the cheek as he and Jimmy ventured deeper into the room. He had his sights set on finding some of Kerry's road crew.

Jimmy contented himself star-gazing. There were famous people here he didn't even know were still alive. But, for all of the glamour, he still couldn't shake the image of the skinny blonde girl running for the door.

"I don't see anyone from the band or the crew," Avery said. "I'm starting to wonder if Carol let them in."

"Are you sure they're not still in England?" Jimmy asked. "They might have had to stay to be available for questioning."

"They may have waited to fly back with Kerry, too. He's due in the morning."

Jimmy worried about Avery referring to Kerry as if he was still alive. He worried, even more, when Avery hid behind him to take a quick nip from his bottle. "C'mon, man, really? You shouldn't even have that stuff in here."

Avery frowned, swishing the liquor around in his mouth a few times before swallowing. "Oh lighten up, Jimmy, damn. I bet I'm not the only one that's brought along a bracer."

Jimmy's eyes bore like lasers. "Let's just get out of here. You can find whoever you're looking for at the funeral."

"No, I'm not leaving yet, old buddy. Somebody here knows something. I'll just have to ask around until I figure out who it is."

The more Avery thought about Carol's security guards, the more it bothered him. There was more going on around Kerry's death than met the eye, of that he was certain. At that exact moment though, he wasn't sure there was a damn thing he could do about it. But he had to try. He owed Kerry that.

After mingling their way through the crowd for the better part of an hour, Avery finally saw someone that piqued his interest. "Hey, wait a second, there we go. There's Jerry Jewell, Kerry's manager. Hang out a minute, Jimmy. I'll be right back."

"Avery...." Jimmy's voice trailed off as Avery lumbered away, leaving him alone in the middle of the room. He looked around feeling completely out of place. He was just an old beat cop. Avery was the only famous person he knew. He had known Avery long before he and Zoe had been embraced by the New York literati, back before Avery's heroin chic notoriety nearly did him in. Jimmy didn't condone Avery's errant behavior and had never once intervened to keep him out of trouble. But, for some crazy reason, Avery kept him around even when Jimmy was in his face. But, perhaps, that was the point. Avery always knew exactly where he stood with him.

As Jimmy watched, Avery's conversation with Jerry Jewell became animated. Avery stepped forward, enraged, as Jerry stuck his finger in his face. Jimmy shook his head, rushing forward to get between them before a fight started.

"Fuck you, Jerry. I've been clean for years."

Jerry glared at Avery with open disdain. "Nobody believes that shit, Clark. Look at you, you're a goddamned mess. Every time Kerry was around you he came back a mess. You got him hooked on that shit and now he's gone."

Jimmy saw the punch thrown before he was close enough to do anything about it. Rage flashed in Avery's eyes as his blow hit its mark.

"Kerry wasn't on junk you piece of shit motherfucker. Somebody did this to him and I intend to find out who it was." Avery towered over Jerry as he cowered curled up on the floor.

Jimmy pulled Avery back just as Carol Merrick's security squad attempted to pile on. Jimmy whipped out his badge and stuck it in the biggest guy's face before they had a chance to lay a hand on him.

"I've got it covered, gentleman, thank you." Jimmy gave Avery a solid nudge toward the door as the mass of people in the room stared at them.

"Get him the hell out of here," Carol screamed as she flung herself down beside Jerry Jewell. "You're going to jail, you son of a bitch. You hear me? You belong in a cage." Avery didn't look back as he made his way to the door. He kept his head down, avoiding the eyes of the crowd. Jimmy followed along, glowering as the crowd parted to let them pass. He resisted the urge to push Avery a few more times as they marched forward.

Just as he and Jimmy reached the door, a wiry looking older gentleman in a Confederate officer's uniform and blue cowboy boots stepped to the front of the crowd. "Keep your head up, Clark. It's about damn time somebody punched that old prick in his mouth."

Avery smiled weakly, nodding as he walked past. "Thanks, Lem."

Then, suddenly, it hit him. Lemmy had just died the winter before. Avery turned back to look again but the old man was gone. He looked over to see if Jimmy had noticed but Jimmy was fully focused on pushing him outside. As soon as they were out on the sidewalk, Jimmy grabbed Avery by the arm and spun him around to face him. "What in the hell was that?"

Avery shook his head, incredulous as he pulled the bottle from his pocket. "I'm sorry, Jimmy. I freaked out. That son of a bitch accused me of getting Kerry hooked on smack! I wasn't even on the shit by the time I met Kerry. Something is fucked up here, man, I'm telling you. None of this is right."

Jimmy could see the frustration in Avery's eyes. And, after everything he had just seen, he was starting to agree with him. "You know what struck me just now was the way Kerry's widow practically dove on him after he went down. It seemed like she was worried about him much more than your average friend."

Avery's eyes widened. "She did, didn't she? What the fuck's up with that? You think they're screwing around?"

"Beats me, but I thought it was peculiar. She sure as hell didn't give off the vibe of a grieving widow. Especially the way she went after that blonde girl. She was just cruel. I wish you'd have gotten a better look at her."

Avery ran his hand down his face before taking a swig from the bottle. He took a long slow pull as he stared out into the darkness. "Something's fucked up here, Jimmy. I can feel it in my bones. Look, man, I'm going to take off. I need some time to wrap my mind around all of this. You go on home. I'll talk to you in the morning."

"No way, I'm not going to run off and leave you here. You're lucky I'm not hauling your ass down to the nearest precinct for punching that guy."

Avery gawked at Jimmy, raising an eyebrow, "Seriously?"

"Seriously, at least that way I'd know you're safe. The last thing you need to do is to go running around the city half-cocked."

Avery started rummaging through his jacket to find a cigarette. "I'm not angry, Jimmy. I'm just hurt. How could anyone seriously think I'd ever do anything to hurt one of my friends?"

Jimmy heard the resignation in Avery's voice. It bothered him knowing that there really wasn't anything he could do to help. The two of them stared into each other's eyes for a long few seconds before Avery turned to walk away. Even though he thought better of it, Jimmy let him go. Avery needed to work things out for himself.

CHAPTER 5

Carol Merrick's face flushed with embarrassment as she realized that all eyes in the crowd were watching her hover over Jerry. She frowned as she climbed to her feet directing her security detail to haul him up off of the floor. She regretted her reaction but had acted out of pure impulse. Now she feared everyone would get the wrong idea. She was here to play the part of the grieving widow. She hoped she hadn't blown it.

Carol turned away from the crowd and rushed to open the door to the anteroom she'd been given access to so the crew could drag Jerry inside. The muted conversations coming from the crowd burned in her ears as she closed the door behind her.

She marched the length of the room, seething, as the guards dropped Jerry askew onto a couch. "Don't let anyone in here. I'll be out in a minute."

As the guards left the room Jerry slowly pulled himself up into a sitting position while rubbing his jaw. His big sad brown eyes followed Carol around the room. She glared at his big red, raw-boned, face and realized that she had made a mistake throwing her lot in with him. He was a shrewd businessman but not the most masculine guy she knew. He didn't even have the balls to defend himself. But, he would do whatever she asked of him. Carol had thought that would be enough.

"So are you going to be alright or what?" she asked before dropping down on to a bench across from him.

Jerry frowned, puzzled by Carol's lack of empathy. "What do you think? That crazy bastard damn near broke my jaw. He should be locked up."

"Don't worry, there was a cop in the crowd that escorted him out," Carol said.

Jerry smirked. "Avery came in with that guy. I very much doubt he's been placed under arrest. But at least now everyone will think he had a hand in what happened to Kerry."

Carol glared at him, "Unless he decides to raise hell about it. Avery knew he never did heroin."

"I just thought he'd make a good scapegoat," Jerry said. "Nobody cares what that washed up junkie thinks."

"I don't need you to think, Jerry. I need you to stick to the damn plan." Carol sighed, looking around at the neutral-toned blandness of the tiny room. "We need to keep our heads down until after Kerry's will is read."

"I don't know what you're worried about, Carol. We've got this all sewn up. The British authorities ruled it an accident. Kerry's body is on its way here, now. Everything's good."

Carol hopped off of the bench and resumed pacing. Everything wasn't good. It was all a big mess. Carol didn't want to think about Kerry. She didn't want to see his face. She didn't want to hear his voice. She didn't want to be reminded of the way she felt, or what she had done. But, she couldn't run away from it. She had loved Kerry more than anyone else in her whole fucked up life. But he had broken her. She couldn't compete with his free-wheeling lifestyle. She couldn't compete with his music. Both were more important to him than she had ever been. No matter what she tried she had always rated third, or worse.

But all of that was all over now. Kerry was dead. She had seen to that. Now she had to live with it.

CHAPTER 6

Sarah scowled as her mother's voicemail message issued, once again, through the receiver. She had spent the better part of the week trying to get her mother on the phone and now it was just getting ridiculous.

"I know you're there, Mom. I know you're avoiding me. I talked to Mrs. Younger. She said you were fine. So whenever you're ready to get this over with, give me a call. There's no point in dragging it out. I love you. Bye."

Sarah shook her head as she set the phone down on the desk. Her mother had to be one of the most stubborn people on the face of the Earth. It was a personality trait they shared. Sarah wondered if her mother was in mourning or just pissed off. She wanted to console her, to gauge how she was feeling. But, in typical Melinda fashion, she had shut Sarah out.

Sarah had to resort to calling her mother's neighbor just to make sure she was all right and ended up spending an hour being regaled by tales of Mrs. Younger's herd of rescued animals. She decided that when she did talk to her mother, she'd make sure somebody was checking up on Mrs. Younger. She was afraid someone would find the woman dead from a feral cat attack. Sarah sighed, running her fingers through her hair. The only way she was going to accomplish anything was to drive out to Arvada and see her mother in person. She didn't want to fight with her but judging from her mother's refusal to speak that's probably what would end up happening.

They had a long history of blowouts. The worst one Sarah remembered was the day Kerry Vance's name came out of her young mouth, the day her mother sent Anna away. She hadn't been prepared for her mother's violent reaction. It was the first time Sarah had ever been truly scared of her. The whole dynamic of their relationship changed that day. And it had been tough going ever since.

Sarah wasn't looking forward to confronting her now. But it had to be done. She needed answers. They both needed closure. Sarah sat forward in her chair pulling up her MP3 list on the computer. She wanted to hear Kerry's voice. She had about an hour before Tracy got home from school. She needed to let everything go for a little while and just kick back and jam. Her brain needed a rest.

C'mon, crank up the radio/The night is at our side/I won't be here forever, honey/ So just lay back and ride....

The first time Sarah encountered her father's music was just a few months after she turned thirteen. As she started the seventh grade and moved to the junior high building, she rode an earlier bus that included the high school kids. It was intimidating at first but all of the older kids turned out to be really cool. They were all just out for a good time.

On the high school bus, on Fridays, their bus driver let them listen to the boom box that Willie Hildebrandt brought to school to record the marching band before football games. Back then, in the '80s, metal was all the rage among the cool kids. There was a lot of it Sarah didn't care for. A lot of it was crude and sexist but there were a few bands she heard more than once that she liked.

One morning they were listening to Iron Maiden, one of the bands Sarah liked because the lyrics spoke to more than sex and partying, when Billy Miller got on the bus with his sister, Mary. Billy was cute. He was tall with long wavy brown hair. His big blue eyes lit up when he talked about music and bands. He was a senior and only rode the bus when his father grounded him from his hotrod '72 Nova.

Every time Mrs. Clepper, the bus driver, opened the door to him she'd ask, 'What'd you do this time, Billy?'

This morning, after telling Mrs. Clepper about the rim he'd bent sliding into a curb while doing doughnuts in his Nova, he pulled a cassette from his pocket and handed it to Willie. "Play this."

Billy, being the alpha dog on the bus when he was there, didn't hear a word of protest as Willie shut down the Maiden and threw in Billy's cassette.

"What you putting on, Wild Bill?" Zack, the minister's son, and all around party animal, asked as Billy dropped down in the seat beside him.

Sarah turned to watch his blue eyes shine.

"Kerry Vance's new album just came out. This motherfucker is badass."

Sarah turned, sliding down in her seat when she heard the name. Anna had told her that her father was a famous singer but didn't elaborate. When Anna confessed to Melinda about her conversation with Sarah their friendship ended. Sarah hadn't seen her in months. As the tape started, Sarah listened intently. The music was eerie. It was so heavy, so intense and fevered, Sarah found it unsettling. She looked back to Billy, his eyes aglow as he played the air drums. The music was unlike anything she'd ever heard. When Kerry's voice joined in, the hair on the back of Sarah's neck rose. It was transcendent.

Sarah decided as the bus pulled up in front of the school that she was going to get a copy of that tape. She was going to get a copy of everything. Sarah loved her father's music. She had been a fan from that day on. But, it left her in an odd position. She quickly grew to understand his rock-n-roll lifestyle. She had no illusions about his use of pharmaceuticals. He was a singular figure.

As she moved into high school, she understood that there wasn't a place for her in her father's world. Kerry was just too wild. She had to distance herself from her fantasy. It galled her to cave to her mother's wishes. The fights they'd had over Melinda's choice of secrecy had sometimes been brutal.

It created a divide between them. But, even so, Sarah knew deep down that her mother was right. She was better off pursuing her own passions. She needed to concentrate on school.

Kerry's lifestyle was not for her.

Now, as the news of his death had settled on her, she had to make peace with her decision. She'd gone online and watched a bunch of his old videos and interviews. She loved the clip of him, along with the author Avery Clark, running around interviewing random people at some spring break concert in Florida. You could tell that they were both hammered but their lust for life was apparent. Something about that gave her a good feeling. She appreciated the need to stop and unwind. Lately, it hadn't happened enough.

When the phone rang Sarah answered it without checking the caller ID thinking her mother had finally relented and called her back. She didn't recognize the woman's voice on the other end but something about it seemed oddly familiar.

"Is this Sarah Koop?"

"Yes, who's this?"

The caller hesitated. It made Sarah suspicious. "My name is Calliope. I'm a friend of Kerry Vance. Do you have time to talk?"

"Look if you're a reporter or something, I don't have anything to say." Sarah couldn't imagine how they could have tracked her down. But it only took a quick instant to decide she was not going to take part in the media circus she'd seen on TV. It wasn't her place.

"No, no, really, honey, I'm an old friend of your father's. I've known him since before you were born. He left me with a message for you and a request."

A chill ran down Sarah's spine. She got up from her desk chair and moved to her husband's recliner pulling her feet up underneath of her as she sat. She felt terrified and elated all once. She was elated to know that her father had known about her and had thought about her, at least, near the end. But she was terrified of what he had to say. She was terrified to know why he had abandoned her. Sarah cradled the phone as she eased into the chair. A moment of reckoning was upon her.

"Okay, I'm listening." She hoped she was ready for what she was about to hear.

She hoped Kerry loved her.

CHAPTER 7

The cooling night air still held a good measure of humidity as Avery sat sweating out on the veranda of the anonymous little dive bar he had discovered. He settled into the shadows, away from the bar and its chattering patrons, cupping his hi-ball glass and staring into its depths. Drinking was the only way he could slow his brain down enough to think properly.

Memories of Kerry came crashing back in waves. Avery had only ever wanted what was best for him. He loved him. He couldn't begin to fathom how Jerry Jewell could believe that he had gotten Kerry hooked on junk.

He was not a junkie.... at least, not anymore. Avery lifted his glass and finished off his bourbon. He was an alcoholic now. It was socially acceptable.

Struck with his own hapless grasp on mortality Avery resigned himself to the fact that everything he'd ever accomplished, ultimately, added up to nothing. He felt like nothing. Avery couldn't escape the cursor blinking endlessly on a blank page. The torrent of words that flowed in his youth had dried up. It left him restless in his own skin. He was staring down the long slow slide into his golden years bereft of his art and alone.

Kerry and Zoe were the only two people in his life who had ever really understood him. Beyond the partying and music, he and Kerry shared a bond that transcended the superficial connections abound among artists. Kerry kept him grounded. He was the rock that kept Avery from cashing in after Zoe died. Kerry looked to Avery for total honesty. Avery was never afraid to tell him when something sucked.

"Well, it sure as hell sucks right now, old buddy."

"I'm sorry. Did you say something, sir?"

Avery was startled as the harried little blonde bartender sat another drink down in front of him, "From the lady at the end of the bar." Avery followed the bartender's gaze then faked a thin smile as he lifted his glass in thanks.

The woman seated at the end of the bar was stunning. Avery took note of her dark eyes as she smiled back from across the dimly lit patio. She was a vision with long coal-black hair highlighted in red with blonde streaks braided at the temples. Her flawless frame was wrapped in a form-fitting white sundress with a red scarf arranged elaborately around her waist. His eyes widened in appreciation. On any other day, he might have been happy to pursue such an enticing opportunity. But today was not the day. Avery settled back into the shadows with his drink. Before he could finish his first taste, the beautiful stranger walked over and sat down across from him.

"Do you mind if I speak with you for a second, Mr. Clark?"

Avery peered across the table and frowned. "I'm sorry but I'd really rather be alone."

To her credit, the woman wasn't deterred by his dismissal. "I was hoping you could help me with something."

Avery was surprised by the statement. It had been a long time since a beautiful woman had just rolled up and propositioned him. He smirked before taking another drink. She probably just wanted an autograph for her mother.

"Look, I don't mean to be rude. It's just that I'm swimming up a shit creek right now and struggling to stay afloat." Avery sighed. "I don't think I could be much help to anyone."

The stranger shot him a sympathetic look then smiled. "Maybe it would help if you talked to someone. I'd be happy to listen."

Avery looked her over. There was something calming about her presence. Or, she was just really flipping hot and he was lonely and about half-buzzed. "I'm kind of leery about talking to strangers. I don't want to find anything I say broadcast all over social media tomorrow. You don't have an agenda, do you?"

"Oh, I have several agendas, Mr. Clark. Plots, schemes, machinations and at least one conspiracy but none of them pertain to you so we should be good."

Avery's laughter rose over the music piped in from the bar. It was the first real laugh he'd had in days. "What's your name, young lady? I'd at least like to know who I'm spilling my guts to."

"You can call me Calliope."

"Calliope. That's a pretty name." Avery grinned. "You have a last name?"

Calliope shrugged. "Not one I use."

Avery grinned again, charmed. She wished to remain an enigma. He knew he was probably setting himself up for a fall but for the moment she was a beautiful distraction. "Well, Calliope, where would you like to start?"

"Well, what I'd really like to know is what you think about all of the mysterious bullshit going on around Kerry Vance's death."

Avery's good cheer vanished as he glared at her across the table. "Who are you? Are you a fucking reporter?"

Calliope leaned over the table to stare him dead in the eye. "No, I'm not a reporter. I am a very old friend of Kerry's and I'm here because I need your help."

Avery held her gaze. She couldn't have been more than twenty-five, thirty at most. She couldn't have been an old of a friend of Kerry's unless she'd known him since birth. But, still, something about her intrigued him. She had a gravitas about her. "I never heard Kerry mention anyone named Calliope. How do I know you're not full of shit?"

Calliope regarded him calmly. "You don't. And I'm not surprised that he never mentioned me. Our relationship was....difficult. But I'm here to tell you that Kerry's death was no accident. I think you know that."

Avery nodded slowly, "That's what I'm afraid of. None of this shit makes sense. What makes you so sure?"

"I got a letter from him two days after he died. He had found out there was something heavy going on between Carol and his manager Jimmy Jewell. They were out to take him for everything he had. He wrote to ask me for a favor in case anything happened to him."

Avery ran his hand down his face and looked away from Calliope. It wasn't a difficult thing to accept given everything that had happened earlier. Carol was a vindictive bitch but he never expected this. "Why do you need my help?"

"Kerry specifically told me to find you." Calliope took a small sip from her drink. "I wasn't sure it was a good idea until I saw you knock Jerry Jewell on his ass earlier."

"You were there?"

Calliope nodded. "I saw the whole thing."

Avery's face reddened. "That crazy son of a bitch thinks that I got Kerry hooked on smack. I haven't done that shit in years. Kerry hated it. He always said that it had taken away too many great musicians. I know he wouldn't touch it."

"You're right. He wouldn't. Somebody did this to him."

"So what do we do? My friend's a cop and he said it'd be impossible to get anyone to look into it, especially since it happened overseas. The Brits ruled it an accidental overdose. What can we do short of getting them to confess?"

Calliope rubbed her finger around the rim of her glass in thought then looked up at Avery. "The first thing we need to do is keep Kerry out of Carol's clutches."

Avery frowned as her words settled into his besotted brain. "Are you saying you want me to help you steal Kerry's body?"

Calliope nodded. "And take him home to Denver."

Avery shook his head before knocking back the rest of his bourbon. "You can't be serious. That's crazy. We'd never make it."

"Trust me, I know it's crazy. But Kerry is the one who planned it, not me. When he found out about Carol and Jerry he filed for divorce and had a new will drafted to cut her out of it. But he was killed before everything could be set into motion. So, we've got to get him out of town and headed towards Denver before she has time to react. Once we're there everything is set up. His lawyer in Denver was an old school chum. He knows about everything that's gone down. We just need to buy a few days until all of the legal stuff works its course."

Avery stared in his glass, swirling the ice around inside it. "So you're saying Carol doesn't know she's about to get screwed?"

"Not a clue," Calliope said.

Avery smiled. "Well, in that case, count me in."

CHAPTER 8

Calliope shifted in her seat for what felt like the millionth time as she and Avery waited for the hearse transporting Kerry's body. The outright ghoulishness of the situation was not lost on her. She had done a lot of bizarre things in her outrageously long life but this was at the top. Still, she was sure she was doing the right thing. She was doing what Kerry had asked of her. No matter what obstacles she'd face she was prepared to see it through.

Calliope yawned staring in the direction the hearse would appear. She had parked about a quarter of a mile down the street from where it would exit the airport close enough that it had no other way around and far enough away to avoid being seen by the guards at the gate.

She had planned it meticulously, but it was taking a lot longer to arrive than she expected. Calliope glanced over at Avery who had dozed off over in the passenger seat. He was a wild card at best and, at the moment, about half-lit. From what little she knew he was a brilliant writer. He was also a drunk, a troublemaker and a former junkie. He had risen to fame as the voice of the heroin-chic rave scene back in the early '90s. He had once been a strikingly beautiful waif. Now he was a graying middle-aged man that was a little soft around the middle. Calliope wasn't sure she could trust him. But Kerry had requested his presence so she would just have to put up with him... for now.

"Hey, are you all right over there?"

Avery jerked awake then tried to stretch out in the confined space. "I'm good, just bored. How long is this going to take?"

Calliope shrugged. "They should have been here by now. Kerry's flight landed over an hour ago."

"And you're sure this is the road they'll take back? Maybe they went out another gate."

Calliope wiped the fog from the door glass as she shifted around in her seat again. "No. This is the route they'll take. I've studied the procedure. We just have to be ready when we see them."

"Well I guess I'm about as ready as I'm going to get given the situation. I never figured I'd be sitting by the side of the road waiting to jack my best friend's body."

"Yeah, me either."

Avery shook his head but didn't reply.

"So you're good with the plan, right?" As she spoke Avery pointed toward a set of headlights cruising down the street. Calliope turned to see the hearse come into view. She reached out and quickly dropped the gearshift into drive then, slowly, inched forward preparing to pull out into the hearse's path. She kept her gaze locked on the hearse timing her jump. "You ready for this?"

Avery laughed; his incredulousness made manifest. "Too late to back out now."

Calliope dropped her foot on the accelerator and jumped straight out into the hearse's path. But instead of the driver stopping short, he kept right on coming barely slowing down before smashing into the side of the rental car. It was a hell of a jolt. The impact knocked their car parallel to the curb as momentum carried the hearse to a bouncing stop atop the opposite sidewalk.

"God Damn!" Avery released his seatbelt as soon as the car came to a stop thankful that he'd kept it on while they waited. He turned to check on Calliope and saw her climbing out through the driver's side window.

Avery forced his door open rushing out after Calliope as she made a bee-line for the hearse.

"What in the hell was that?" Calliope yelled, arms waving in the air, as she rounded the driver's side of the hearse.

Avery caught up with her just as she snatched open the driver's side door. Inside was a tiny little old man wrapped in an ill-fitting black suit. He looked to be in his eighties, if not older. The expression on his face was one of pure shock as he sat motionless with his hands still on the wheel.

"Did you not fucking see us?" Calliope said leaning over him down inside the car.

Avery was afraid he might have to step in to keep her from smacking the old guy around. She was livid. The old gentleman turned his head slowly to stare at them distress evident on his face. "I'm sorry, ma'am. I can't see so good at night anymore. There's usually not anyone down here this early."

Avery laughed, rubbing his eyes as the ridiculousness of the situation struck. His heart went out to the old man. He was just trying to do his job.

Calliope turned to face him. "You find this amusing?"

"If I found it any other way, I'd be crying right now. So what are we going to do?"

Calliope shook her head stepping around the door to go look at the front of the hearse. Avery stopped to help the old gentleman out of the car before following along.

"It doesn't look too bad," Calliope said. "The grill and bumper are smashed, but it's not overheating or leaking fluid."

"That's the good thing about these old Caddies," the old man said. "They were built to last, not like that junk they make now."

"You think it'll drive?" Avery asked.

Calliope looked from him to the old man. "We're about to see. We need to get out of here before the cops show up."

"What are you talking about?" The old man said. "We need to wait for them."

"No, we really don't," Calliope said. She stepped closer to the old man looking him dead in the eye. "Look if you want us to drop you off somewhere, you're more than welcome to ride along but, one way or the other, we're taking this hearse."

Calliope's expression was menacing. It occurred to Avery that he wasn't at all sure who he was dealing with. She may have been a friend of Kerry's but she seemed dangerous. He'd have to keep his eyes open.

The old man stood motionless staring up at Calliope. After a second he dropped his head and nodded. "Well, if that's the case, I guess you better drop me off at a hospital. Because when my boss finds out about this, I'm going to need one."

Calliope smirked before walking away to move the rental car out of the street. Avery put his arm across the old man's shoulders and guided him toward the passenger side of the hearse. "Are you sure you're okay?"

"I'm a little banged up but I'll be fine. By the time they get me settled into a room and get a cop there to take my statement, you two will be long gone. I figure that's what you want, right?"

Avery smiled. "It is. I appreciate your help."

The old man shrugged. "Ah, well, with any luck they'll keep me for a few days. It'll give me a break from my wife."

Avery laughed as he helped the old man into the seat. "It'll be a win for both of us."

CHAPTER 9

Jimmy sat up with a jerk, startled awake, as his cellphone sprang to life beside the bed. He snatched the phone off of the nightstand squinting in the darkness against the glare of the screen.

[19ᵗʰ Precinct]

"Aw, shit." Jimmy dropped back down on to his pillow. He really didn't feel like going into work early. He let the phone ring for a fourth time before he accepted the call, "Werner."

"Jimmy? Hey man, it's Zap. Look, we've got a situation here. Nolan wants to see you in his office A.S.A.P."

Jimmy rubbed his eyes and yawned, "Now? Why in the hell is he even there this early?"

"Look, Jimmy, I don't want to go into detail over the phone. Just get here as quickly as you can. And maybe turn on the T.V. while you're getting ready, huh? I'll see you soon."

Jimmy dropped the phone on the nightstand. If it had been a real emergency Zap would have read him in over the phone. But something heavy had to have gone down to be summoned to his Captain's office at six o'clock in the morning. Jimmy fished around in the covers for the T.V. remote as he sat up and stretched. As soon as the screen lit up, he knew it was going to have a very bad day.

'Again, Eyewitness 7 News has learned that the hearse carrying Kerry Vance's body was stolen shortly after departing JFK early this morning.'

Jimmy snatched his pants from the chair beside his bed as he glared at the TV screen, "Son-of-a-bitch."

CHAPTER 10

The throng of reporters outside of precinct headquarters far surpassed the group that had covered Kerry Vance's memorial service the night before. Jimmy scowled as he pushed his way past them. The thought of all this time and energy being wasted on a dead rock-n-roll singer was ridiculous. There were far more pressing issues in the world.

Jimmy wondered why they were here in the first place. He figured they'd be out swarming the 113th where the hearse had actually been stolen. He had a feeling that had everything to do with the reason Captain Nolan had called him in. Jimmy walked up the stairs into the squad room preparing himself for whatever was about to go down.

"Damn, Jimmy, what'd you do, fly down here?" Luiz "Zap" Zapata rose from behind his desk to meet Jimmy in the middle of the squad room.

"Didn't figure it'd be a good idea to keep Nolan waiting," Jimmy said. "What's up with all of the reporters outside?"

Zap smirked. "They have Kerry Vance's widow in there. She's a real ballbuster, that one."

"Brother, you're not kidding," Jimmy said. "Why is she here, though? I thought the hearse was stolen over in Jamaica."

"Evidently she lives somewhere in Lenox Hill. I guess she didn't want to schlep all the way out to Queens. So she and her lawyer met their detective here." Zap winked, "Fame has its privileges, you know."

"So what does this have to do with me?" Jimmy asked. "Why did Nolan drag me in here?"

"Sorry brother," Zap said, clapping Jimmy on the shoulder. "I have not a clue."

Jimmy looked over to see Nolan standing at his office door waving him in. "Well, I guess I better not keep him waiting. He doesn't look happy."

"He never looks happy," Zap said. "Don't sweat it, Jimmy. I'm sure it can't be that bad."

Jimmy laughed. "Yeah, right, after the past few days I've had, I'm ready for a vacation."

"Let me know," Zap said. "I can always hook you up with my cousin, Carla."

Jimmy walked away without saying anything. He'd seen pictures of Carla. There was no way that was ever going to jump off.

"Have a seat, Sergeant Werner."

Jimmy sat down on the couch as Nolan closed the door behind him. Seated across from him was a short little bald man that Jimmy guessed to be the detective from Queens. The cheap gray suit and thrift store tie were a dead giveaway.

"Werner, this is Detective Barlow from the 113th. He's here to interview Carol Merrick. There are a few things we'd like to ask you about that came up during the course of the investigation."

Jimmy looked from Nolan to Barlow and nodded. "Sure. What do you need to know?"

"Well, first off, sergeant. Are you friends with Avery Clark?" Barlow asked.

Jimmy's heart sank. Was Avery in on this? "Yes, sir. We've been friends since grade school."

Barlow looked up at Nolan as he circled around to sit behind his desk. Jimmy knew that look. He didn't like it.

"And you were with Mr. Clark yesterday evening?"

Jimmy looked Barlow square in the eye. He didn't want to give the impression he was hiding anything. "Yeah, I went with him to Kerry Vance's memorial service."

Barlow looked Jimmy over, sizing him up. Jimmy returned the favor. He seemed affable enough other than his terrible taste in suits.

"Well, sergeant, it's come to our attention through Ms. Merrick that there was an altercation at the memorial between Mr. Clark and a Jerry Jewell?"

Jimmy watched Barlow flip through his notebook. He couldn't muster the patience to wait for the old man to practice his Colombo impersonation. "And you're wondering why I didn't collar Avery for decking the guy."

"Yes," Nolan said.

Jimmy nodded. "Well, first off, the guy deserved it. And, secondly, I wasn't exactly setting precedent. I removed Avery from the situation and sent him on his way."

Barlow looked around at Nolan. "We can't exactly fault him there. How many fights have we broken up over the years and not hauled anyone off?"

Nolan released a sharp sigh and sat back in his chair. "True."

"Am I missing something here? What does this have to do with the theft of Kerry Vance's body?"

Nolan picked a picture up off of his desk handing it to Jimmy. "This was taken by a traffic camera about a quarter of a mile down the street from where the hearse exited the airport facility."

Jimmy picked up the picture. There, standing on the sidewalk next to a weathered-looking older gentleman, stood Avery. They were both staring at something out of view of the camera, but there was no denying that it was him. He was wearing the same T-shirt and sport coat he had worn for the memorial service.

Jimmy dropped his head to stare at the floor. "Ah, fuck." He knew he should have made good on his threat to Avery. He should have stayed with him. Now, it was all a big goddamned mess and there wasn't a thing he could do to protect him.

Barlow leaned forward and tapped his notebook against Jimmy's leg. "Look, son, I'm not here to jam up you. I just want a clear picture of how this went down. What happened at the memorial?"

Jimmy took another long look at the picture trying to figure out just exactly what in hell Avery was thinking. He looked at Barlow and sighed. He wouldn't lie to him. But, hopefully, he could spin it so Avery didn't come off as a complete head case.

"Avery is convinced that Kerry Vance's death wasn't an accident. He went to the memorial looking for someone that was with Kerry in London to find out more about what happened."

Barlow perked up in his chair. "What made him think that?"

"Avery said that Kerry never did heroin, ever. He hated it. Avery has told me before how Kerry counseled him to make sure that he never went back to it. So, anyway, Avery spotted Jerry Jewell and approached him. The two of them started arguing and before I could get between them, Avery slugged him."

"What were they arguing about?" Nolan asked.

"Jewell tried to pin Kerry's heroin use on Avery. And I can fully appreciate why Avery went off. He's been off of heroin for years, over a decade. Avery and I actually reconnected after he got clean. Trust me, I wouldn't be anywhere around him if I even suspected he was still using."

Another look passed between Barlow and Nolan. Jimmy wondered if they had been partners at some point in their careers. They had an easy rapport. Jimmy just hoped they believed what he was telling them.

"Did Clark speak with anyone else while he was there?" Barlow asked.

"He spoke to a lot of people while we were there. The room was packed. Probably the longest conversation he had was with a younger brunette right after we got there. I think she was a model or an actress or something. She looked familiar. They were just recalling stories about Kerry, though. He didn't share his suspicions with her."

Nolan picked up another photograph and handed it to Jimmy. "Is this her?"

Jimmy glanced at the picture. It looked like it was taken by the same camera that had caught Avery over in Queens. It had the same oblique angle. Whoever she was, she was much more attractive than the woman at the memorial. "No. Who is she?"

Before Barlow could reply a woman started yelling outside in the squad room.

"What the fuck is this? Get away from me you son of a bitch!"

The shrill voice cut through the door of Nolan's office. Jimmy recognized it immediately. Carol Merrick. She had a tuneless bleat that could warp steel. Nolan hopped up from his desk and rushed toward the door with Barlow hot behind him. Jimmy stayed back only going to the door for a peek. He didn't want to get close enough for Carol to recognize him.

"What the fuck is this, Parker? Did you know about this?" Carol held up a summons in the face of a slick-looking hipster in a Fioravanti suit.

Jimmy guessed him to be Carol's lawyer. He bore the right mix of arrogance and befuddlement. Nolan and Barlow rolled up in an attempt to calm Carol down. Then, as she took a turn berating the two of them, Jimmy saw the beautiful young blond he'd spotted at the memorial service standing behind her.

The girl was breathtaking.

She watched the proceedings with a pained embarrassment apparent on her face. Whatever her connection to Carol, Jimmy suspected the girl's patience for it was wearing thin. She shook her head in disgust and turned to see him standing in the doorway. Jimmy was taken by the urge to rush over and ask her name. Instead, he stood frozen in the doorway grinning like a fool. The girl smiled faintly before rejoining the fray. As his good sense reasserted itself, he realized she was way too young for him. He doubted she was much older than eighteen. But, she was a striking creature. He felt bad that she was caught in Carol's orbit. Finally, Nolan and Barlow managed to get Carol and her entourage moving toward the door. Jimmy stole another quick glance at the blonde girl before returning to his seat. After a few more minutes spent alone pondering her, Barlow and Nolan returned.

"Man, that broad is a piece of work," Barlow said as he followed Nolan into the room. "If I was married to her, I'd be dying to get away, too."

Jimmy arched an eyebrow as Barlow returned to the chair across from him.

"She was just served divorce papers and the notice of a new will. She didn't take it well."

"Yeah, I noticed," Jimmy said. "Divorce papers, huh? That's a bit of bad timing," Jimmy was also struck by the notice of a new will. Carol's GQ lawyer should have at least known something about that.

"No doubt," Nolan said. "OK, Werner, look, I'm going to put you on administrative leave until this all blows over. We may need to call on you again depending on where all this leads. So take some time off and relax but keep your phone turned on."

"And if you hear anything from Avery Clark let us know, immediately," Barlow said. "If he gives this little stunt up and turns himself in he'll save us all a boatload of trouble."

Jimmy rose from his chair. "Sure, I can do that. Hopefully, he'll arrive at that conclusion on his own." As he left Nolan's office Jimmy realized there was a lot more going on than he had a handle on. Barlow and Nolan definitely knew more than they were telling. Jimmy considered asking again about the identity of the woman in the picture but thought better of it. He doubted he would get a straight answer. He'd just have to track Avery and his mystery woman down on his own.

CHAPTER 11

Carol and her niece, Daisy, arrived home from the precinct to find another gaggle of reporters loitering outside of her home. Carol's rancor seethed in the camera's eye as the litany of questions blurred into a tuneless chatter around her. She pushed Daisy forward into the house then quickly slammed the door behind them. It felt so good to do so that, after gently placing her purse in the hall closet, Carol slammed that door several times as well.

"Goddamn it! Goddamn it! Goddamn it! That son of a bitch has screwed me over again!" The vibration from the door knocked a Baccarat vase off of its shelf to shatter on the floor. Carol stopped. She stared at the scattered shards cast across the floor before slowly resting her head against the door. Tears poured from her eyes before she could even think to fight them. Every second of the past week hung like a dead weight from her heart. But, she did what had to be done. She couldn't watch Kerry suffer. Kerry Vance had to go out on top. His legacy would've kept her flush forever. But, somehow, he still had found a way to defy her. Carol bumped the door with her head, then let loose and cried. It had been a long time coming.

Daisy, her ungrateful bitch of a niece, sat watching from the couch over the pretense of her cellphone. The girl was a constant reminder of the lousy family Carol had been born into and a walking testimonial to just how far her junkie sister, Pam, had been willing to go to stay high. It was a miracle the girl hadn't been permanently damaged.

"I need a drink," Carol said, at long last, slowly gathering her wits and wiping her eyes. She glared at Daisy as she crossed the room. "I gather you're enjoying this."

It had been Kerry's bright idea to take Daisy in after her mother passed. Guilt, Carol assumed, from having abandoned his own daughter to pursue stardom.

"Not as much as you'd think," Daisy said, rising to follow Carol into the kitchen. "Now that Kerry's not here to protect me I figure my days are numbered."

Carol nodded in approval. If Kerry's plan was to leave her penniless, there was no need to squander resources maintaining her. She was an adult now.

"You're a smart girl," Carol said. "That's how I know you'll do just fine out there on your own. You want to be a singer now, don't you? Maybe it's time you suffered for your art a little."

Daisy did her best to appear indifferent. "Perhaps. There's really no reason to stay, anyway. I realized a long time ago which one of you really wanted me here."

Carol scowled. She wanted to protest, but there really wasn't any point. Daisy was no one's fool. If Carol had no other feelings for the girl, she could at least take solace in the fact that she had a hand in giving her a little backbone. That was about as nurturing as she was capable.

"You're right," Carol said, pouring herself a drink. She took a long sip of bourbon then sighed. "And, since we're being honest here, I want you to know it's not your fault. Your mother and I had a lot of issues. Some I'll never be able to forgive. I let that taint my feelings toward you and I'm sorry. But, hell, Daisy, you've got to give me a little credit here. I could have said no."

Daisy's eyes widened. It wasn't like Carol to be apologetic. This was the first time in a long time that they'd had an actual conversation. Carol usually just shouted orders at her. Kerry's death had taken a toll. If it sparked a change in her aunt's demeanor, Daisy decided it might not be a bad thing. She could stand to be nicer.

"I know," Daisy said, "And I'm sincerely glad you didn't. You've given me opportunities that I never would have had in Blacksville. I am grateful for that."

"Blacksville," Carol spat the word as if it tasted of shit. "Your grandparents weren't capable of taking care of you. They were too fucked up to raise their own kids. Even if I had decided against taking you in, Daisy, I'd have made sure you were never left with them."

Daisy stared at her aunt. This was the first time she had ever gotten a real sense of just how badly Carol hated her family....their family. "I've always wondered what my grandparents were like. I don't remember them."

Rage flashed across Carol's face then, just as quickly, subsided. "Trust me, you're better off. That house is no place for a little girl."

Daisy nodded, deciding not to question Carol further. Whatever had happened in their childhood had damaged Carol just as much as her mother. It never occurred to Daisy before. Her aunt was always a pillar of strength, always in control. Kerry once remarked, in admiration, that Carol had more balls than a room full of rodeo clowns. Daisy never considered that her aunt could be vulnerable.

"I'm sorry it was so difficult for you," Daisy said.

Carol turned with a sharp gaze. "Some things are just better left in the past. Remember that." Carol took another sip of her drink trying to keep Kerry out of her mind. She was determined not to miss him. Her love for him was best left in the past, too. Carol gazed around the kitchen. She had loved the room from the moment she first saw it. The alabaster tile and quartz countertops gave the room a warm luminescence. But now, the energy of the place seemed diminished. As if Kerry's absence had stolen its essence. Carol found the thought disturbing. She had to stop obsessing. She'd made her choice.

"You know when Kerry bought this place for me we barely knew each other. He used to come to watch me dance at a club I worked down in midtown. I didn't know who he was. I'd heard of him and loved Zephyr, but I hadn't put it together. I just thought he was another old pervert slinging money around to try and look important. When I found out who he was, I set out to scam him for everything I could get." Carol looked Daisy in the eye. "That's how I survived back then. Of course, Kerry was on to my little scheme instantly."

Carol smiled, recalling the memory. "He thought it was cute. So he gave me a couple of grand one night then disappeared. I didn't hear from him for a good while after that so I just wrote him off and went back to the routine.

Then, about six months later, he stops by the club and asks me to go out with him after work. He said he had a present for me. That's when he brought me here."

Carol rubbed her fingers across the countertop. "After he gave me a tour of the house, he brought me in here and lifted me up to sit right here on the counter. That's when he told me he'd bought this place for me. No strings attached. I was barely twenty years old."

Daisy sat speechless. Carol had never opened up to her before. She wasn't sure how to react.

"I was dumbfounded," Carol said, smiling, before finishing her drink, "Then, I'd thought he'd lost his damned mind. Who buys a complete stranger a fucking house? It was ridiculous. Then, while I'm raising hell with him about it, he looks me in the eye and says; 'This is what you need the most. All of the other good things in your life will rise from here.' It stopped me dead in my tracks."

"Kerry was good to his word, too. He left me alone and kept the lights on while I made the transition from dancing to modeling. I never asked for his help, although I do think now that he whispered my name in a few ears. He had that kind of influence."

"So when did you get together?" Daisy asked.

Carol grinned, blushing. "Not for almost another two years. It really started as a publicity stunt. My career was just starting to make waves and I, in my youthful impatience, was looking for a way to put it over the top. So I talked Kerry into taking me to the Grammy's because he was up for an award. He didn't win but we still had a lot of fun celebrating. We were together from then on and married a year later." Carol's expression turned mournful. "Back then, I thought it meant something."

Carol stared at Daisy admiring her, her long thick blond hair and willowy limbs. She had her mother's deep-set amber eyes and a wide mouth with dimples. But the thing Carol envied most was the girl's youth. "Don't ever make the mistake of tying your happiness to any man. If you aren't happy with yourself and who you are inside, you'll never find happiness with someone else, even someone as great as Kerry."

Daisy nodded, nearly moved to tears. She reached out to rest her hand on Carol's shoulder. Here was the aunt she'd always wanted. It wasn't fair that she had to lose Kerry to gain the woman in front of her now. All Daisy had ever wanted was a loving family. Before Daisy could confess her wish, someone started ringing the doorbell, rapidly, as if in a panic. Carol followed Daisy as she went to the door, stooping to look through the peephole. "It's Jerry."

A look of disdain gathered on Carol's face. "Oh, let the dumb son of a bitch in before the reporters beat him up."

Jerry rushed past Daisy without a word and went straight to Carol's side. "Are you okay? What in the hell happened? Why didn't you call me?"

"I had enough to deal with without you hanging around being a damned nuisance." Carol stepped out of his embrace to drop on the couch. "Why are you here, Jerry?"

"Why do you think? Where the hell is Avery Clark? "

Carol bristled at his tone. A subtlety only Daisy saw. She winced.

"How the fuck am I supposed to know? Go ask the damn cops. The detective I talked too looked like he was about fucking eighty. That fat son of a bitch couldn't catch a turtle. So, I'm not holding out much hope that they'll run across Avery Clark any time soon."

Jerry stared at Carol with a mix of anger and agitation. Daisy decided there was more to it than Carol chiding him.

"The cops think he's hiding in the city somewhere," Daisy said.

Carol snorted, "Yeah, like that helps any."

Jerry paced across the room, stopping to stare at the broken vase next to the hall closet. "This isn't good. We really need to discuss some things." Jerry glanced over at Daisy. "Alone."

"Oh, just go ahead and talk," Carol said. "Daisy already knows how big a pain in the ass you are."

Daisy grinned. She was enjoying being in Carol's good graces. "It's not much of a secret."

Daisy had always thought that Jerry was a buffoon, even when she was a child. He fancied himself a rocker, a scene-maker, and Daisy supposed he was, about forty years ago. But, to his credit, he had helped Kerry take his solo career to the pinnacle of fame. So he wasn't completely useless, just creepy. Jerry ignored her jab and kept pacing around the room. "I'm serious, Carol. This thing with Clark has to be handled."

Before Carol could say anything, Daisy snatched her phone from the coffee table. "It's cool. You all go ahead. I'll go chill in my room. I need to figure out how I'm going to pack it all up anyway."

Daisy headed for the stairs intent on listening from the banister. It was a habit she had cultivated ever since moving in with her aunt. She had received a salacious education over the years from doing so. She wanted to know why Jerry was so jumpy. Something was up.

"So what the hell is wrong with you?" Carol asked. "What are you so damned antsy about?"

Jerry stopped pacing and looked around the room. His gaze followed Daisy's path up the stairs. He moved closer to Carol to keep his voice just above a whisper. "We've got to get to that coffin before the cops do. I stashed damned near a quarter of a million dollars in it."

"You WHAT?"

Daisy couldn't hear a word Jerry said. Carol came through loud and clear.

"Why in the hell would you do that?" Carol asked.

"It's the money I told you I had stashed. There was no way I could transfer it without the cops over there asking a lot of questions. And I sure as hell didn't want the Feds to know, especially now."

Carol glared at Jerry. "So why am I just hearing about this now? Were you planning on keeping it all?"

Daisy inched closer to the edge of the landing. *Keeping what?*

Jerry ran his hand over his shiny bald head. That was the plan. "No," he said. "I wanted it to be a surprise. It was supposed to be a slush fund for us until the estate is settled."

Carol's eyes blazed. "There is no us, Jerry, you stupid motherfucker. There never was. And, now, there's not going to be any estate, either. I just got served divorce papers and a notice of a new will. So, if your plan is to leech off of me, you might want to rethink it."

Jerry sat down on the couch, stunned. "You don't think Kerry knew what we were planning, do you? Christ, Carol, do you think he just let it happen?"

Jerry's words hung in the air as Daisy's mind clamped down on them. They planned this? Daisy's stomach dropped. A wave of nausea hit her like a punch in the gut. She got up slowly, not wanting to be discovered. She crept down the hallway to her bedroom in a daze.

Carol and Jerry Jewell killed Kerry. They had planned it together. Daisy dropped on her bed fighting the urge to hyperventilate. The changes she had seen in Carol earlier, the changes she'd *welcomed*, were evidence of her guilt. The enormity of what she had done was eating at her.

Daisy hoped it ate her alive. She was a monster. Daisy was determined not to spend another second under her aunt's roof. She wasn't safe. If Carol and Jerry knew she'd overheard their conversation they could just as easily kill her, too. Daisy hopped off of her bed racing around the room tossing clothes into her backpack. She climbed out of her bedroom window and shimmied down the drainpipe at the back of the house. As she came out of the alley she pulled the hood of her sweatshirt up over her head and skirted the crew of reporters lingering out in front of the house. She didn't know where she was going. She only knew what she had to do. There was no way in hell Carol and Jerry were going to get away with this.

CHAPTER 12

Avery sat quietly numb in the passenger seat of the hearse watching as the first slim arc of sun illuminated the cloudless sky. It had been a while since he'd been lucid long enough to watch the sunrise. The last time he could remember he had been on the roof of his brownstone crying on Kerry's shoulder. The night after Zoe died. He took a deep breath and pushed the memory aside. Intellectually, he was acutely aware that he should have been able to move on from Zoe's death. That each day shouldn't still carry the burning edge of tears that still lingered just below the surface. As he took in the slow brilliance of another dawn, he could have broken down and cried all over again just like he had that morning on the roof with Kerry. Kerry.... Kerry, whose mortal remains lay restless in the big metal box behind him. The reality of his end was so far beyond reason Avery still couldn't wrap his head around it. He couldn't accept that Kerry was really gone.

Three weeks ago they had been sitting at the bar in Navarro's wasted on a mad torrent of vodka as Kerry propositioned nearly every woman in the room with a ridiculous Russian accent. The two of them caused such a ruckus that the bouncers finally had to escort them out. Then they got into a screaming argument over who was going to foot the bill at the funky little diner just down the street because neither wanted the other to do so. Avery wiped a tear from his eye as he caught a glimpse of his reflection in the window. Whoever was responsible for taking Kerry away from him was going to pay.

"Are you okay, Avery? You've been awfully quiet."

"Huh? Oh, yeah. I'm sorry. I'm just lost in my thoughts." Avery shot Calliope a quick glance before turning his attention back to the horizon. "How far is this place? It's not going to take much to spot us now that the sun's up."

"We're almost there, actually," Calliope said. "It's only about ten more miles."

Avery nodded as he stared out into the distance. "Good. Hopefully, we won't pass any cops before we get there. I bet we're all over the news by now."

Calliope nodded. "Have you checked your phone?"

"No, I can't get a signal out here."

"Well, I guess we'll hear all about it once we get where we're going." Calliope slowed the hearse to turn onto a narrow country road that stretched even further out into nowhere.

"And where exactly is that? It doesn't look like there's much out here." Avery said.

"I don't have much more than an address."

As the sunlight grew around them, all Avery could see were corn and bean fields that seemed to roll on for miles. He found all of the empty space nerve-racking.

"It just seems like a long way to go to switch vehicles," Avery said.

"I agree, but this is the guy Kerry told me to go to. He said we could trust him."

Calliope hadn't shared much information about their trip to Denver. Of course, Avery hadn't asked a lot of questions either. He was just happy to be involved in something that would help Kerry. Now that sobriety had settled over him once again, he hoped he hadn't acted rashly. He just had to take it on faith that Calliope could be trusted.

After another few jarring minutes spent racing across the vastness of the wild Pennsylvania countryside, Calliope finally pulled up in front of an ancient, weathered, white farmhouse. Avery took in the sight of the dilapidated house and the rows of rusted metal buildings lining both sides of the barnyard and started feeling even more uneasy. It didn't look like there had been any kind of farming going on here in quite some time. The place looked like something out of a horror movie. Out across the road, the wind picked up and waved through the tall grass in the fallow field beyond. It was a beautiful landscape but felt bleak somehow in the pale morning light. Avery imagined that living here would have been lonely enough to be depressing. He couldn't see himself thriving in all of this empty space.

"Wait here and don't get out until I call for you. Kerry said this guy can be a little trigger happy."

Avery raised an eyebrow as Calliope pushed open the door. He sat forward in the seat and took a deep breath. "Great."

Calliope was greeted on the porch by a tall, well-muscled, specimen of humanity dressed in camouflage pants and a black tank top. He was bald with a big bushy salt and pepper beard. As the big man looked toward Avery, he could see a smile shining underneath the beard. That, coupled with a wry twinkle in his eyes, put Avery a little more at ease. Of course, it didn't hurt that Calliope was as attractive as she was. Most men probably couldn't help but smile in her presence. Calliope laughed at something the big man said before motioning for Avery to join them. Before Avery could lift the doorknob the door at the back of the hearse was thrown open. He jumped, turning to see four huge, gnarly-looking, biker types removing the coffin. Avery climbed out of the hearse and watched as they shouldered the coffin. He noticed that all of the men wore pistols strapped to their hips. Avery didn't know a lot about Pennsylvania country boys but it wasn't exactly a welcoming party.

"Avery, I want you to meet Daniel Martin. Dan this is Avery Clark." Avery reached out to shake hands. Dan's hands were massive, but his grip wasn't overpowering. Avery saw a sharp intelligence in his eyes. He was no mere brute. But, he was intimidating.

"It's nice to meet you, Avery. Kerry spoke highly of you."

Avery smiled. "It's nice to meet you, too. How did you know Kerry?"

"We grew up together," Dan said. "I was in Kerry's first garage band."

"Oh, no kidding? What do you play?"

"I used to play around on the drums. I was never very good at it, though."

Avery didn't think there was a drum kit on Earth that could stand up to this guy beating on them. "So you didn't run off to California with Kerry?"

"No. Kerry and Mark were the real musicians. I joined the Marine Corps right after high school."

"Mark?" Avery asked. "I don't think I ever heard Kerry mention him."

A grim look crossed Dan's face. "I guess I'm not surprised. Mark was Kerry's younger brother."

Avery looked at Calliope. She looked like she was about to cry. "What happened?" Avery asked. "Did they not get along?"

Dan looked past Avery, out across the field. "C'mon, let's go inside."

The interior of the farmhouse stood in stark contrast to its rugged exterior. It was well-appointed with ornate scrollwork bordering the walls and staircase. The living room was furnished with large, overstuffed, black leather couches and recliners, a logical choice given the size of the men who occupied them. There were three large TV's resting on and mounted above the huge entertainment center at the front of the living room. Below them rested an older component stereo that was jacked into four large PA speakers situated in the corners of the room. The stereo, when cranked up, could produce the raw decibels of a rock concert. Now, it was turned low to talk radio on an AM station.

Dan motioned them toward one of the couches then sat in the chair at the center of the room. He rubbed his hand over his beard as he gathered himself to talk. "Everyone knows the story about how Kerry moved to LA and got the gig singing for Zephyr. But, originally, Mark and Kerry were set to move there together. Their parents made Mark stay until he graduated high school. They weren't convinced that either of them had the talent to become professional musicians. They hoped that by asking the boys to wait a couple of years before leaving that they would change their minds and stay closer to home."

"During the two years between Kerry and Mark's graduations, though, the two of them saved money like mad for the trip. Kerry worked full time at a junkyard crawling in the mud to pull car parts and Mark worked after school as a stock boy at the supermarket. On weekends the band played every school dance and backyard party in the county. We had a lot of fun."

Dan smiled as the memories flooded back. "About a month before they were set to take off we played a huge graduation party. There were kids from at least ten different schools. It was going to be the band's last hurrah. I was reporting to Parris Island in August and Randy Green, our bass player, was starting college that fall."

"Anyway, after the party we were all shit-faced. Kerry was the worst. He was absolutely polluted, heartbroken over some married chick he'd been involved with. Mark decided to drive them both home in Kerry's car."

Dan looked away, out through the window to the right of his chair. "They didn't make it. Mark ran off the road and hit a tree a couple of miles from the party. He was killed instantly. Kerry was thrown from the car as they left the road. He walked away with barely a scratch."

"After Mark's funeral, Kerry disappeared without a word to anyone. He just vanished. His parents were so worried that they finally resorted to hiring a private detective to track him down." Dan looked at Avery and shook his head. "He eventually went on to L. A. but there was about a year there that I don't know anything about. I never could get Kerry to talk about it, either."

Avery stared at the big man like he had just punched him in the gut. Kerry never talked about himself much and now Avery was starting to understand why. There had been a lot of pain hiding below the surface.

He turned to find Calliope staring off into space. Her expression was haunting. The news had come as quite a shock to her, too. Avery was curious about the nature of her relationship with Kerry but was afraid to ask. There'd be more than enough time for that later. They still had a long way to go.

"Are you okay, ma'am?" Dan asked.

Calliope looked up slowly. "Yeah, I'm fine, just trying to process all of this."

Dan rose from the chair. "It's a lot to take in, I know. Look, you all just sit back and relax for a bit. I'll go and get some coffee."

Calliope looked up at the big man and smiled. "Thank you. Hey, do you mind if we turn on the T.V.? We need to take a minute to see what we're up against. I have a feeling there might be something about us on there."

A smile emerged beneath Dan's beard. "Sure. The remote for the big TV is on the table there in front of you."

It only took a single flip of the switch to find coverage. All of the major news organizations were running full-tilt with the story. Avery was taken by surprise when he saw surveillance footage of himself standing next to the old man out in front of the hearse. He'd have never guessed there'd be cameras out in that part of town. There really wasn't anything there to look at. Even more curious was Calliope's absence. They had omitted her entirely.

50

The focus was entirely on him. They even went as far as to dig up a few of his old mugshots while reporting a near libelous account of his career. It was galling.

"Well, it looks like they think I've pulled this caper off all by myself," Avery said.

Calliope frowned turning the volume down with the remote. "Yeah, what's up with that? If that surveillance camera saw you it had to have seen me too."

"I'd say they have plenty of pictures of both of you," Dan said, returning with a decanter of coffee and mugs on a sterling tray. "The cops do that shit all of the time. It's a way to weed out the crazies. They can test whomever they're dealing with to see if they're legit."

Avery nodded. "It makes sense. I've used something similar in one of my books. It's just different when they're doing it to you."

"At least we have one thing going for us," Calliope said. "They think we're still hiding in the city somewhere. That gives us a healthy head start."

Dan shook his head as he poured the coffee for his guests. "I wouldn't trust that, either. They have cameras on every route in and out of Manhattan. They have since 9/11. It may take them a while to dig through the footage but they'll find your path out, eventually."

"Well, hopefully, we're a few hours ahead of them," Calliope said. "Now that we have a new vehicle, we'll just have to make sure we press our advantage."

Dan nodded as he handed Calliope a cup. "True. You should be good to go here in a few minutes. As much as I like having pleasant company about, I wouldn't linger long."

Calliope nodded. "As soon as it's ready, we're out. I want to make Cincinnati by dusk."

"Cincinnati?" Dan looked up from his mug and frowned. "That's a bit out of your way, isn't it?"

"I have a few things Kerry wanted me to take care of down that way," Calliope said. "Plus I think it might be better if we stayed away from the obvious route. I mean who in their right mind would think to look for us there?"

Dan let out a big hearty laugh. "True."

Avery took in the new information silently and wondered about Kerry's business in Ohio. He took a few slow sips of his coffee trying to recall what he knew about Cincinnati. Just then, one of the gnarly-looking guys who'd removed Kerry's coffin from the hearse came in through a back room and called Dan over to the doorway. As grateful as Avery was for Dan's help in getting Kerry home, he couldn't help being curious about the big man's set-up out here in the boonies. The place had a weird vibe. It seemed more like a biker's compound or a militia headquarters than an actual home. Not that it mattered. But Avery really didn't feel at ease here.

Avery and Calliope both turned to watch as Dan's conversation with the gnarly guy grew heated.

"No, we're not, goddamn it. You just go get the shit ready and let me worry about it."

The gnarly guy slunk away with a sour expression as Dan came back in the room. It wasn't hard to tell who was in charge, but at that moment, the gnarly guy didn't exactly seem enthused with the pecking order. The dynamic set Avery on edge.

Dan sat down with an expression like he couldn't decide whether to be pissed-off or amused. Avery kept a close eye on him in case it was the former.

"Well, folks, it looks like we've got a bit of business to discuss. Did either of you know that there's about two hundred grand in cash stashed in Kerry's casket?"

"What?" Calliope sat her coffee mug on the table. "Where the hell did that come from?"

Dan stared at her as she looked on agog. "You tell me."

"I don't have a clue." Calliope returned Dan's gaze, recognizing his suspicion. "Look, man, I'm telling the truth. We haven't touched it. Whatever is in there has been with him since he left England."

Avery and Calliope exchanged glances. "Jerry."

Dan looked from one to the other. "Who?"

"Jerry Jewell, Kerry's manager," Calliope said. "We think that he had something to do with Kerry overdosing."

Avery frowned. "I think that motherfucker had everything to do with Kerry overdosing. I bet he knew that Kerry was going to leave Carol. Kerry was suspicious of them. Why else would he plan all of this?"

"The cancer?"

Calliope and Avery stopped cold and stared at Dan. "What cancer?" Avery asked. "He never said anything about having cancer."

Dan glanced at both of them and shook his head. "Christ, he really didn't tell you people anything, did he? Kerry was diagnosed with liver cancer about three months ago. He called me right after he got the diagnosis. I went and met him in the city so we could talk."

Avery stared at Calliope. He wanted to believe that Kerry hadn't told him in order to keep him from worrying. Or perhaps Kerry wanted to protect himself from being treated like an invalid. But, after everything he'd heard today, he had to wonder if Kerry considered him as good a friend as Avery viewed him. It was a troubling thought but it may have very well been true.

Dan stroked his beard and let out a deep sigh before speaking again. "Kerry told me then that he was leaving Carol. But I don't think he knew about an affair. If he did, he didn't say anything. I think he set all of this up to make sure he would get home in case he passed before the divorce was final. It was plain that he didn't trust Carol to abide by his wishes. When I heard that he overdosed over in England I just figured the pain got to be too much for him. Now I'm starting to wonder."

"Bloody hell," Avery said. He rubbed his eyes as a tension headache built behind them. "I just can't see Kerry giving up like that especially turning to heroin. He's railed against heroin as long as I've known him. But I don't know man. Fuck. None of this makes any sense."

"Well, whatever happened, somebody saw it as an opportunity to smuggle money into the country," Calliope said. "Jerry Jewell is the only logical choice."

Avery nodded. "The question is; How far is that snake willing to go to get it back?"

"It doesn't matter," Calliope said. "Once we get to Denver, the truth of all of this will be out in the open. If Jerry Jewell has any sense at all he'll be looking for a place to hide."

Avery lifted an eyebrow. "Yeah, well, I don't credit him with that much sense. So we better keep an eye open just in case."

"You sure you don't want me to send one of my guys along?" Dan asked.

Avery wasn't crazy about the prospect of driving across the country with one of the gnarly-looking dudes in tow but held his tongue as Calliope shook her head.

"We'll be fine," she said. "I have a few tricks up my sleeve."

Dan smiled as he led them toward the door. "Yeah, I bet you do. So what do you want to do about the money?"

Calliope shook her head as she considered it. "Well, if it is Jerry Jewell's I don't mind giving some away. Take what you need, Dan, for setting us up."

"No way, man, I don't want any part of it. If this Jewell character did have something to do with Kerry's death, I think it'd best be used as evidence. If not, you could always donate it to charity or something in Kerry's name."

Calliope's eyes lit up. "That's a fantastic idea. I'll keep that in mind."

Dan beamed as Calliope wrapped him up in a hug. "Well, if you two do need anything, don't hesitate to call me. I'll get someone to you as quickly as I can."

"Thanks, Dan," Avery said. "You don't know how much we appreciate it."

Dan shook Avery's hand as a tear formed in his eye. "Just get my boy home, Mr. Clark. Set him to his rest."

CHAPTER 13

Sarah brought her car to a jarring stop in front of her mother's place still reeling from the news on the radio; someone had stolen Kerry's body. How in the hell could someone just steal Kerry's body? The news didn't seem to have a firm handle on the situation just yet. But it sounded to her like somebody planned it. It was just too bizarre to have happened otherwise. Who in their right mind would car-jack a loaded hearse? Sarah's heart went out to Kerry's widow. The poor woman had to have been going through hell. She couldn't imagine what it was like having to go through all of this exposed in the public eye. It couldn't have been easy. Kerry had asked that she and her mother attend his funeral. Now it looked like that wasn't going to happen anytime soon. Sarah looked along the path leading up to the front porch. Perhaps it was better this way. She would probably need the extra time to convince her mother to go. But, come hell, high water, an earthquake or asteroids, Melinda was going to be there even if Sarah had to hogtie her to do it.

Sarah took a deep breath as she opened the car door. She didn't want to fight. Though she was sure that was exactly what was going to happen. Her mother had never been the easiest person in the world to deal with. As Sarah started up the porch steps the front door opened. Her mother stood leaning against the jam with a bemused expression.

"I was starting to wonder if you were going to get out of the car."

Sarah shrugged. "I was listening to something on the radio."

Her mother lifted an eyebrow before turning out of the doorway. She walked back into the house without a word.

Sarah looked skyward shaking her head. "Hi, Mom, it's good to see you, too."

She followed her mother to the kitchen where a cup of coffee and a cigarette sat awaiting her return. The morning paper was still rolled up in its orange plastic wrapper on the table beside a bouquet of fresh-cut lilies from the garden.

Melinda sat down pushing the chair beside her out with her foot. She took a long drag off of her cigarette before crushing it out. Sarah sat down with a wan expression looking around the room. She looked at her mother and smiled trying to gauge how best to start.

"You might as well say your piece, Sarah. You didn't drive all the way out here to admire the kitchen."

"So I take it you heard what happened," Sarah said. "I hoped you weren't ignoring me on general principles."

Melinda frowned. "You'd have to be living on another planet not to hear about it. It's been all over the news for days. And I wasn't ignoring you, young lady. I had stuff going on."

"Really?"

Melinda picked up her coffee cup from the table. She stared off into space for the briefest of moments. "What do you want me to say, Sarah? That I was sad? Well, OK, I was. I needed time to process it. It's brought up a lot of things that I didn't want to deal with, like the conversation we're having now."

"Well, I'm sorry, Mom. But you know damn good and well we should have had this conversation long before now."

Melinda got up from the table with her coffee cup in hand. She crossed over to the counter, shaking her head. As she sat her cup down, she dropped her head and sighed. "I know, baby girl, and I'm sorry."

Sarah stared at her mother as she poured another cup of coffee. She could see the pain lingering in her eyes. Whatever had happened between Kerry and her had left one hell of a scar.

Melinda was the strongest woman Sarah had ever known. Here she was just a few weeks shy of her sixty-first birthday and she still looked more like Sarah's sister than her mother. She still pulled forty plus hours at the power plant and still found time to volunteer at one of the local hospitals. The woman was a dynamo.

Sarah often felt overwhelmed by her example.

"So what happened, Mom? I need to know everything."

Melinda smirked as she sat back down at the table. She took a long sip of her coffee then fidgeted with the cup after returning it to the table. "You don't need to know everything. But you do deserve some answers."

Sarah reached out and rested her hand atop her mother's smiling as tears formed in her eyes. "Tell me."

Melinda pursed her lips. She stared out across the kitchen for several seconds as she gathered the words. When she spoke, she focused her gaze outside toward her garden.

"I fell in love with Kerry Vance when I was 10 years old. His family lived behind ours on another street and our back yards bordered each other. Back then our neighborhood was packed with kids. There were ten or twelve kids on our block alone and all of us were roughly the same age. Most of the time the boys all gathered in Kerry and Mark's back yard. There was always a baseball game or a football game going on. It was always loud and boisterous and Kerry was always at the center of it. He was a natural leader. The boys all looked up to him. One day your Aunt Karen and I were sitting out watching the boys play baseball when I got hit in the head by a foul ball. It knocked me out cold. The next thing I remember I woke up in Kerry's arms as he was carrying me into the house. I looked up to find myself staring into those deep blue eyes and, even though my head was pounding, I just felt safe, like that's where I belonged. Kerry came to my house every afternoon for a week after that to make sure I was feeling better. I was smitten with him from then on."

Sarah smiled, taken with the memory and the soft expression on Melinda's face.

"It was a lot later. After I started high school before we actually dated. It really wasn't anything serious though, at least for him. A lot of the girls in school swooned over him especially after he and Mark started the band. He had a lot of options to explore and, trust me, he did. It drove me crazy. It wasn't until after I graduated that things changed. By then I was already engaged to Ken. Ken and I had been together for the better part of a year by the time we graduated. Our future was pretty much laid out for us. Ken's dad had jobs waiting for both of us at the car lot. He had a rental property ready for us to move in to. It was stable. It was what I thought I wanted. I knew by then that Kerry was just too wild. Deep down, I knew he was destined for greater things. He was always busy with the band. After he graduated, I hardly ever saw him. Then one night I saw him at the movie theater. I went out by myself that night because I was pissed off at Ken. Back then Ken spent a lot of time out running around with his dumbass friends. We had made plans to go to the movies together. But, at the last minute, he bailed on me because he just had to go work on Bobby Blake's piece of shit Ranchero. It was really an excuse to hang around and watch Bobby work on his own car while he and his friends stood around drinking beer and talking shit. I was beyond livid. So there was Kerry, larger than life. He had on black leather jeans and a white Nehru shirt. He looked just like Jim Morrison. He looked like a rock star, even then. When he saw me his eyes just lit up. An actual chill went up my spine when I caught him staring at me. So, he walked over, looking around for Ken. *'Where's our fiancé tonight?'* And, God help me, Sarah, I was so mad and Kerry just looked so goddamned good I just shrugged and said, *'Who cares?'*

Sarah stared at Melinda doing her best not to react. She didn't want to interrupt.

"Kerry and I started seeing each other behind Ken's back. And Ken, being the way he was, gave us plenty of opportunities. I knew that I should have broken up with him. I should have done the right thing and called off the engagement. But that would have meant moving back home. It would have meant losing my job. And, worst of all, it would have meant that all of the wagging tongues around here would have kicked into overdrive at the scandal. I couldn't deal with it. I knew I couldn't count on Kerry. He and Mark were already planning their move to California. The last thing they needed was me being the third wheel. So I just enjoyed our time together because I knew, eventually, it was going to end. It needed to end. I loved Kerry but even if he had stayed, we couldn't have gone on like we were."

"But then you got pregnant with me?" Sarah said.

Melinda nodded, pausing to take a sip of coffee. The look in her eye seemed haunted for the space of a breath before she turned to Sarah and smiled. "And believe me, honey, I don't regret it. Not for a second. You're the best thing that's ever happened to me. But that's not to say we didn't get off to a hell of a start."

"What happened?"

"Well, when 1 first found out, 1 freaked. It happened just about a week before Ken and 1 got married. You see, 1 knew it wasn't his. Ken was sterile from a bad bout with the mumps when he was a kid. We had discussed maybe adopting at some point but we were so young it was far from being a priority. We just wanted to be out on our own, to be in control. 1 had no illusions about how Ken was but 1 thought 1 could live with it. 1 thought he would change. 1 hid it, from both of them. 1 didn't know what else to do. 1 didn't tell Kerry because 1 didn't want to stand in the way of his dream. He was far too talented to get stuck in Arvada raising a kid. And 1 knew when Ken found out that it was going to be a mess. The only person 1 told was Anna."

A wave of sadness overtook Sarah at the mention of Anna's name. After all these years she was still ashamed over the trouble she'd caused. "1 miss Anna."

Melinda reached over and patted Sarah's hand. "1 know. 1 miss her too. 1 do know that she lives over in Utah somewhere. Somebody told me she married a rancher out there."

"We should try to get in touch with her."

"No. 1 don't think that's a good idea." Melinda removed her hand from Sarah's to grab a cigarette. "1 could never apologize enough for what 1 did to her. I'm just glad to hear that she's happy. Everything else is best left in the past."

"That seems to be a theme with you." Sarah blurted out the words before she had a chance to measure them. But she realized she didn't regret it, either. It was absolutely true. Sarah was surprised when her mother laughed. It was nice to see the smile on her face.

"Yeah, 1 suppose that's true. But seriously, Sarah, 1 did it to protect you. You were my priority."

"And you were heartbroken. 1 don't think 1 fully appreciated that until now. So how did Kerry find out about me?"

Melinda arched an eyebrow. "How do you know he did?"

"1 didn't. 1 grew up hoping he didn't. It was easier for me believing that Kerry hadn't chosen his career over me. But when that Calliope woman called me the other day, I found out that he knew about me before I was born. I just need to know how it all went down."

Melinda scowled. "Calliope called you? When?"

Sarah took a deep breath. "A few days after Kerry died. She's helping handle Kerry's affairs. She called me to tell that Kerry had named me in his will and asked if we would come to the funeral."

Melinda's scowl deepened. The expression made her look her age. It also made Sarah extremely uneasy. "What the hell is she doing involved in this?"

"I don't know, Mom. All I can tell you is what she said. How do you know her?"

"Let's just say we've crossed paths."

"C'mon, Mom, what are you not telling me? You said it yourself. I deserve answers. So just come off of it, please."

"Calliope is the reason Kerry was never involved in your life. That woman is trouble. I don't want anything to do with her. I don't think you should either."

Sarah shook her head. She knew this had been too easy. "C'mon, mom, all of that happened over forty years ago. It seems to me that she's trying to make amends. Maybe Kerry was going to reach out to me. Maybe he died before he had a chance to do it. I don't know. Look, you can do whatever you want. I'm going to get to the truth of this one way or the other. I'd prefer to have your help. We have a lot of hurt to navigate."

Melinda stared at Sarah. She couldn't begin to guess what was going through her mother's mind. She was happy that she had gotten as much out of her as she did. But they still had a long way to go.

"You're right," Melinda said. "We do. It's time to put all of this to rest."

CHAPTER 14

Avery sat quietly, dead sober and shaking, watching as the last fiery arc of sunlight dipped below the slow horizon. Its absence left a breathtaking wash of violet and gold flowing low across the sky. It stirred hope in him that his first day on the run would soon be at an end. He needed a stiff drink and a soft place to crash. Avery had no poetry left in him. The past twenty-four hours had whizzed by in a blur. His mind kept going back to the host of secrets Kerry never bothered to share. Why did Kerry not tell him he had cancer? As Avery fought against the shakes that seemed to emanate from his very damned bones, he realized that the answer was staring him in the face.

Kerry thought he was weak.

It was a bitter pill to swallow. He had let his passion for life follow Zoe to the grave. Kerry tried to help him but must have decided that he was a lost cause. That thought hurt the most. Kerry had lost respect for him. Kerry did trust him enough to try and pull off this little escapade. So perhaps he wasn't a total loss. He just needed something radical to happen to get his head back in the game.

Avery smiled. This was definitely that. Kerry knew it, too. Across from him, Calliope had a thousand-mile stare locked on the road. Her dark eyes shone with haunting depth as she navigated the rolling length of river valley. Calliope had a presence that was both terrifying and comforting. Avery felt safe with her at the wheel. But he had also quickly learned that it wasn't a good idea to piss her off. As kind as she had been to him, the way she went off on the hearse driver stuck in his mind. Outside the windshield, the lights of Cincinnati grew brighter. Avery took a deep breath trying to dismiss all of his worries as he exhaled. He eased back in the seat and yawned.

"Hey, don't fall asleep over there. We'll be at our first stop in about 20 minutes." Calliope stretched her arms above her head as she came to a stop at a traffic signal. "I don't want to be here any longer than I have to."

"I'm just ready to get out and stretch my damn legs," Avery said. "My ass has been numb for a couple of hours."

Calliope laughed. "Yeah, I'm right there with you."

"So what's on the agenda?" Avery asked.

"The first thing we need to do is find a Mega-Mart. I need to buy a burn phone and let these people know we're in town. We're just here to deliver some old photo albums and band memorabilia to a roadie friend of Kerry's and then drop off a check for 50 grand to some stripper so she can quit her job." Calliope grinned. "No big deal."

Avery let out a long low whistle, "Wow, 50 grand? That must be a hell of a stripper."

Calliope shrugged. "I'm told she used to be. Now she's pushing 40 with a worn-out old ass."

Avery laughed, surprised by Calliope's description. "You paint a hell of a picture."

Calliope reached over pushing Avery's shoulder. "It was in the notes Kerry sent me. He said Jill Emory is to get the money; 'before her old ass gets too worn out to show off anymore'."

"Yeah... that sounds like him. So did he leave a dossier on everyone you're to meet?"

"No, not a dossier, just a few notes to get me in the door, I've already talked to both of them. I'm going to try to get them both to meet us at this Jill chick's strip club so we can knock both of them off the list at the same time."

Avery raised an eyebrow. "Well, now you are speaking my language. It sounds like a great place to unwind."

Calliope rolled her eyes seeing the enthusiasm on Avery's face. "Don't get too wound up there, killer. As I said, we're not going to be there long."

Avery kicked back in the seat. "Yeah, I guess it's just as well. I'd probably be asleep before I could pull off anything, anyway."

"That's good because I don't want to be exposed any longer than necessary. We need to keep a low profile."

Avery yawned shifting around in the seat. "You're right. But at least I can get a quick peek."

After gas, grub, a wholly disturbing bathroom break in a gas station toilet and an exhilarating walk around the local Mega-Mart, Calliope made contact with their quarry. A quick game of phone tag managed to get them all lined-up and headed in the right direction. Then, after a longish jaunt out of the river valley, Calliope finally pulled into the parking lot of their destination; The Red Kitty Saloon. When Avery looked up and saw the faded glory of the gaudy old-school neon sign, he started grinning all over. It was the most gnarly-looking strip club he had ever seen. It reminded him of the old organ-grinder dives on Times Square before Giuliani ran them off.

As they pushed through the door Calliope huffed in derision as she pointed at the slogan over the playbill: *The Red Kitty Saloon; "If your Kitty ain't red, you aren't using it enough."*

Avery laughed, suddenly manic. It seemed he had gained his second wind in anticipation as he paid their cover and strolled inside. The inside of the Red Kitty was the kind of garish neon nightmare that put Avery right at ease. The room was packed. The perverts around him were so rapt with the show that you could have shot any one of them in the head and no one would have known what happened until after the music stopped. Avery took a look along the low catwalk that divided the center of the room. On the pole, a tall brunette, dressed in a white cowgirl outfit, made skillful use of the apparatus. She twirled around the pole effortlessly, spread eagle above the heads of the mesmerized crowd. He counted himself lucky to get in at the start of the show. The woman had skill.

Calliope rolled her eyes as she watched Avery became as entranced with the show as the rest of the zombies around her. She grabbed him by the arm. "Come on and sit with me at the bar. I want you to meet Mr. McGee when he gets here."

Avery turned to gawk at Calliope. "We're meeting Clyde McGee? Suicide Clyde?"

Calliope shrugged, "Yeah. Do you know him?"

"No. But Kerry used to talk about him all of the time. He's a fucking legend. He was a roadie for Buddy Holly." Avery followed Calliope to the bar. "He worked for Kerry for years."

"Oh. Well, I had no idea we were meeting a legend."

Avery noted Calliope's sarcasm. "Well, he is in music circles. Bands used to try and outbid each other to get Clyde to work for them. Kerry once told me he was the best-connected person in the business. He said Clyde could find you anything you wanted in any city you were in."

Calliope was unimpressed. "A must on any tour, I suppose."

Avery shrugged and turned back to the show. There, the brunette, who already had all of her goodies on display, was going buck wild on the pole swinging around like it was an Olympic event. Avery wondered if she hadn't twirled the rest of her clothes off.

"Now this is the place to have a damn meeting. Hey are you, Calliope?"

Avery turned at the sound of the gruff voice. The man approaching them was a sight to behold.

Suicide Clyde McGee was a tall man, at least 6'6", and about as thin as a broom handle. His long course gray hair was pulled back into a braided ponytail that hung down to the waist of his ripped up black denim jeans.

He had on a *Rob Zombie* T-shirt with various necklaces, bracelets, rings, belts, studs, and buckles. Up top, a thin wisp of red dye ran through the center of his long gray goatee which tapered to a devilish point at his chest. He was nearly eighty-five years old and still pure rock-n-roll. Calliope stood to shake his hand. "Yes, sir, I'm Calliope and this is my friend Avery Clark."

Clyde frowned, his wrinkles piling up on his forehead, "The writer? Yeah, I've read your stuff. Kerry said you were a good man."

Avery was humbled. "Wow. Thanks. It's nice to meet you, Clyde. Kerry always said you were the best old dude on the planet."

The old man shook his head, smiling, as he took a seat at the bar. "Well, I'd call him a lying S.O.B. if it weren't wrong to speak ill of the dead." His expression faded as he turned to look toward the door. "So he's really out there, huh, waiting to get back to Colorado?"

"Yes, sir," Avery said.

Clyde tilted his head back as he caught the bartender's eye, "I guess you all don't have liquor here, do you?" He frowned as the bartender shook his head. "Well, give us all a Coke then and don't skimp on the damned ice."

Calliope grabbed her cellphone and slid off the barstool. "I'm going to try to call this Jill chick again. She should have been here already.

"Avery nodded absently watching as Clyde pulled a flask from one of his pockets and knocked back a quick shot. As soon as the bartender sat his soda down in front of him, Clyde poured a healthy dose of it into his glass, too. Then, without asking, poured a generous shot into Avery's glass as well.

"Bourbon," Clyde said. "I hate to drink alone."

Avery winked at the bartender who pretended not to notice the flask. "Well, hell, thanks, Clyde. I've been waiting for one of these all day."

Clyde nodded, lifting his glass as Avery hastened to meet it, "To Kerry. I hope all of the crazy shit you went through on this planet was worthy of the ride, little buddy. I'll miss you."

Avery bowed his head.

Clyde drained the 12-ounce plastic cup like it was a shot glass. He slammed it down on the bar and pointed from the bartender to his glass. As soon as he had the bartender's attention, he turned to look Avery in the eye. "It's a goddamn shame that boy thought junk was the only option he had available. I don't understand any of this Mr. Clark. I really fucking don't."

"Well, I'll be honest with you, Clyde. I don't buy it." Avery slugged back a good portion of his drink. "Kerry never would have touched that shit. Somebody did this to him."

The sudden scowl on Clyde's face was menacing. "You think somebody murdered him?"

"I do," Avery said. "And I'm pretty damn sure I know who it was."

Clyde's eyes narrowed, "Carol?"

"She was in on it, but Jerry Jewell was the one in London with him."

Clyde erupted nearly knocking his cup off of the bar. "Jewell, that son of a bitch, I told Kerry not to sign with that motherfucker. I'll kill that prick bastard with my bare hands if I find out he had anything to do with this."

"Jerry and Carol were having an affair. I think Kerry planned the divorce and changed the will because he was ready to give it all up and go back to Denver for cancer treatment. I think Jerry and Carol wanted him to go out in a blaze of glory so they could capitalize on his legacy."

Clyde shook his head, disgusted. "That's the dirtiest damn thing I've ever heard, Clark."

"Please, call me Avery," he said, motioning to the bartender for a repeat. "At least Kerry had time to plan all of this in case something went wrong. The only thing that gives me any solace is knowing that when Carol finds out about this new will, she's going to know she's fucked."

"Man, that is some fucked up shit," Clyde said doctoring their drinks again. "That's the kind of shit that boy always had to deal with. There was always someone trying to screw him over."

Calliope appeared reclaiming her barstool. A pensive expression overtook her as she looked at Clyde. "Kerry?"

Clyde nodded, his eyes cast to the bottom of his cup. "Yes, ma'am. I've known Kerry for over 40 years. His life was always chaotic. The only time that man had any peace at all was when he was on stage."

Calliope nodded slowly. The pain in her eyes was obvious. Whatever her connection was to Kerry, Avery could see that it was true. In the grand scheme of things that was all he really needed to know.

"So what's the deal with our stripper?" Avery asked.

"She's on her way." Calliope said, arching an eyebrow "She's having a bad day."

"She's about to get fifty grand," Avery said. "How can that be a bad day?"

Calliope chuckled, watching as the crowd tithed the bare goddess set before them. "Just wait, you'll see."

"Fifty grand? Who the hell is getting fifty grand?" Clyde asked.

"This stripper buddy of Kerry's," Avery said. "You don't know her?"

Clyde shrugged. "It's the first I heard about it." He smiled, stroking his beard. "Doesn't surprise me though, there's probably a dozen more of them stashed around the country."

"Yeah, well, I only have stuff for two more people. So if there are more of them out there, they're out of luck." Calliope said.

Avery was just getting steady after his fourth boost from Clyde's flask when he heard someone burst into the room behind him.

The tone of the voice stopped him cold. "You're fucking A right, fat boy. You're never going to see me in life again. How's that grab you?"

The woman's whiskey-laced voice raised the hair on Avery's neck.

"There she is," Calliope said. "It's about damned time."

In the slow shadow of the club's black-light reality, the woman Avery saw was flawless. She was tall, long-stemmed, with raven black hair and soulful dark eyes. Avery stared like a concupiscent fool as she walked toward the bar. When she caught him staring, she smiled, stopping at the corner of the bar between him and Calliope.

"You're Calliope, right?" The woman reached out to shake hands. "It's nice to put a face to the voice on the phone. I'm Jill."

"It's nice to meet you," Calliope said. "This is Clyde and that's Avery there behind you."

Jill nodded to Clyde, "Nice to meet you, sir." When she turned to Avery she looked him over from head to toe then paused to stare him dead in the eye. She turned back to Calliope tilting her head in his direction, "Yours?"

Calliope laughed. "Nope, he's a free agent."

Jill turned back to Avery and winked. "Good to know."

"So if you're ready, Jill, I have your check out in the van. I didn't want to carry it around with me."

"Well hell yeah, honey, let's get the fuck out of here," Jill said. "I'm sick of looking at this place."

"Hold up a second," Clyde said. He leaned in close to Calliope. "Homeboy up in the box office there just slid out and said something to the bouncers after Jill came in. We may have trouble getting out of here."

"Don't worry about it," Calliope said. "Those meatballs aren't keeping me from leaving."

Avery couldn't hear their conversation as the music ramped up for the next act. But the look of surprise on Clyde's face was apparent.

Calliope caught up to Avery as they headed for the door. "We might have trouble. Be ready to move."

As Avery considered her statement the bouncers sitting on either side of the door stood up and blocked Jill's way. She didn't take it well.

"Get the fuck out of my way, boys. I'm not taking any more shit off of that fat son of a bitch and if you had any sense you wouldn't either. Now move!"

The pair didn't budge.

"Not until you pay the boss, Jill." The smaller of the two, a long-haired, wild-looking, Samoan cat kept his cool and spoke calmly. Jill didn't.

"I don't owe that motherfucker shit. He's just trying to con me because he knows he's going to lose his ass when I'm gone." Jill stood on her tiptoes leaning against the bouncers to scream into the hallway. "Why don't you haul your fat ass out of that box office and do your own dirty work, Bill. I'm not giving you a damn dime. Do you hear me?"

Avery heard Clyde chuckle beside him. He glanced back at Avery and shook his head. "I'm glad I stuck around. I haven't seen this much action in years."

Avery scowled. He wasn't as enamored with the situation. Then, sure enough, out of the box-office came Bill. He was a short, sweaty, chunk of a man, nearly as round as he was tall. He rounded the corner, livid. He pushed past the bouncers to jump right in Jill's face. "Listen, you ungrateful bitch..."

As soon as Bill reached out to grab Jill, Calliope rushed past her in a blur. With one deft move she grabbed Bill's arm then whirled away out of reach of the bouncers. When they came to a stop, Calliope had a ten-inch dagger slid up under the arm she had wrapped around Bill's neck pointed right at his throat. It happened so fast Avery thought he was hallucinating.

"Alright, this is how it's going to be, folks. I am in no mood for a bunch of silly shit. I'm tired and I want to go to sleep. So, first off, you security guys are going to back the hell off and go lay down on the floor. Then, Jill, you are going to keep your big mouth shut and walk out of that door." Calliope squeezed even harder on Bill's chokehold. His face reddened to a sickening shade of crimson. "And you, Mr. Funny Fat Man, if you think Jill owes you money then go hire a fucking lawyer."

Avery stood with his jaw dropped open as the bouncers held up their arms and backed away. All noise in the club ceased as everyone stopped and stared. Avery looked around to see that Clyde had produced a snub-nosed pistol from somewhere and had it aimed at the bouncers. The old man had a big shit-eating grin on his face.

"Alright, you heard the lady. Let's get this show on the road."

The two groups slowly revolved around each other until the four of them had their backs toward the door. Calliope released her grip on Bill then shoved him down beside the bouncers. She held up the dagger and waved it over the crowd. "If anyone sticks their head out of this door in the next five minutes, they're going to find themselves having a really bad day."

Clyde covered their retreat as they pushed their way through the door. Jill and Clyde followed Avery to the passenger side of the van as Calliope ignited the engine. She pulled out of the parking lot gingerly then, after clearing the scene, stepped on the gas to move out. Avery lay back in his seat taking a series of deep breaths to try and get his heart out of his throat. It was, without a doubt, the craziest thing he'd ever been through. Now that they were out of it, he felt electrified. He glanced over at Calliope amazed as they disappeared into the night. "So much for keeping a low profile, huh?"

CHAPTER 15

The ungodly cacophony of a screaming heavy metal band assaulted Jimmy's ears as he pushed his way into the secluded underground club down in the Bowery. On stage, a mountain of angry man advocated extreme violence in a grating guttural rasp delivered from behind a big bushy multi-colored beard. His voice reminded Jimmy of Froggy from the Little Rascals. After the image struck him the singer's calls for bloody revolution didn't quite pack the same punch.

Jimmy made his way through the tattooed mob to an empty stool at the end of the bar. He looked carefully out over the crowd but didn't see Glenny Ewes anywhere among them. He should have been easy to spot. Glenny had a penchant for dressing extravagantly. Plus, he was thirty years older than everyone else in the room.

Communication with the bartender proved tedious as the assault from Froggy and company raged on. Jimmy pulled a pen from his blazer pocket and wrote on a napkin. "*Do you know Glenny Ewes? Is he here?*"

The bartender nodded, smiling. He picked up the pen and flipped the napkin over. "*Booths over on the far wall, halfway down. Can't miss him.*"

Jimmy winked dropping a twenty on the bar before pushing back through the crowd. Thankfully, Froggy announced that the band was taking a break. The crowd started moving toward the bar leaving Jimmy room to maneuver. As soon as he got close to the booths, he spotted Glenny. He was resplendent in a powder blue suit with a checked shirt and wide corduroy tie. Jimmy smiled. Glenny seemed even more incongruous to the room than he did. Of Avery's coterie of colorful friends, he liked Glenny the most. The poet had a wicked sense of humor and charming old-school manners.

He just had shitty taste in music. If anyone knew the workings of Kerry's inner circle it was him. He had been on the scene since the beginning.

As soon as Glenny saw him, he stood letting Jimmy slide into the booth next to a tall exotic redhead wrapped entirely in red latex. As she turned to regard him Jimmy noticed that she had the word *Lust* tattooed on the right side of her neck.

"Jimmy, I was surprised to receive your call. I figured you'd be out chasing Avery down with the rest of the NYPD."

Jimmy took another good long look at the redhead, who winked at him, before turning to engage Glenny. "I was put on paid leave. I was with Avery right before all of this shit went down. They're afraid of bad publicity."

"I heard things got heated at Kerry's memorial. I assume you were the officer who escorted him out?"

Jimmy nodded. "I went with him. I had to jump in before Carol's security detail used him for a punching bag."

Glenny shook his head before taking a long swig of the neon pink cocktail in front of him. "So he goes out and steals Kerry's body in retaliation? That's not our dear Avery."

Jimmy let out a long sigh watching Froggy haul himself down from the stage. "No, it's not. None of it makes a damned bit of sense. That's why I called you. Avery had a woman with him when Kerry's body was taken. She's a tall, absolutely gorgeous, brunette with a Greek or eastern Mediterranean look. I wondered if it wasn't someone connected to Kerry, a vengeful girlfriend or something. You knew him better than I did."

Glenny smiled. "Well, now, I suppose Kerry had more than a few vengeful women scattered around the country but no one local that I'm aware of, none that he or Avery ever mentioned. How come I didn't hear about this woman on the news?"

"Strategy. It helps weed out the kooks on the tip lines. When I was at the precinct, I got the impression they hadn't identified her." Jimmy looked at his watch. "They probably have by now."

"But you would like to know too," Glenny said.

"I would," Jimmy said. "Carol was served divorce papers when she was at the precinct this morning. I'm wondering if the woman with Avery wasn't the reason for it."

Glenny raised an eyebrow. "I'd say that has more to do with Carol's affair with Jerry Jewell than any of Kerry's extracurricular activities. And, more to the point, I think he did it to protect his business concerns more than any big jealousy issues over Carol."

Jimmy nodded slowly, considering it. "So they are having an affair. You know the reason Avery approached Jewell was that he was looking for more information about Kerry's death. Avery was convinced that Kerry would have never used heroin and that there was more to the story than he was getting."

"He would know better than anyone," Glenny said. "Kerry stayed after him to leave the shit alone, especially after Zoe died. That's why I find the whole thing to be suspicious, too. But, of course, you never know what a person will allow themselves to do when they are facing that kind of pain. It may well have been suicide."

Jimmy stared at Glenny a little lost in the flow. "What kind of pain?"

Glenny's eyes widened as he finished his drink. "Kerry was diagnosed with liver cancer a few months back. Avery didn't know this?"

"Not as far as I know," Jimmy said. "Kerry's death came as quite a shock to him. I really don't think he knew anything was wrong."

Glenny hung his head, shaking it slowly, staring into his empty cup. "I guess I'm not really surprised. Avery's a brilliant man but not the sturdiest of spirit, not after everything he's been through. Kerry probably didn't want to worry him."

"I believe it," Jimmy said. "Avery's been in really bad shape since the anniversary of Zoe's death. To lose Kerry in the space of a year may have well sent him over the edge. I hate to contemplate that but how else could you explain this? It makes absolutely no sense."

Glenny dropped a fifty on the table in front of the redhead sending her off for another round of drinks. "I certainly hope there's more to it than that. Avery's always been impulsive but not to such an extreme degree. Perhaps if you can get a picture of this mystery woman, we can get closer to the center of things. There are plenty of people I can show it to."

Jimmy's expression soured. "That may take a bit of doing. I just can't roll into the precinct and ask for one. But I may be able to call in a favor. If I can get ahold of one, I'll give you a call."

Glenny smiled as Jimmy slid around and out of the booth. "I'll help in any way I can, Jimmy. We can't just leave our boy to the wolves."

Jimmy furrowed his brow noticing Froggy and company heading back toward the stage. It was definitely time to go. "I'll be in touch."

CHAPTER 16

Cori Asteri smiled through the creeping pain in her lower back as she lugged another case of liquor up the stairs to her harried bartenders. Her nightclub was filled to capacity. The dance floor was packed and the booze flowed in torrents. It had taken her a lot of years to attract the A-list clientele she now catered to. Now that she'd found success, she wasn't about to complain about a few sore muscles. Cori handed the case over to one of her bar backs and headed back down to check the levels on the beer taps.

Before she got to the door her head bartender, Lisa, rushed over to stop her. "Hey, Cori, there's somebody here that says he needs to see you. He said it's urgent."

Cori frowned. She could barely hear the girl over the music. "Urgent? Yeah? So what? I'm a little busy here, Lisa. Who is it?"

Lisa leaned in closer to yell in Cori's ear. "Some guy named Harry? I sent him back to your office."

Cori tilted her head back and dropped her shoulders, "Great. That's just what I need."

Lisa pulled Cori into the stairwell shutting the door to baffle the music. "What's the matter? Is he your ex or something? He's pretty hot."

Cori shook her head before wiping sweat from her brow. "Good lord, no. He's family."

Lisa's face brightened, "Oh, no kidding? Cool. Well, when you're done, let him know what time I get off work, would you? I could use a little action."

Cori laughed in spite of herself. "Geez, Lisa, horny are we? Look, do me a favor, go on down there and check the beer taps for me. I'll go see what he wants."

Lisa turned as she dropped down onto the first step. "I'm serious, Cori. I think we had a moment just now. At least give him my number."

Cori rolled her eyes. Lisa had a lot of "moments" especially with gentlemen who looked like they had a little money. "Trust me. You don't need that kind of trouble. Now, go on, get to work, huh? You'll meet someone better in no time."

Lisa stuck her bottom lip out in a fake pout before descending the steps. "If you say so, boss."

Cori walked around the bar to weave her way through the crowd. Harry was the last person she wanted to deal with right now. He was always a downer. But he was also the head of the family. He had kept Cori and her sisters safe for more years than she dared remember. She couldn't just ignore him no matter how much she'd prefer it.

She found Harry sitting behind her desk flipping through her mail. If it would have been anyone else she'd have gone off but when Harry looked up and his dark eyes focused on her she knew better.

"Hey, if you really want to help out you could pay a few of those bills for me."

Harry scowled motioning for her to take the seat across from him. "I don't know why you waste your time with this, Terpsichore. You don't need the money."

Cori grinned. "It's not about the money, Harry. I like to entertain people."

Harry's expression turned grim. "Oh, yes, I'm quite aware. You girls and your thespians and your bards, just like in Athens and Rome, Constantinople, Paris, always chaotic, always wrought with debauchery. Well now, once again, we find ourselves at risk of being exposed and I find myself having to clean up the mess."

Cori frowned. "What in the hell are you talking about?"

"Calliope!" Harry threw her mail down to scatter across the desktop. "Her face is all over the media. You can't tell me you haven't seen it."

Cori sat up in her chair. She knew Calliope was headed for trouble when she walked out of her office that day. She also knew there was no way in hell she'd have been able to talk Calliope out of going, either. Calliope followed her heart sometimes to the exclusion of her common sense. No amount of time was ever going to change that about her.

Cori did her best to stay steady as Harry glared at her. She didn't dare confess to having seen her. "I haven't heard anything. I've been working my ass off around here. I don't even own a television."

Harry didn't believe her. She knew the look.

"I'm serious, Harry. I put in 16 hour days around here. I haven't been out in months. What happened?"

Harry stood then walked around her desk to sit on the corner of it in front of her. "She has stolen the dead body of one of your beloved rock-n-roll singers. She and some third-rate novelist are currently trapesing across the country assaulting anyone that opposes them."

"WHAT?" Cori shouted. She felt her heart drop in her chest. "That's just not possible, Harry. That's insane."

Harry lowered his eyes to stare at the floor. "It is, Cori. It's madness. Unfortunately, it is also true."

Cori rose from her chair to pace around her desk. "So what are you going to do? How can I help?"

"The first thing we need to do is find out where they're going. If I can find her I can extract her from the situation before she's arrested."

Cori stopped pacing and turned to stare at him. "It might not be as easy as all that. There has to be a very good reason why Calliope has done this. It won't be easy to convince her to quit before her task is accomplished. You know how she is."

Harry's eyes flashed. "She will do as she's commanded, Terpsichore. I will not let her misguided obsession with these minstrels endanger the Oikogeneia."

Cori took a step back surprised by Harry's outburst. "Now hold on a second, Harry. Calm down. Let's not get ahead of ourselves here. What makes you think that we risk being exposed?"

Harry took a deep breath then exhaled a long slow sigh in an attempt to keep his anger in check. "You know as well as I do that our identities rest atop a house of cards. If the federal authorities really start digging into Calliope's past in the course of their investigation it won't stand up to scrutiny. All of us will run the risk of being exposed."

"Perhaps as frauds," Cori said. "There's no way they could find out anything else. We've taken far too many precautions to allow that to happen."

"That might have been true in the past but now, with the advent of all of these computers, information is all too easy to come by."

"Yeah, but even so, they'd have to be willing to believe it." Cori grinned. "You know how they are, Harry. They fancy themselves far too clever to believe in something that would upset their place at the top of the food chain."

Harry smirked. "Well, that's certainly true."

"So let's not focus on it. We just need to find Calliope and save her from her better nature again."

Harry ran his hand down his Mephistophelian beard. "You know this is really starting to get old, Cori. Calliope needs to control these impulses."

"Perhaps," Cori said, stopping to stand before him. She rested her hand on his shoulder and looked him in the eye. "But I think that part of her has a lot to do with why you love her so much."

Harry looked away shaking his head slowly. It also had a lot to do with why they could never be together. "Just find her for me, please?"

Cori heard the sadness in Harry's voice. His love for Calliope had tortured him for centuries. She knew full well that Calliope's heart would never be his. She suspected he did, too. Whatever mess Calliope had created for herself Harry would be there to help her just like he always had. And Calliope, from whatever twisted sense of feeling she had for him, would welcome it. Cori had seen it too many times.

"I'll call you as soon as I know something."

CHAPTER 17

Calliope moved with weary urgency as the group filled the limited space inside the van with supplies. After the incident in the club the growing acrimony in the media and the two new passengers bent on accompanying Kerry on his last trip, Calliope decided to move on in one mad dash across the country. Jill's apartment was far enough out of the city to offer a few hours rest and time to get organized before the police rolled in.

Calliope seethed silently, angry over losing her composure with the club owner. She had let the worst part of her nature take over. Her hatred born in the terrified girl lashing out under threat of Harry's berating voice. Her innocence shattered as his bloodlust forced her to the kill. He had broken her heart trying to teach her strength, to survive their life spent on the run. But his methods had earned her contempt as well.

Calliope took a deep breath stopping to look up at the stars.

That had been ages ago in another life when violence was the only currency for survival. Calliope hadn't raised a hand in anger for a very long time. But now, as the chips stacked against them, there was no question of her resolve. She was taking Kerry Vance home and nothing was going to stop her.

Calliope watched Avery and Clyde laughing together as they placed the last of the supplies in the van. She had no doubt that they were both good men. She just wondered how far they'd be willing to go to if things went wrong. She frowned hearing Harry's voice in her ear. That was the way he thought. But Calliope had to admit in times like this, it served.

"All I'm saying is that it should have a name." Clyde placed the last bag neatly on top of the pile at the back of the van. "It is a holy vessel."

"You're right," Calliope said staring at Kerry's coffin. "It is."

Avery nodded in agreement. "So what do you think we should call it, Clyde?"

"The Sonic Temple," Jill said. She looked at Clyde. "The first album Kerry did with Raimey."

Clyde smiled, a deep sadness settling in his eyes. "Raimey Hall, man, talk about a player. Another one partied into an early grave." He looked at Jill and nodded. "That'd be perfect, ma'am."

Calliope kissed her fingers then lay them reverently on Kerry's coffin, "The Sonic Temple, it is."

They stopped and held a moment of silence. As Calliope pushed the doors closed a fine cold mist began to fall. The sky wept with them. Calliope turned to Clyde as they climbed in the van. "When did you first meet Kerry, Clyde? I want to hear that story while I get us moving."

Clyde grinned as he settled in, resting his hand against the coffin. "That, my dear, went down a very long damned time ago. I had just been hired to be the road manager for Zephyr when Kerry came in to audition. The band's first singer, Jarvis Gray, freaked out and joined some acid trip cult up in Oregon just as their first album started making waves. The band was stressed out and fighting. It got to the point where I started putting out feelers for another gig of my own. I didn't think the band was going to make it. But Chip Reed, their manager, lined up a couple of singers to come in to try and help them regain momentum.

"The first guy, I can't remember his name, was horrible. He looked like Glenn Campbell and sang like Ethel fucking Merman. I thought Chip was putting us on. This guy was from the goddamned moon. Then, after a bunch of bitching, pissing and moaning over the first guy, Kerry comes in. Now you have to remember this was 1976. Kerry was only 22 or 23. He was a kid. He had the look but he was green as grass. So the band, being the assholes they were, decided to fuck with him and started playing 'White Rabbit' by *Jefferson Airplane*. That's a hell of a song for a dude to pull off. Kerry didn't even blink, man. He stepped up to that microphone and just fucking killed it. He set that song on its ass. As soon as it was over I told Chip, 'If you don't sign that kid, I'll put together a band for him.' But I didn't have to. The band knew they'd found their voice."

Avery listened intently to Clyde's story. He needed to be writing it down! "Kerry told me once that he never felt at ease around those guys. It sounds like you weren't crazy about them either."

"Yeah, Kerry had a lousy few years with them," Clyde said. "They treated him like hired help. Kenny Carney, their bass player, was the worst. He and Jarvis were best friends. He resented the hell out of Kerry being there. I had to put him in his place more than a few times over Kerry. Ultimately, he was the reason Kerry quit. Right after Kerry beat his ass in the middle of Sound City's parking lot. I quit on the spot and left with him."

"That's awesome," Jill said. "He never told me that story. Kerry was too good for those guys, anyway. I always thought their guitar player sucked."

Clyde smiled. "Yeah, well, he was a big-time rock-n-roll star, you know. He couldn't be bothered to practice. That's why he sells car insurance out in Palo Alto now."

"So you helped Kerry put the Bastards together?" Calliope asked.

"Not really. Kerry found those cats on his own. I just hung out and paid the bar tab. He knew what he wanted. He had it all worked out in his head. His music was magic. It was intrinsic to his nature."

Calliope nodded solemnly. "Yes, it was."

"He was a mystic of the highest order," Clyde said.

Avery was so tired he thought Clyde was having a joke at their expense. "Kerry Vance, a mystic? OK, you've got my attention, Clyde. Tell me that story."

Clyde furrowed his brow. Avery saw the savage intelligence at play in his eyes. The old man had something heavy to convey. When he spoke he had their full attention.

"The medium upon which the whole of creation is based, Mr. Clark, is a harmony, a tonal, musical harmony. It is created from the resonance of the underlying cosmic currents which define the void. It is the matrix of a static universe."

"This resonance, this pulsation, scrambles the matrix to create matter and energy. The essential tone, the frequency which contains the lot of us, is based on a three-beat pulse in the key of C-430. It is the mother of both rhythm and tone."

Avery shot Calliope a quick glance of disbelief. Calliope grinned, shooting him a wink.

"Kerry understood this on a genetic level," Clyde said. "All of the great musicians do. They are born to the task. Unfortunately, from everything thus observed and Kerry notwithstanding, it's a rough life. Creating and performing are the only things that matter. To souls that sensitive and intelligent, everything else is a disappointment. Nothing else rings true."

"That's why Kerry never really stopped to enjoy his success. It wasn't what he was after. It was the freedom of the stage that he needed, it was the music. That was where he escaped into the peace of the Universal tone. Kerry's best grooves are all based on it. That was what set him apart from the beginning, his whacked-out cosmic groove. Nobody had ever heard anything like it."

Clyde smiled but his eyes were awash with tears. He patted the side of Kerry's coffin. "Kerry made a good life for himself, not because of the money, but because of the good he did for others, the man he became. That's why we're all here, isn't it?"

Calliope, Avery, and Jill sat silently for a long time sifting through their own visions of Kerry. The truth was absolute.

"So how did you meet Kerry, Mr. Clark?" Jill asked.

Calliope glanced over from the driver's seat. "Yeah, I want to hear that story, too"

Avery looked around at Jill, grinning, "Please, call me Avery. Mr. Clark was my grandfather." Avery rubbed his eyes with his fingertips as he tried to ignore how insanely attractive Jill really was. "I first met Kerry at a friend's party about 1992, I think. He was a bit beleaguered by the crowd and jittery."

"Probably all the damn cocaine," Clyde said.

"Yeah, well, that's why we were all at the party." Avery grinned. "It was actually a few years later before we became acquainted after a stern exchange at a photography studio."

Calliope raised an eyebrow along with a sly smile. "You two argued? Wow."

"Yeah, and it was Kerry's fault, too." Avery laughed. "See, I was sent to this photography studio for publicity stills right before my second book was released. I had to rush to get there and I was pissed off because I was running late. So I blow into this loft in midtown to find, dead in front of me, a pair of fucking tigers snuggled up against two naked chicks in body paint. Between them was Kerry, sitting on a throne waving a sword around while two guys in the shadows fanned dry ice vapor around the room."

"Ooh...That's the back album cover of 'Transistor,' Jill said. "That was in '96?"

Avery nodded, "Sure was. So, anyway, as soon as I bust in, everything stops dead and everyone turns to glare at me. Kerry jumps up on the throne and points the sword at me, 'What the fuck are you doing here?' And I'm already pissed off from being late, right? So, without thinking, I snap right back, 'I was supposed to be here twenty minutes ago, why the fuck are you still here?' And Kerry starts cracking up laughing at me. So the mood in the room eases and he said, "Alright, let's get this shit wrapped up people. Evidently, this young man has business here."

"Oh my God," Jill said. "That's crazy. So you were standing in the periphery when that shot was taken? That's awesome."

"Well, I'm not sure," Avery said. "They sent me up to the roof with one of the photographer's acolytes to do my shots. Anyway, right before I'm done, Kerry comes up on the roof and waits for me to finish. Someone told him about my book. So he asked me about it and then we talked about literature for a while, our favorite authors. Kerry's knowledge surprised me. We ended up standing there and talking for about half an hour. We just hit it off. Then, right before they hustled him out, he had someone in his entourage give me tickets and backstage passes to his show that night. Zoe and I watched the whole show from the side of the stage."

"At Madison Square? Oh, I wish I could have seen him there," Jill sighed. "I never went to many of his shows. Staying at my place was his asylum from all of that."

"So how did you get hooked up with the old coot, Jill?" Clyde asked. "You're just a baby."

Jill's smile held Avery's attention as she reached over to push Clyde's shoulder. "And you, sir, are full of shit."

Calliope looked up in the rear-view mirror to catch a glimpse of Jill. She was surprised by the sudden wave of jealousy she felt over Jill's time with Kerry. It was petty.

"I first met Kerry when I was thirteen," Jill said, turning to lean back against the side of the van. "I grew up behind the bar of my grandmother's roadhouse."

"No shit?" Clyde said. "Kerry and I have run through quite a few of those. What was the name of it?"

"Nona's, it was on Highway 3 between Venice and East St. Louis," Jill said

"Hell yeah, I remember that place," Clyde grinned. "That was a cool spot to hang."

"The best roadhouse in Illinois," Jill said. "Everybody passed through there at one time or another. I've met a lot of great musicians growing up there. But Kerry was the one that always stood out for me. I was in love with that man since the first time I laid eyes on him."

"Yeah, well, the silly son of a bitch never did have any trouble getting his noodle wet," Clyde said. "The chicks loved him."

"It was nothing but a schoolgirl crush back then," Jill said. "I was just a skinny teenager flipping burgers in my grandmother's kitchen. The first time I remember talking to him he wasn't even in town to perform. He was there hanging out with Maven Kohl."

"Maven Kohl, that crazy motherfucker, I haven't heard his name in years." Clyde shook his head as the memories flooded back. "That was another guitar-playing son of a bitch, right there, and another one gone too goddamned soon."

"My grandmother sure loved him," Jill said. "I think she and Maven had something going on at some point but I never could get the details out of her."

Calliope glanced over at Avery and smiled. Having the two of them along might not be a bad thing. "Did Kerry hang out there a lot?"

"Whenever he was in town," Jill said. "He always bragged about my cooking. He'd drop outrageous tips for me which my grandmother would then sock away. I would always go out and shoot the shit with him if I wasn't busy. He would tell me crazy stories from the road and tell me about the new places he'd been."

Jill ran her fingers through her hair, grinning. "I would pine over that man for days after he left. Not long after that my grandmother got sick and had to sell the roadhouse. I kept up with Kerry's career and hoped one day I would see him again. Then, years later, after I'd married and dumped my dumbass first husband after we moved here to Ohio, I was dancing at a club over in Newport. One night, out of the blue, Kerry walks in with some of his band and a big entourage. I didn't even know he was in town but there he was big as life."

Jill flashed a crooked grin. "He recognized me as soon as he saw me. He started shaking his head and giving me the 'shame, shame' finger gesture before splitting back to the V.I.P. room. When I cornered him later he said he couldn't stay and watch me because I was like a daughter to him. It hurt my feelings a little. But we were solid friends from then on. Whenever he was in town I'd make him a home-cooked meal and have a few drinks."

"He never touched you?" Clyde asked. "That's fucking crazy. Look at you."

Jill erupted with a boisterous laugh. "Well, thank you, Clyde, I appreciate that. But, seriously, Kerry never thought of me that way. I guess he always saw the gawky little girl in pig-tails behind the counter. It used to bother me. But now that he's gone I like it a lot better. I know that I really meant something to him."

Calliope glanced away out of the window as a tear formed in her eye. She regretted letting Kerry get away from her, too. Harry had forced that decision on her. And she had been too frightened to defy him. That had caused her last emotional tie to Harry to be severed. Calliope loathed herself for ever giving in to him. But all that was over now. Kerry was gone. All she could do now was find solace in sharing his memory and get him back to Denver.

Avery reached over and put his hand on her arm. "Are you OK, Calliope?"

Calliope forced back tears as she turned her gaze steady on the road. "I will be, once he's home."

CHAPTER 18

The taste of cheap bourbon burned in Carol's throat as she lay curled up on the couch in front of the television. She choked it down galled that she'd had to resort to buying it when her favorite brand called out from its place on a higher shelf. It had been a very long time since she had to keep such a close eye on her finances. But it was only a temporary inconvenience. She would get what was rightfully hers as soon as she could get into court and contest Kerry's will.

All of Kerry's resources were now tied up in probate leaving her to fend for herself on the accounts in her name alone. It didn't amount to much. If she'd have seen this coming she could have easily padded her own accounts for the battle ahead. Kerry had really managed to blindside her. He had never given a damn about money except for having enough cash in his pocket to drain the contents of a tavern.

What really bothered her was in not knowing where he'd wanted the money to go. Was he leaving it all to his bastard daughter in Denver? Carol didn't know anything about her. Kerry had always been tight-lipped where she was concerned and Carol thought it best not to dig. When riding high on the gravy train it is best not to nibble on the biscuit wheels.

Carol frowned. It was a bullshit copout. The truth was she really didn't care. She knew Kerry hadn't sent the girl a dime in all of the years they had been together, so why sweat it? It was just another of the numerous mysteries that had surrounded the late great Kerry Vance and a minor one as far as she was concerned, until now. Carol took another long swig of the noxious bourbon. She was going to have to be cautious as she maneuvered through the next few weeks. The deck was stacked against her.

Her biggest problem was finding Daisy. The girl's disappearance was unsettling. She had left with a few clothes but the rest of her stuff remained untouched. Carol had to assume that she had heard every word that that idiot Jerry had said. Daisy had a long history of eavesdropping on private conversations. She was a bit too nosey for her own good just like her mother. The only thing Carol had going for her was that the girl had no proof. But that didn't mean that Daisy couldn't convince the police to start digging. Daisy knew too much about Carol's machinations.

That was a problem.

Jerry, in his eagerness to remedy his five-star fuck up, had sent people out looking for her. But that did little to ease her worry. Jerry didn't have the mental acuity to find a set of tits in a strip club. She doubted any of his brain-dead associates would fare much better.

Carol still could not fathom what had possessed her to sleep with him. Aside from his undying loyalty, his skill sets were all sorely lacking. She found that out the hard way. At some point, very soon, Jerry would have to be eliminated. If things went wrong for her with the court case and the embezzled money in Kerry's coffin, he would be the one to take the fall. Or, failing that, Jerry would soon thereafter be forced to take a long walk on a short pier, preferably in concrete shoes. He was simply too dumb to be a suitable partner. She couldn't trust him to keep his mouth shut.

As she knocked back the last of her drink her cellphone rang. Jerry had to buy her a new one after the press had somehow managed to get the number to her old one and started blowing it up with requests for interviews. He was the only one that had the new number. Carol stared at the screen for a second wondering if that could be used to her advantage.

"What do you want Jerry?"

"Well, good morning to you, too, love. Are you near the TV or a computer?"

Carol frowned. She was in no mood to watch all of the rehashed shit about Kerry's abduction. "I have the TV on. I'm watching a movie."

"Well turn it over to Channel Two. Clark and his accomplice nearly killed a club owner in Cincinnati last night."

"What?" Carol snatched the remote control off of the coffee table and changed the channel. "Why in the hell are they in Cincinnati?"

"Beats me, perhaps...."

Before Jerry could finish his sentence, it hit her. "Denver! They're taking him to Denver."

"I guess it's plausible," Jerry said. "But why go through Cincinnati? It seems a bit out of the way."

"Well, hell, Jerry, would you think to look for them there?"

Jerry sighed, "No, I guess not."

Carol stared at the screen as she maneuvered the DVR back to the beginning of the story. The faces of Clark and his accomplice appeared on the screen. The new image of the woman was a lot clearer than the one she had been shown at the police station.

"There was a surprising twist today in the Kerry Vance abduction case as Avery Clark and his still unknown accomplice assaulted the owner of a strip club in a suburb of Cincinnati. Officials inside the NYPD wouldn't comment on this new development other than to say that the FBI is now leading the investigation."

"Man, I know I've seen that chick before," Carol said, "But I cannot for the life of me remember where."

"If I'd have seen her, I think I would have remembered it," Jerrys said. "She's hot."

Carol rolled her eyes, always thinking with their dicks. Of course, in Jerry's case, it might be an upgrade.

"Well, she certainly has brass," Carol said. "I'd admire it if I wasn't the one she's trying to screw over."

"So what are we going to do?" Jerry asked. "If they're back on the road they could be in Denver by tonight."

Carol stared at the ice in her glass. Maybe there was a reason they went to Cincinnati. Kerry knew people all over the damned country. They might have gone there for shelter or help of some kind. "I doubt they're heading there directly. I think we might have a few days. Just the same book me a flight to Denver, Jerry. It's time I paid Kerry's family a visit. I think I should get to know that daughter of his."

Jerry paused for a long moment before speaking. "What are we going to do about Daisy?"

Carol smiled. "I have an idea. Have your secretary book a TV interview. I think it's time we crank up the heat a little on Daisy. And while all eyes are on her, I'll get the hell out of town."

"OK, I'm on it," Jerry said. "I'll let you know as soon as it's all...."

Carol clicked the phone off. She couldn't stand the whine of Jerry's voice for another second. She had research to do. She wondered if Kerry's daughter's last name had ever been Vance.

CHAPTER 19

Jimmy walked into precinct headquarters through the public entrance keeping a close eye out for any reporters that might still be hanging around. The theft of Kerry Vance's corpse had turned into a media frenzy. It was only a matter of time until someone in the press figured out who he was and sought him out.

He resigned himself to the fact that there really wasn't a whole hell of a lot he could do for Avery now. The media was ripping him apart in the court of public opinion. Jimmy wanted very much to stand by his friend but he needed answers. He needed to look Avery in the eye and hear the truth for himself. Jimmy just had to find out where Avery was hiding and talk some sense into him. The woman in the surveillance footage was the key.

"Jimmy, what in the hell are you doing here? I thought you were on vacation."

The desk sergeant, Eddie, called him out as he had attempted to slip by and go up to the squad room. Jimmy smiled, taking a quick glance around before strolling up to the desk. "I wish I was on vacation. I sure as hell wouldn't be here. How are you, Eddie?"

Eddie shrugged. "Alright, I guess, same shit, different day." Eddie leaned forward over the desk resting his elbows on it so only Jimmy could hear him. "I heard about what was going on. I just wanted to give you a heads up before you went upstairs."

Jimmy looked at the older man and frowned. "What's up?"

Eddie looked around to make sure no one was within earshot. "A bunch of Feds headed up there about twenty minutes ago. Something's going on but I don't know what."

"Are they here about the Kerry Vance case?"

"Beats me," Eddie said. "You know the drill. I just log them in and issue their passes. They don't tell me shit."

Jimmy nodded. "Great. Well, I guess I'm not going up there. The last thing I need is one of those guys asking questions."

"Probably a good idea," Eddie said. "Nolan's been a cagey prick the past few days anyway. He reassigned Zap and Randy Toons to the task force the chief set up to investigate the Vance case. They've been running around like a couple of madmen."

Jimmy ran his hand down his face, frustrated, as he considered his options. "Hey, Eddie, you don't happen to have copies of the surveillance pictures of Clark and his accomplice, do you?"

Eddie shook his head. "No, and I couldn't give them to you if I did, Jimmy. You need to stay as far away from this as you can. I know you want to help your friend but if shit goes wrong, he'll drag you down with him. You need to think about that."

Jimmy sighed. "I know. But I can't just sit around on my hands. I've got to do something. Look, do me a favor, have Zap to call me, okay? Maybe I can get him headed in a direction he hasn't thought of yet. Will you do that for me?"

"Sure, I'll tell him," Eddie said. "But that's no guarantee he'll call especially if the Feds are breathing down his neck."

"Just do what you can, huh? Thanks, Eddie."

Eddie smiled. "Go on. Get the hell out of here before Nolan sees you. I'll talk to you soon."

"Yeah, I'll see you, Eddie."

Jimmy pushed through the door considering what Eddie said. This thing with Avery had the potential to ruin him too. His actions at the memorial service alone were enough to get him hauled in front of the disciplinary board. If he ignored Nolan's orders now he could find himself busted all the way down to meter maid, or worse.

Avery's actions mystified him. Jimmy could not wrap his head around the few scraps of information he had. Avery had done some wholesale silly shit over the years but Jimmy would have never drawn a line from that to this. Something was missing. He had to know what it was.

If it wasn't for Avery, Jimmy would have never made it through high school. Avery would spend hours after school helping him muddle his way through his homework. Sometimes, when Jimmy just absolutely could not get the gist of his lessons, like algebra, Avery would do it for him. He would screw it up just enough for Jimmy to pass and avoid raising suspicion. In return, Jimmy protected him from the all of the wannabe tough guys hanging around Hell's Kitchen.

Back then they were inseparable, spending summer nights on the roof of Avery's walk-up while his Mom worked double shifts to keep the two of them afloat. Jimmy would stay up there until all hours to avoid the wrath of his alcoholic father. Avery would make them turkey sandwiches and Jimmy would boost soda-pop from the old Coke machine in front of the bodega down the block. They would sit up there and look out over the lights of the city and dream of their future. All that they really had back then was each other. And, for Jimmy, the same was still true now. Avery was all he had.

When the woman's scream rang out ahead of him, Jimmy jumped, startled. He had been so wrapped up in his own thoughts that he failed to see a woman being mugged in front right of him.

"Let me go!"

Jimmy took off running as the woman clawed at her attacker's hand, desperate to pull away. When she turned, Jimmy realized it was the wispy blonde that worked for Carol Merrick.

The panic in her eyes set him ablaze.

Jimmy quickly closed the gap between them. He dashed in full force, blind-siding the guy with a body check. The momentum sent her attacker crashing over the curb and into a light post. The attacker, a dirty dark-haired punk in camouflage pants and a Sex Pistols T-shirt, landed in a heap, blood flowing from a scratch on his forehead. Anger flashed in his eyes as he pushed himself back to his feet. Jimmy descended upon him, kicking his legs out from under him before he could regain his balance. The attacker hit the sidewalk again with a sharp thud as his head smashed against the ground. Jimmy towered over him resisting the urge to kick him a few more times just to soften him up. "You better stay down, motherfucker, NYPD."

Jimmy heard the siren check as a patrol car pulled up behind him. Jimmy flipped the punk over on his belly and locked his arms behind him. He was glad they'd been close. He didn't have any handcuffs on him and he really didn't feel like wrestling the bastard all the way back down to the station.

"Geez, Sarge, fighting crime in our free time, are we?"

Jimmy looked up, grinning when he saw his favorite rookie, Percy Lowe, roll out of the car ahead of his partner. "Wasn't my idea, this genius here thought it was a good idea to try and mug someone right in front of a police station. Why don't you two get acquainted?"

Percy grinned. "Yes, sir."

Jimmy kept his knee in the punk's back as Percy slapped on the cuffs. He looked around for the girl hoping she hadn't run off. He had a feeling she wasn't down here by accident. Jimmy helped Percy raise the punk to his feet. As he stood, he saw the girl leaning against the side of a bus stop shelter. An elderly lady in a blue pea coat was comforting her while handing her a tissue out of her purse.

Wiping at the tears smeared her mascara. It gave her eyes a hollow look. She looked like a lost little girl. Jimmy had thought about her more than few times since he'd first seen her storm out of Kerry's memorial service. She was practically a baby. But something about her haunted him.

"Excuse me, miss. Are you okay?"

"I will be, I guess." She wiped at her eyes again, thanking the elderly lady as she walked away. "I don't know where the guy came from. I didn't see him until he grabbed me."

Jimmy watched Percy do a pat-down while his partner, Gil, ran his I.D. "Did he say anything to you?"

The girl hesitated before speaking. It was a cue that all cops were trained to look for. She was fabricating an answer. "He said something but I was so freaked out I didn't hear it." She looked up at Jimmy and squinted. "You were at the station yesterday day when I was there with my aunt. Weren't you?"

Jimmy nodded. "Yes, ma'am."

Carol Merrick was her aunt? That put a new spin on things.

Gabe Gil, Percy's training partner, walked over to them taking his hat off to wipe away the sweat on his brow. "Hey, I don't want to step on any toes here but I can't have you working this case, Jimmy. Nolan will have my head on a platter."

The girl looked at Jimmy questioningly as he turned to Gil and grinned. "It's all yours, old buddy. I was just seeing if she was OK."

"Daisy," she said, touching Jimmy's arm. He turned to find her staring him dead in the eye. "My name is Daisy."

Up close the depth in her sky-blue eyes was stunning. There was no way Jimmy could just leave her here. He needed to find out all he could about Jerry and Carol. "But I do think I should tag along back to the station to give a statement."

Gil sighed. "There really isn't any need, Jimmy. I'd just as soon keep you off paper if it's all the same to you. There's less of a chance of Nolan giving me a headache that way."

"I'd say that opportunity just passed you by, Gil." Jimmy lifted his chin, smirking as Captain Nolan closed in on them.

"Jesus, just my fucking luck," Gil said as he turned to watch Nolan approach.

Jimmy watched Nolan take in the scene. He didn't look angry but Jimmy had learned over the years that the old man was a wildcard. Most of the time appearances didn't serve. As soon as Nolan recognized Daisy his expression changed. It wasn't pleasant.

"What's going on here, Gil?" Nolan may have addressed Gil but he was staring straight at Jimmy.

Jimmy repressed the urge to smile and wave. "As far as I know sir, Sergeant Werner here stopped a mugging. My partner and I were pulling up in front of the station when we saw him take the guy down."

Nolan frowned. Jimmy could tell he didn't like the answer, but he'd accepted it, for now. "And you're the victim, miss?"

Daisy glanced at Jimmy before speaking. "Yeah, but it was a hell of a lot more than a mugging. That guy was trying to drag me into the alley. I didn't know what he was going to do."

"You're Carol Merrick's personal assistant, aren't you?" Nolan asked.

A look of terror flashed across Daisy's face. Jimmy saw it. Nolan had too. "Not anymore," Daisy said, as tears formed in her eyes, "After everything that's gone on the past few days I couldn't stay with her a minute longer."

Nolan expression turned sympathetic as he handed Daisy the handkerchief from the breast pocket of his jacket. "It's all right, ma'am. You're safe now. Why don't you go with Officer Gil here and give him your statement. I need a word with Sergeant Werner."

Daisy glanced at Jimmy before following Gil inside the bus shelter. Jimmy saw her glance over at him again before she sat down.

"So just exactly what in the hell is really going on here, Jimmy? I'm seeing a lot of coincidences piling up." Nolan pulled a cigar from his shirt pocket and lit it, "In my experience that's usually by design."

"I just came down to get a picture of the woman Avery was with when Vance's body was taken. I reached out to a mutual friend of Avery's and Vance's hoping he'd be able to identify her." Jimmy ran his hand over his head in frustration. "I wanted to get to Avery first and talk him into turning himself in."

Nolan nodded slowly as he listened. Jimmy couldn't begin to guess what his reaction would be. "Well, I guess if I was in your place I'd have probably done the same thing, too." Nolan took a long draw on his cigar. "But, for future reference, just remember that ignoring my orders isn't the wisest career move."

"Yes sir," Jimmy said.

"So what's the deal with the girl? What's she doing here?"

Jimmy shrugged. "I honestly don't know, Captain. I didn't even notice her until she started screaming. That guy had a pretty good grip on her arm and was trying to pull her over toward the alley there. She was putting up a good fight by the time I got there. After talking to her, though, I don't think it was entirely random. She didn't want to tell me what the guy said to her."

Nolan chomped on the end his cigar as he watched Gil write down her statement. "I doubt she was down here by accident, either."

"I was thinking the same thing," Jimmy said. "She said that she had left Carol Merrick. Maybe she was here to share information."

"Or start trouble," Nolan said. "Not that it matters, now. It's not our problem anymore."

Jimmy furrowed his brow. "What do you mean?"

"The F.B.I has taken over," Nolan said. "The case has taken a turn."

Jimmy frowned. "What the hell happened?"

Nolan removed the cigar from his mouth. He held it out in front of him gazing at it. In the interval, Jimmy knew he wasn't going to like what he about to hear.

"Clark's not in the city anymore. He and his accomplice assaulted the owner of a strip club in Cincinnati. I wasn't told all of the details but it's not looking good for him."

"Cincinnati? Why the hell is he in Cincinnati?" Jimmy felt the sudden urge to pound his head against a wall.

"The Feds are fairly certain that they're on their way to Denver. That's Vance's hometown."

Jimmy shook his head in disbelief. "So they stole the body to take him home?

"That's the theory," Nolan said. "It seems that Vance cut Ms. Merrick completely out of his will. My thought is that Clark and his accomplice are trying to get him interred before she can contest the will."

"What good would that do? It doesn't make any sense."

"Well, if it were you or me, it wouldn't," Nolan said. "But when you're a big star like Kerry Vance being buried on your Virginia estate would be a big tourist attraction."

Jimmy's eyes opened wide as the connection was made. "Merrick wants to turn it into some kind of fucked-up Graceland. She wants to capitalize on his death."

Nolan took another long draw on his cigar, "Bingo."

"That's crazy. But I feel better knowing that Avery is actually trying to do something noble."

"Not the way he's going about it. He's looking at some time."

"There has to be a way to spin this so that Avery doesn't come across as the ghoul the media is making him out to be."

Nolan shook his head. "I don't know. But, if I were you, I'd keep my distance and let the Feds sort this out. Making him out to be a folk hero could backfire on you."

Jimmy wondered if that was veiled advice.

Nolan pinched the fire off his cigar before tossing the butt into a garbage can. "Anyway, it looks like Gil has things sewed up here. So, I'm going to go and get lunch. You care to join me?"

Jimmy watched Daisy as she and Gil came out of the shelter. She smiled at Jimmy and headed straight for him. "Thanks for the offer, Captain. I think I have other plans."

Nolan grinned before turning to walk away. "Just make sure you're back at work first thing Monday morning."

CHAPTER 20

Sarah snapped awake to find her husband, Ronnie, standing over her. He snatched his hand back startled by her response. "Sorry, baby, I didn't want to wake you. Your Mom is on the phone."

Sarah frowned, squinting from the light in the bathroom across the hall. "What the hell does she want?"

"Beats me. She sounds pretty upset."

Poor Ronnie was always up and out of the house well before dawn. Normally, he made it a practice not to wake her before leaving. Sarah had always been a night owl and did well to haul herself out of bed in time to get Tracy ready for school. It was way too early for her to function properly.

Sarah sat up and took the phone. "Mom, is everything okay?"

"Sorry to wake you up, sweetie. I know you're not a morning person. But, I just saw some really messed up shit on the news. I need to talk about it. I'm flipping out over here."

Sarah threw the covers back and slid to the edge of the bed. She looked up at Ronnie raising an eyebrow. Ronnie smiled, reaching over to rub her shoulder before leaving the room.

"What is it? Something to do with Kerry?"

"It was Calliope. They're all over the news again because, apparently, she attacked a club owner in Cincinnati. But that can't be her. There's no way it could have been her. She looks like she hasn't aged a day since the last time I saw her. That was in 1974, Sarah, four months after I had you."

Sarah slid down onto the floor trying to get her feet stuffed into her slippers. If she didn't know better she'd have thought her mother had slipped a cog. "What are you talking about?" She could hear her mother sigh. It was a sign of her impatience. She always did it when Sarah was a little slow on the uptake. It pissed Sarah off every single time and it sure as hell was too early for it now.

"They have surveillance footage of Calliope and Avery Clark inside of a strip club. Apparently, Calliope attacked the club's owner with a knife. Here's the thing, though, Sarah. That's the very same Calliope that Kerry lived with after he left Arvada. I hated that woman so much that her image is burned into my memory. I know that's her. But she still looks like she's twenty-five years old. She hasn't aged. Something is fucked up. There's no plastic surgery in the world that works that damned good."

Sarah pulled the phone away from her ear and shook her head. She worried that her mom's memory might not really be what it once was. Her mother had always been so strong that the thought of it scared her.

"OK, well, it couldn't have been her then. It had to have been her daughter or something. There's no point in letting it upset you."

"Goddamn it, Sarah, I'm not kidding. I've been nose to nose with that woman. She was wearing the same kind of hippy sundress flouncy shit that she wore back then. I know it was her."

Sarah rubbed her eyes, yawning. Whatever her mother had seen it definitely had her spooked. "OK, mom, if you say so. If it is her things really are screwed up. She sounded on the phone like she was representing Kerry's estate not planning to steal him. There has to be more going on than we know."

A long silence fell across the line. Sarah could almost hear the gears turning in her mother's mind. "I think there's a whole lot more going on than we know about and it's been going on for a very long damn time. I knew something was off about that woman since the first time I laid eyes on her. It brings into focus a few things Kerry told me about her back then, too."

"What are you talking about?"

"Don't worry about it, honey, not yet. I want to think about this before I say anything. Call me tonight after you get things settled. I want to check out something."

Sarah threw her hands up in the air. The conversation would have been aggravating at any normal time of day. Right now, before the cold crack of dawn, it was just plain maddening. "OK, Mom. That's fine. I'll call you later."

"I'm sorry I woke you up, honey. Go ahead and get some sleep. I'll talk to you later."

"Good-bye, Mom." Sarah hit the button on the phone before tossing it over on Ronnie's side of the bed. She threw her arms out and arched to stretch her back. There was no way she going to be able to go back to sleep now. She grabbed the T.V. remote off of her nightstand and hit the switch. She wanted to see what Calliope looked like for herself.

CHAPTER 21

Jimmy stared into the depths of his favorite coffee cup dead tired and angry as the waxing light of dawn fell unnoticed over his shoulder. His mind had raced in so many different directions over the course of the past few days that sleep had proven impossible. After the events in Cincinnati he'd been forced to assume that Avery's plan was in motion long before Kerry's memorial service. From everything he'd discovered the theft of Kerry's body was too organized to be perpetrated on the fly. Avery and his accomplice had driven a stolen hearse across the width of New York City at dawn and no one noticed.

Jimmy couldn't shake the feeling he'd been played for a fool. He shook his head watching shadows creep across the floor. That Avery had fooled him was unsettling enough. But what really stung was wondering if Avery hadn't gotten over on him by allowing him to fool himself.

Jimmy bore a measure pity where Avery was concerned. It went all the way back to when they were children. Avery had always been fodder for bullies. He was so small, so quiet and unassuming that he was an easy target. Jimmy had taken pity on him then, taking him under his wing to protect him. Jimmy had taken pity on him again, thirty years later, in the days after Zoe's death. Her loss triggered a breakdown that Jimmy feared would consume him. He reconnected with Avery then to keep from losing him while pitying him, again, for being weak.

Ultimately, his influence held little sway. Avery had a wild streak that Jimmy didn't understand. He reveled in the hedonism orbiting Kerry Vance. Right or wrong, Jimmy never wanted anything more than to protect Avery. He was a brilliant man with a truly peaceful soul. If Avery knew the truth of how he felt then he also felt ashamed. Avery would always be his friend. He would still do what he could to help but it wasn't easy. He just hoped Avery was actually doing the right thing.

Across the room Daisy stirred, breaking the silence as she popped up abruptly from under the covers on Jimmy's couch. "Geez, man, are you always up this early? What time is it?"

"It's just past six-thirty." He watched closely while Daisy ran her fingers through her tangled hair. "Sorry if I woke you. I couldn't sleep."

"It's cool," Daisy said, settling back against the couch. "I really should get out of here. I've troubled you enough."

At the shallowest level, Jimmy was as attracted to her as any woman he had ever laid eyes on. Her face haunted him. She was also barely nineteen years old. The age difference was scandalous. "Trust me. You're the least of my worries. Stay as long as you need to."

Daisy grinned pulling the blanket up around her. "Oh my god, I thank you! I really didn't feel like getting up yet. I haven't slept more than an hour or two in the past couple of days. This whole thing with Kerry is insane."

Jimmy nodded, weary, before draining his coffee cup, "Boy, that's no lie."

Daisy tilted her head returning his gaze. "Were you working on the case?"

"Not exactly," Jimmy said. "It's more complicated than that."

He paused, unsure of how to broach the subject. Daisy had been too distraught the night before to say much of anything. The attack rattled her. Jimmy suspected there was more to it than she had said. But he didn't want to pressure her. She'd been through enough.

"You mean more complicated than it already is?" Daisy smirked. "That's doing something."

Jimmy watched Daisy stretch out on the couch. She had a swimmer's body, long and lean, muscular, not reed-thin like most women her height. She certainly didn't look a thing like Carol Merrick. But she definitely came from sturdy stock. Jimmy looked away, back down into the singularity of his empty coffee cup. His apprehension over pursuing a relationship was predicated on the false assumption that this starry-eyed girl would ever entertain the notion. He was just a middle-aged beat cop and, if Avery was to be believed, without a cool bone in his body. He probably reminded her of her father. Still, she had accepted his invitation for dinner and an offer to crash. It occurred to him that it was only because she had no place else to go. At the very least she felt safe with him. That was enough.

"You ever meet Avery Clark?" Jimmy asked. He rose from his chair and crossed into the kitchen to pour more coffee.

"Oh, sure, I used to see him all the time. He's a charmer, always so funny and upbeat. Kerry always seemed relaxed when they hung out. Avery kept him laughing." Daisy paused, fidgeting with the edge of the blanket. "I'm not sure why Avery did what he did but I'm certain he had a good reason."

"You really think so?"

"I think he's doing exactly what Kerry wanted," Daisy said.

The statement hung in the air. Jimmy was more than happy to entertain the idea. But it seemed a little far-fetched. "I don't know. That seems a bit out there. Why would Kerry plan the theft of his own body?"

Daisy leaned forward tears forming at the edges of her eyes. "Because he knew they were going to kill him. I think he let them do it."

Jim glared at her, thunderstruck. "Carol?"

Daisy nodded, the tears spilling over to tumble down her cheeks, "and that bastard, Jerry Jewell."

"Why on earth would he let them? That's crazy."

Daisy wiped her eyes. "Kerry had cancer. He'd been seeing an oncologist. I booked his appointments."

"I'd heard that," Jimmy said. "I don't think Avery knew."

Daisy shrugged. "I don't know. I didn't think Kerry told anyone besides Carol. I don't think he wanted to burden anyone. Things had been tense between Kerry and Carol for months before he was diagnosed. But I didn't know the whole story. Kerry was pissed over how much Carol had spent remodeling their farm in Virginia. Carol and Jerry Jewell were planning on producing a reality series there about her and Kerry. Kerry hated the idea and refused to do it. I saw a couple of arguments break out over it. It was ugly.

"Not long after the cancer diagnosis Kerry quit staying at the house in Lenox Hill. He must have filed for divorce and changed his will before leaving on the European tour."

Daisy wiped her eyes again looking away through the window. "I don't see how he could have gone over there knowing what they were planning. I don't know. Maybe he was in pain and just ready to let go."

Daisy's tears weighed on Jimmy's heart. He rose from his chair to go and sit beside her. "It's a hell of a thing to contemplate, isn't it?"

"The only thing I can fathom is that he wanted to go out on top," Daisy said. "Hell. That may be why Carol planned it. She wanted to secure his legacy. She probably figured it'd be the easiest way to line her pockets."

"I take it she had full control of his assets," Jimmy said. "Before Kerry changed the will."

Daisy nodded. "She was set to bury him on the farm in Virginia. I think she wanted to turn it into some kind of fucking shrine. Probably make a buck off of that, too, if I know her."

"You mean like some kind of knock-off Graceland?" Jimmy scowled. "That's ghoulish."

Daisy looked Jimmy dead in the eye. "It is, isn't it? That's how Carol is. She's all about the dollar. She has to have the best of everything."

"Wasn't she a supermodel? Didn't she have her own money?"

Daisy laughed, her dimples capturing Jimmy's attention. "She was a joke. Kerry's connections drove her career. She blew all her money trying to become a real estate mogul. After that, she started concentrating on Kerry's career. She started hitting him up with all these lame ideas trying to capitalize on his fame. Kerry wasn't having any of it. He was all about the music. I don't think Kerry ever really liked being rich or famous. Not to the extent that he was. All he wanted to do was play. That was what mattered to him."

Jimmy was beginning to see why Avery had such a deep connection with him. They were both artists with genuine depth. Despite his wild ways, at heart, Kerry had integrity.

He paused to gaze into Daisy's eyes feeling suddenly self-conscious about being so close. "You don't happen to know who Avery's accomplice is, do you?"

"I only caught a brief glimpse on the news. She didn't look familiar. Why?"

Avery rose from the couch. "I'm just trying to put it all together. As far as I know, she's a wild card. Nobody seems to know who she is"

"That's what I gathered," Daisy said. "I've been trying to contact them. But it hasn't happened yet."

"How are you doing that?"

Daisy grabbed her phone off the coffee table. "I'm the one who ran all of Kerry's social media stuff. I've been on there trying to drum up support for Avery using Kerry's official pages. I'm hoping they'll get in touch."

"This is where I lumber off into the land of the dinosaurs. I don't know anything about that stuff."

Daisy gazed at him, grinning. "You don't have any social media accounts?"

"I don't even own a computer other than the one on that damned phone. I can barely use it."

Daisy giggled. "There's not that much to it. I can show you if you like."

Jimmy's face flushed. He must have come across like a senior citizen. "I'd be more interested in seeing what you're up to. Maybe I can find a way to get Avery's attention."

Daisy studied Jimmy with an appraising glance. "You're a friend of his, aren't you? That's why you wanted to keep me around."

Jimmy smiled. *That wasn't the only reason.* "I am. We've been friends since we were kids. I was with him at Kerry's memorial service. That's why I was barred from the investigation."

"I remember seeing Avery. I thought about going over and saying hello. Carol was being such a bitch though I didn't want to piss her off any more than she already was. But I managed to anyway."

"I saw you storm out." Jimmy said. "Your aunt is a piece of work."

Daisy's eyes widened. "Ah, man, you have no idea. That's why I need to stay a step ahead of her. I didn't tell your cop buddy yesterday but that guy on the street worked for Jerry Jewell."

"Why didn't you tell them?"

Daisy jumped up from the couch. "They're not going to do anything. Even if they do manage to get Jerry's name out of that knucklehead, he'll just deny it. He has money. So, they'll take his word for it and move on. I'm going to need hard evidence before I get the police involved. That's the only way they'll do anything."

Jimmy was taken by the fire in her eyes. "Yeah, I guess that's a fair assessment. You're going to need something pretty damning. Do you want some help?"

Daisy's eyes lit the room. She took a step closer meeting Jimmy eye to eye. "I was hoping you'd ask."

CHAPTER 22

Carol's pulse quickened as she was hustled from the green room to a chair out on the studio set. There, a make-up artist assailed her once again bent on wiping away all traces of the glow of healthy skin. She ignored the powder puff assault and focused instead on the mousey little intern chattering beside her.

"Just remember to ignore the cameras, Ms. Merrick. Focus all of your attention on Donna. The camera will catch you if you stare off-set."

Carol smirked. "This isn't my first interview, honey."

The intern ignored her and continued undaunted. "Your segment will last approximately four minutes. At 3 minutes our producer will signal the host giving you time to summarize and finish on schedule. Do you have any questions?"

Carol eased back in the chintzy canvas chair then jumped, startled, as a sound man snuck up behind her. He smiled, embarrassed, as he ran a microphone cord up through the chair to clip onto her jacket.

Carol ignored him, frowning, as she turned back to the intern. "Four minutes isn't a lot of time."

"Trust me, Ms. Merrick, when the lights and camera go on it'll seem like an eternity."

Donna Day smiled as she came from behind the set's backdrop to take the seat beside her.

Donna's *Evening Wrap* was one of the few news shows Carol ever bothered to watch. She had an acerbic wit and a take-no-prisoners attitude Carol loved.

Carol nodded. "It's just been a while since I've done any interviews."

"Just relax," Donna said as she shuffled through her notes. "I'll try not to make it too painful."

Carol smiled but the statement raised a sudden pang of suspicion. Before Carol could ask what she meant by it the lights on the set ignited. Three seconds to air. Carol took a deep breath and pulled herself together.

"Welcome back. Tonight, we have as our guest former supermodel, Carol Merrick. Carol is the widow of rock-n-roll legend Kerry Vance and at the center of the firestorm surrounding the mysterious abduction of his body. This is her first interview since the abduction. Carol thank you for joining us during this difficult time."

Carol gathered her composure and issued a thin smile. She had to play the grieving widow role to perfection. To do that, she had to set her real emotions aside. There was too much at stake. "Thank you for having me, Donna. I wish it was under better circumstances."

"So take me through the events that led up to the theft of your husband's body. He allegedly overdosed on heroin while on tour in England, then what happened?"

"Well, Kerry's body was kept in England for about a week while an autopsy was performed and an inquiry held. Then, after his death was ruled an accidental overdose, the State Department arranged for his body to be flown home. From what I understand the hearse from the funeral home was stolen shortly after it left the airport."

"And Avery Clark and an unknown accomplice stole the hearse?"

Carol looked Donna in the eye and nodded. It was common knowledge. Carol wondered where the brassy blonde was leading her. "I still can't fathom it. At first, I thought it was some kind of sick joke. Clark's career is in the gutter anyway but I'd never dreamed he'd go this far to gain a little publicity."

As soon as she finished speaking Carol saw a glimmer in Donna's eye. "Is it true you received divorce papers and a notice of a new will shortly after your husband died?"

Carol's eyes narrowed. "Yes. The day after his body was taken. Things weren't perfect but I had no idea he was ready to give up on us. It came as quite a shock."

"I can well imagine. So let's get back to Kerry's rumored drug use. Are you aware of the massive social media campaign that's refuting claims that Kerry was a heroin addict? It seems to have started on your husband's own social media apparatus."

Carol attempted poorly to mask her surprise. *Daisy!* She was going to have to put that little bitch in check. "I wasn't aware. I don't spend much time on the internet. But I can understand his fans' frustration. I really don't think Kerry was a heroin addict. I don't know what went wrong in London but it was completely out of character for him. He was a drinker more than anything."

"But doesn't that contradict claims that Kerry's manager, Jerry Jewell, made against Avery Clark? That Clark had been supplying Kerry with the drug?"

Carol looked at Donna Day with a blank expression for the smallest of moments. Who in the hell had she been talking to?

"Jerry suspected it. But I think he's way off base. Kerry and Avery Clark certainly had a toxic relationship but I'm not convinced that was what was going on. Jerry and Kerry had worked together for years. I think Jerry was just hurt and grasping for answers. He was never a big fan of Avery Clark anyway. He was a troublesome influence."

Carol found herself forced to improvise.

"And why was that?" Donna asked.

"Well, his opinion held a lot of weight with Kerry. Sometimes he would influence decisions that were bad for business."

Donna shot Carol a quizzical expression. "Okay, hold on. Let me make sure I'm clear on this. You're suggesting Avery Clark had undue influence over your husband?"

Carol's face flushed. Donna Day had taken her completely off-topic. "No, not exactly, Kerry was pretty strong-willed. I just think there were times when Clark played on Kerry's apprehensions."

"I'm not sure I understand, Ms. Merrick. What did Avery Clark stand to gain from doing this?"

Carol took a deep breath trying to keep her anger in check. "I don't think there was anything to gain other than some sort of sick satisfaction at keeping Kerry from capitalizing on his fame."

"Ms. Merrick by all estimates your husband's net worth is over a hundred million dollars. How exactly was Avery Clark holding him back?"

Carol's face reddened. In the camera's eye, she looked like a big juicy tomato. "He talked Kerry out of licensing songs for commercials. Avery also talked him out of doing the reality series we had in the works."

"Ah, now I think we're closing in on the truth. You and Jerry Jewell were set to produce the reality series. So when Avery Clark talked your husband out of it that cost you quite a bit of money, did it not?"

Carol glared at Donna Day. "I'm not answering that."

"Is it true that you and Jerry Jewell are having an affair?"

Carol ripped the microphone from her lapel and tossed it to the floor. It was all she could do to keep her from reaching across and slapping Donna Day in the teeth. "I'm not going to dignify that with a response."

Carol hopped out of the chair and stormed off set.

Donna Day remained unperturbed as she watched Carol go. She smiled gracefully turning back to face the camera. "It would seem that there is much more to the Kerry Vance case than we all first believed. I would urge all of my colleagues to keep an open mind as this story develops. We will be sure to keep you all up to date as it progresses. For all of us at Evening Wrap, this is Donna Day, signing off. Goodnight."

CHAPTER 23

"Fucking Kansas, man," Clyde looked back at Avery from the driver's seat and shook his head, "Four hundred long odd miles of nothing. I used to hate driving this piece of I-70 back when Kerry was touring. It's lonely out here."

Avery nodded but didn't speak. Calliope was curled up beside him sound asleep. After all the miles she had racked up over the past three days he didn't want to wake her. She was completely spent by the time they arrived in Kansas City. But it still took quite a bit of convincing before she agreed to let Clyde take the wheel. She was hell-bent on getting Kerry all the way home. After all of her protesting, she was asleep before they even got out of the city.

Now they were off across the width of Kansas with Suicide Clyde at the helm. He piloted the Temple like it was a rocket ship. Avery was glad he'd given up the passenger seat to Jill. He really didn't want to know how fast they were going.

His nerves were shot. He needed a drink.

His brain was crowded with ghosts. His thoughts kept returning to Zoe and to Kerry and sometimes even to his own father.

It was the strangest thing seeing his father's face now after so many years. His father had died when he was a toddler. The only way Avery remembered him at all was from the fading photographs his mother had hanging on their walls at home. But he was there moving through his thoughts as if he, Zoe and Kerry were all together somehow and calling out to him. It was as if they were trying to get a message through. It was haunting.

Avery pushed the thought away and focused on the moment. He took a deep breath and gazed out of the window watching as the highway signs passed at breakneck speed. The speed didn't seem to faze Jill. She had her legs pulled up in the seat sitting Indian style while playing around on her phone. She was truly a beautiful woman, more so as he watched her in the fading light of dusk.

The lights inside the club in Cincinnati had created a fantasy. There she was a native goddess cast from light and stardust. But here, as the shadow fell long over the empty prairie, the delicate lines on her face showed her age. She was no longer a fantasy. She was something more rare and precious. She had a subtle grace Avery found entrancing. It belied her brash personality.

"Hey, Avery, do you know someone named Burner?" Jill asked.

Avery sat forward. "Yeah, we used to call a good friend of mine Burner when we were kids. His real name is Jimmy. Why?"

"I was just looking at Kerry's Mugshot page and, Jesus, there's a whole lot of action going on there."

Avery took another deep breath. "Yeah, I figured as much. What's that got to do with Jimmy?"

Jill turned in her seat to face him. "Well, there's an official post on there from whoever runs Kerry's page that says; 'If Avery Clark reads this please be advised that Burner is in the loop and needs you to call'."

Avery smirked. "Well, I'll be damned. I wonder how he managed that."

Clyde looked at Avery in the mirror. "Didn't Carol's niece run all of Kerry's internet shit?"

"Daisy? Yeah, I think so, why?"

"You might want to be careful," Clyde said. "It might be the cops trying to pull some shit to track us down."

Avery laughed. "Jimmy *is* a cop, NYPD. I doubt he'd be in on the investigation, though. He's not a detective. He's a shift supervisor, a beat cop."

"Yeah, but he has an in with you. That's all they need," Clyde said.

Avery leaned back against the side of the van. He wondered what Jimmy thought about all of this. "Yeah, but I doubt anyone knows him by Burner.

No one's called him by that name since junior high. I'd say that's his way of being incognito."

"Hold on a second, check this out," Jill handed Avery her phone. "Read through that. Whoever is running Kerry's page has posted a lot of stuff about Carol's actions since his death. There's some really shady stuff on there."

Avery scrolled down through the posts. It seemed Carol was doing her best to liquidate as much of Kerry's stuff as she could as quickly as possible. "Hey, it says here she was trying to sell off his studio gear before he even died. Do the cops know that shit?"

Jill shrugged. "Yeah, you'd think that'd raise an eyebrow somewhere, huh?"

"I guess by killing him overseas she figured it'd just look like another business deal." Avery could feel the heat rising in his face. If there was ever anyone on this earth that he'd like to slap in the mouth it was Carol Merrick.

Avery reached over and touched Kerry's coffin. He couldn't begin to imagine what she'd put him through especially at the end. "There has to be a way to make sure Carol and that son of a bitch Jerry Jewell get what's coming to them."

Avery handed Jill her phone back. "Maybe I should get a hold of Jimmy. Could you drop a comment on that thread and ask 'Burner' why his sister couldn't take ballet lessons?"

Jill arched an eyebrow, "A test?"

"Yep, and if it's really Jimmy, he'll know the answer."

"Good idea," Jill said. "At least it looks like whoever is running Kerry's page is trying to make some noise. Maybe if we add some of our own stuff somebody will start paying attention."

"Yeah, I think it's about time we share our side of the story," Avery said. "That should draw plenty of attention."

"Do you have a Mugshot page?" Jill asked as her fingers tapped madly on the screen of her phone. "I can't find one."

"Yeah, look up Malevolent Endeavors. It was the last book title. I doubt it will do us much good, though. I don't have anything to do with it. My publicist runs it."

"Wow." Jill looked at Avery and grinned. "It looks like the crazies didn't have any trouble finding it."

Avery held Jill's gaze. "Why am I not surprised?"

"The same message about Burner is posted on here as well," Jill said. "Whoever is looking for you is certainly thorough."

"That sounds like Jimmy."

"He must be a hell of a friend," Clyde said. "As crazy as all of this shit is he'd be putting his job on the line by trying to help you."

Avery dropped his head. Jimmy had been looking out for him for most of his life. And now here he was, once again, trying to bail him out.

"Yeah, you're right, Clyde. I can't let him do that. I owe him too much already."

Clyde watched him for a long few seconds in the mirror. It was an appraising stare. At the speed Clyde had the Temple howling across the face of Kansas it was a good thing the road ahead of them fell in a straight line.

"So how the hell did he get stuck with you?"

Jill reached across and slapped the old man's shoulder. "That's not nice at all, Clyde."

Clyde looked over and winked. "I never claimed to be nice, little lady. I was just wondering how a big city cop got to be friends with the Wildman, back there. That's a story I'd like to hear."

Avery scooted up between the front seats. He took a quick glance at Calliope as she rolled over beside him and kept his voice low. "Jimmy's been looking out for me since we were kids. I think he got tired of seeing me getting beat up every afternoon after school."

"Aww, that's awful," Jill said. "Why'd they pick on you?"

Avery shrugged as he gazed into the dark depths of Jill's eyes. "I guess I was an easy target. I was really small when I was a kid. I didn't weigh a hundred pounds until after I was in high school. Plus, I did well in school and was into weird shit like horror comics and Dungeons and Dragons and stuff."

Clyde snorted a dry, wheezing laugh. "Well, hell, it ain't no wonder you got your ass beat. Did you grow up in the city?"

"Yes sir, right in the middle of Hell's Kitchen, West 45th and 11th Avenue."

"Wow," Clyde said, "Tough neighborhood."

"It used to be. It's all corporate now. The building I grew up in was torn down years ago. There's an office supply store there now. Whenever I get homesick I go there and stare at the color copiers."

Jill shook her head and rested her hand on Avery's shoulder. "So you and Jimmy have been close a long time."

"We were inseparable all the way through school but gradually lost touch after I left for college. We actually didn't reconnect again until after Zoe died."

Avery was embarrassed by the sympathetic look in Jill's eyes and looked away. "Everyone was so afraid that I was going to fall apart and relapse that one of my cousins called Jimmy and had him meet us for dinner one night. I guess they figured if Jimmy was back in the picture it would keep the bad influences away."

"Well having a cop around will sure do that," Clyde said. He looked up to catch Avery's gaze in the mirror, "If you're willing to let them."

Avery arched an eyebrow then looked away out of the window. "True enough. I tried really hard not to let any of them down especially Jimmy. But it didn't work. I did fall apart after Zoe died. I went right off the deep end."

"As much as I love Jimmy though, he really isn't the nurturing type. He didn't understand what I was going through. He never said it but he thought I was weak. I think he's always felt that way. So, I shut him out a lot of the time. I didn't want to be a burden to him and I sure as hell didn't want his pity."

Jill reached over again and gave Avery's shoulder a gentle little squeeze.

"Well you have to give the guy credit," Clyde said. "He's stuck around. He's still trying to help."

"That's true. I'm really not sure why."

Clyde laughed. "I'm sure as hell not seeing it."

Avery shook his head, flipping Clyde off via the rear-view mirror. "Truthfully, I think it's because we're really the only family each other has. Neither of us had siblings and all of our parents are gone. Jimmy never married. So, really, I guess I'm all he's got."

Avery waited for Clyde to pop off with another smart-assed comment but then the old man sighed as he stared out at the road.

"I can dig that," Clyde said. His voice sounded suddenly weary. "My only real family's lying in that box there behind you."

"I'm sorry, Clyde. I didn't know." Jill said.

Clyde stared out at the road. "That boy was something special. He's taken a lot better care of me over the years than he ever should have. And if there's a way we can make that hillbilly bitch pay for taking him away from us I say we pull the trigger."

"Hillbilly?" Avery looked up. "Carol? The socialite supreme?"

Clyde nodded. "That's the one. I take it Kerry never told you the story of how he found her, did he?"

Avery chuckled. "No. He never talked about Carol. It was a sore subject."

"Yeah, I can imagine. You see, our dear Ms. Merrick is originally from a tiny little town in West Virginia called Blacksville. It's just a dot on the map from what I've heard, pretty much a gas station and a post office along the way to someplace better. Carol took off for New York when she was still a teenager. All she really had going for her was a pretty face and a nice set of tits, so after getting her hands on a fake I.D. she started stripping in a club down on Times Square. Kerry said she wasn't even sixteen yet."

"Good lord." Jill said, "She was a baby."

"I doubt she was ever that innocent," Clyde said. "From what I gathered her own father molested her and her sister since they were little. It destroyed her sister. She turned out to be a junkie. She died of an overdose when Daisy was about six. I was still working for Kerry when that all went down."

"Wow." Avery stared out into the gathering twilight trying to process the information. "It's kind of hard to hate her after hearing all that."

"I guess it wasn't easy to love her, either," Clyde said. "But Kerry went stark raving ape shit for her the first night he laid eyes on her. I was there. The club she worked in was a shit hole. It was one of the worst organ grinders on the square. Kerry liked to go there because no one ever bothered him. And Kerry, being the way he was, went out and bought her that fucking house in Lenox Hill on the condition that she quit stripping. He got her hooked up with the modeling gig and eventually married her."

Avery watched as a frown gathered on Jill's face. It was subtle.....but formidable. It was as clear how much she loved Kerry. She was jealous of what he'd done for Carol. She felt cheated. Avery couldn't help being attracted to her but it was a ridiculous notion to ever dare act on it. She had her own ghosts to deal with. She wasn't ready to take on his kind of crazy. And Avery wasn't sure he had anything more meaningful to give.

"What year did they meet?" Jill asked.

Clyde's brow furrowed. He looked over at Jill and said, "Eighty-five? I think we'd just come off of the *Jaded* tour."

Avery watched Jill internalize this. He guessed it softened the blow to her ego knowing that it all went down long before she had come on the scene. But it was just a guess.

"Geez," Jill giggled. "I guess he always did like them young."

"No. Not always," Clyde said. "When I first met him he was all broken up over some older woman he knew up in Oregon. He was a mess over that one. He shied away from women for a long time afterward. But I think that also had a lot to do with getting thrown into the deep end with Zephyr. He had a lot to deal with."

"What was her name?" Jill asked.

"He never told me and I knew better than to ask. He needed to put it behind him." Clyde looked out at the rear-view mirror on the door of the van. "Jesus Christ, where did that son of a bitch come from?"

Avery hopped up on his knees to see over the casket and out of the back window. There was a classic black Mustang closing on them at an insane rate of speed. Before Avery could get a good look, it darted into the inside lane and passed in a flash. "Damn," Avery said. "That crazy bastard has to at least be going a hundred and fifty."

"Right?" Jill said. "Did you see the California license plate?"

Clyde shook his head. "No. But the motherfucker must be in a hurry to get back there, if he doesn't splatter himself all over the goddamned highway first."

The Mustang vanished into the distance.

As Avery sat back down, he noticed that Calliope was wide awake with tears running down her cheeks. "Hey, you OK?" he asked.

She wiped the tears out of her eyes and stared out into space.

Jill peeked around the seat. Avery tilted his head toward Calliope and shrugged.

"Calliope, honey, are you all right? You need anything?"

Calliope sat up quickly wiping at her eyes again. "I'll be fine. But I think you need to slow down some, Clyde. Something's off."

Clyde let off of the gas pedal as they topped a rise. As soon as he did, he nailed the brakes. "Son of a bitch!"

Out ahead of them, stopped dead in the middle of the road sat the black Mustang. It was turned sideways blocking both lanes.

"Holy shit, hit the exit," Jill said.

Clyde swerved quickly onto the exit ramp. The sudden shift caused the rear of the van to kick out sideways. Avery grabbed the back of the driver's seat trying not to freak out. Clyde proved a deft hand at the wheel as he turned into the slide and set the van straight in the road. As soon as he did he brought it to a full stop.

"What the fuck was that shit? Stupid motherfucker," Clyde said. He threw the gear shift up into reverse and started to back up. Avery was afraid Clyde had decided to chase the Mustang down. But, as soon as they started moving, the tire underneath Avery flopped wildly beneath them, flat.

"That's just fucking great," Clyde said. He pulled the gear shift back down into drive and crept forward off of the exit ramp and onto the shoulder.

Out on the highway, the Mustang came alive again. Smoke poured from the tires as it slid back around straight in the road. Avery swore he heard an inhuman wail come from inside the car as it raced away.

He glanced at Calliope who appeared to be having a full-metal meltdown. Her brown eyes were feral. Then, just as quickly, the tempest faded. She tilted her head as if someone had whispered something in her ear. She closed her eyes in response to it and sighed.

"Well this sure as hell isn't good," she said. "We need to find a place to hide, quickly."

Clyde frowned. "I don't want to risk trying to go too far. If the tire rolls off of the rim we run the risk of tearing it up. Then we'll really be screwed."

Avery surveyed the sparse landscape and spotted a big barn off by itself a good way up ahead of them. "Do you think we could make it there?"

Clyde looked then turned back to them and shrugged. "I guess if we're really careful. Folks around here are usually pretty friendly. Maybe they'll at least let us pull it off of the road to work on it."

"Did anyone happen to catch what exit that was?" Jill asked, looking at her phone. "Hopefully we're not that far away from a town where we can get it fixed."

"I don't know," Clyde said. "It's already dark. Most of these small-town businesses close for supper. I doubt we're going to get it fixed tonight. We'll probably have to crash here and hope the cops don't find us."

Avery looked around at the group. None of them seemed keen on the prospect of spending the night at the edge of East Jesus' unplowed field. But it seemed they didn't have much of a choice. All they could do was hope they didn't get caught.

"I say we head for the barn," Calliope said. "Keep your eyes open. If we can find a pull off closer we can hide in one of those fields. The fewer people we have to deal with here the better."

Everyone nodded in agreement as Clyde inched the van forward. Avery watched the stars as dusk finally gave way to the full expanse of night. Hopefully, out here in the middle of nowhere, he'd be able to rest. No one on the outside had a clue where they were and he felt at ease with the people around him. After everything they'd been through they all could use a good night's rest.

Tomorrow would see Kerry home. Avery wanted to be ready.

CHAPTER 24

Sarah sat staring at her phone gathering the courage to call Anna Colvin. It had been such a long time she was afraid of how she'd be received. She worried that her mother had created a rift too far to bridge. She found herself hesitant to punch in the number.

Anna Colvin, once upon a time, had been Sarah's favorite babysitter. But really Anna was much more to her than that. She was Sarah's surrogate big sister, teacher, confidant and the person Sarah most wanted to be like when she grew up. Anna had watched over Sarah from the time she started kindergarten. She never would have been anyone's first choice as a caregiver but to Sarah she'd meant the world.

Anna had been a runaway. She was a recovering addict and had once worked as an exotic dancer. She came back to Arvada burned-out and flat broke after her drug dealer boyfriend was sent to prison down in Vegas. That Sarah's mother had allowed Anna to watch over her was beyond the reckoning of a lot of people.

With Melinda's help, Anna slowly put her life in order. She and Melinda had a bond as strong as any family tie. Sarah loved both of them beyond measure. Everything in their world went along fine, for years, until the day she told Sarah the truth about her father.

In truth, it was an accident, a slip of the tongue. If Sarah hadn't pushed the issue the situation may have been avoided. But she wouldn't let it go. She pressured Anna for the truth.

Sarah already knew, long before then, that something about her life was off. Her parents divorced about the time she started kindergarten. It didn't take long to notice that the man she thought was her father never came back to visit her. Some of her friends would spend every other weekend and holidays with the parent that they didn't live with. Sarah hadn't seen hers since the day he walked out of their house as her mother screamed and threw a vase at the closing door.

If Melinda had come clean then and told her the truth it could have all been avoided. Instead, her mother doubled down on the deception and only cursed Ken's name. Melinda was unwilling to open any door that would allow Sarah to discover the truth.

Melinda saw Anna's confession as a complete betrayal.

Anna had taken her into the city that day to visit the big cemetery there, the Fairmount. She said that it was a special day and that they were going there to take flowers to a friend she'd lost. Sarah remembered being intimidated by the sheer size of the place and the thought of all those dead people lying silently around her.

They went into a huge mausoleum that loomed over the cemetery grounds. Sarah's eyes adjusted to the cool shade of the building listening intently as their footsteps echoed on the marble floor. Then, Anna paused. Sarah followed her gaze up to one of the headstones lining the walls of the cavernous room.

"Mark Vance? Is that who we're looking for, Anna?"

Anna nodded. A single tear ran down her cheek as she placed star lilies into a vase hanging beside the headstone.

"Mark was such a great person, Sarah. I wished you'd have known him. He was so funny and smart. He had such a gentle soul." Anna choked up as the memories flooded back. "I loved him with all my heart."

Anna rested her hand on Sarah's shoulder as the tears ran steady now down her face. "He'd have been a great..."

Then Anna stopped, cold.

"A great what, Anna?"

Anna wiped the tears from her face. She shook her head and squeezed Sarah's shoulder. "Nothing, sweetie, don't worry about it. It's just me wishing that things were different, that's all."

Sarah stared at Anna. Something about the expression on Anna's face compelled her. "What is it, Anna? Tell me. If it's in your heart it deserves a voice."

It was something Anna had always said to her. It was how she had helped Sarah work through her feelings about Ken.

Anna smiled. Sarah could see the love in her eyes. "I'm afraid that's not always true, my dear. As you get older you'll learn that sometimes the truth is the cruelest thing you can say. I'm afraid this is one of those times."

Sarah remembered her heart dropping in that moment and the frustration she felt.

"You brought me here for a reason. I wish you would just tell me the truth. I'm not a little girl anymore."

Sarah remembered the pain that came to Anna's eyes. She had grown to realize by then that there was something heavy between Anna and her mother that loomed over all three of them. There was something they purposely left her out of. She was tired of not knowing.

"Okay, its fine, Anna. You don't have to tell me. I'll just ask Mom. I know you're only protecting her."

Tears erupted from Anna's eyes. She wrapped Sarah up in a big hug and cried on her shoulder. Sarah felt so bad for causing it that she started crying, too. They stood there for a long time as the tears fell between them. Sarah didn't want to cause Anna any pain but she had to know the truth. She deserved it.

Anna guided Sarah to one of the benches that ran down the center of the room. They sat there in silence as Anna stared up at Mark's headstone. Then, after several long minutes of quiet deliberation, Anna told Sarah about her and Melinda's relationships with Mark and Kerry Vance. Anna artfully dodged the part about Kerry being her father or how her mother had cheated on Ken with him. It was much too heavy a story to drop on a twelve-year-old. But it didn't take Sarah long to put it together.

"He's my father, isn't he?"

Anna turned, astounded. "What makes you think that?"

Sarah could sense Anna was afraid. Most likely of what her mother would say if she found out.

"Who else could it be? I know Ken's not my father. He's never wanted anything to do with me. And I guess Ken is the reason the other guy's not around, either."

Anna reached over brushing the hair out of Sarah's face. The look in her eyes was haunted. Sarah remembered being so frustrated at that moment. She couldn't fathom why no one would just tell her the truth.

"Sarah, honey, it's a lot more complicated than that. And it's not my place to tell you. You need to have this conversation with your mother."

Sarah stiffened pulling away from Anna. "Yeah, like that's going to happen. She won't tell me anything. She thinks I'm still a baby."

"No, she really doesn't. Melinda is all too aware of how old you are and just how much you've matured. I think the reason she's kept this from you is that she's still too hurt and too embarrassed by what happened back then. I think she's afraid you'll think less of her for some of the decisions she's made."

It was the first time Anna really spoke to her like an adult. "I could never do that. I love her."

Anna smiled wrapping an arm around her shoulder. "I know you do. And that's what we need to impress on your mother. It's time for all of this to be brought out in the open. That way all of us can deal with it and move on."

Unfortunately, that's not how it went down. When Anna told Melinda what happened and what she'd told Sarah her mother lost it, big time.

The ensuing argument was one of the nastiest Sarah had ever witnessed. It was that argument, the way she spoke to Anna that made Sarah wary of her mother. Anna was only trying to help. She should have never been treated that way. That moment drove a wedge between Melinda and Sarah that still existed. It was Sarah's lingering guilt from causing it all that kept her from contacting Anna after she'd grown.

Now, with Kerry's death, it was time to reach out. It was time to set things right. Sarah knew her mother would never do it. Melinda was too proud and way too stubborn. As distraught as her mother had become since Kerry's death Sarah hoped that Anna could help, if she was willing. There was only one way to find out.

Sarah dialed Anna's number and hit send.

CHAPTER 25

The acrid smell of rain-soaked asphalt rose to greet Jimmy as he opened the door to his Juliet balcony. The sudden influx of air wrapped him in a cool embrace as lightning flashed across the sky. The muted glow of the uptown skyline shimmered as the storm raged across the island. Jimmy drew in a deep breath savoring the storm. After the last few days of stifling heat, it was a change worth appreciating.

As was the storm of emotion Daisy's presence created. Jimmy cherished the opportunity to be close to her. Her beauty, charm and wild sense of humor were captivating. She had been a gracious guest. She cooked for them and cleaned up around his apartment while lampooning him for being a typical male slob.

Jimmy knew better than to read too much into it. Daisy was just trying to make the best of the situation she found herself in. The fact that she hugged him as they watched Carol meltdown on the Donna Day show was of no significance. Though it had him walking on air it also left him feeling very much like a presumptuous old fool. He just hoped that when this madness was over Daisy would be able to find closure and make a new start. All he wanted was for her to be happy.

Now, as he waited for Daisy to finish getting ready, he hoped they were pushing a little closer to that goal. They were set to have dinner with Zap.

Now that Zap was officially off of the case he seemed eager to talk to Jimmy about what he had learned. Jimmy welcomed the opportunity. He hoped Zap could tell him more about Avery's mystery woman. Though, really, it wasn't a lock that knowing her identity would yield the desired result. But something about that woman's face stuck with him. Something in his gut told him she was the key to everything.

"So what do you think, Jimmy? Do I look presentable?"

Jimmy turned at the sound of her voice. As soon as he set his eyes on her he was spellbound. It was the first time Jimmy had seen her with her hair and make-up done. The short navy blue dress she was wearing hugged her curves like a second skin. That Jimmy couldn't stop staring was probably more than creepy. But he didn't care. She was stunning.

"So, I'll take that as a yes?" she asked, breaking the silence.

Jimmy blushed. "I'm sorry, Daisy, but words fail to describe how great you look right now."

Daisy's smile left Jimmy weak. "Ah, thank you. I just wanted to look sharp. It's been a while since I've actually gone out on a date."

"Why's that? Did Carol keep you on a short leash?"

Daisy's smirk was also wildly appealing. "I guess you could call it that. She certainly did her best to discourage me from dating. I was absolutely forbidden to have boys over to the house. Kerry paid for me and my girlfriends to go to spring break in Daytona last year as a graduation present. I'm pretty sure he did it just to piss her off."

Jimmy bristled at the thought of what Daisy had endured at the hands of that woman. It seemed that Kerry's influence was the only thing that kept her balanced. Jimmy was grateful for that, grateful to him. He was starting to wish that he'd been able to see past all of the hype and rumor surrounding Kerry and actually taken the time to get to know him. He had let his jealousy over Avery's attention cloud his judgment. Although there were aspects of Kerry's lifestyle he could never agree with, he could have at least tried to understand him. It seemed he had missed a worthwhile opportunity.

"So Carol just kept you cooped up at home? That doesn't sound like much of a life."

Daisy giggled. "Hardly, Carol used to drag me everywhere. Concerts, clubs, I've been going to nightclubs with her since I was like fourteen. No one ever bothered to card me, either. No one wanted to incur her wrath."

"I think Carol's been able to get away with shit for so long she's deluded herself into thinking she can get away with anything," Jimmy said.

"She's had a more than a few run-ins but they never affected her. She got arrested once for biting a waiter. They didn't do anything to her. Kerry's lawyer got it dropped."

"She bit a waiter?"

Daisy's expression was a messy mix of admiration and disgust. "Yeah, we were at a party and the guy kept bumping into her as he was serving drinks. I think he was trying to flirt. The last time it happened he made her spill her drink. So, she just turned around and bit the guy right on top of the shoulder. She was about dead ass drunk when it happened. But he still filed charges. Evidently, she took a pretty good chunk out of him. He needed stitches."

"Jesus. That's just fucking crazy." Jimmy said.

"I know. That's how she is sometimes. She can be vicious."

Deep down Jimmy could tell Daisy really loved Carol. Her betrayal of Kerry had left Daisy adrift. It made her fragile. She was trying to put on a brave face but Jimmy could see how just quickly those frailties rose to the surface.

"She's not going to get away with this is she, Jimmy? I mean she can't, right?"

Jimmy went to her wrapping his arm around her shoulders. "I don't want to lie to you, Daisy. What we're doing is a longshot at best. But it's not impossible. We just have to keep at it. We've already rattled Carol's cage. With a little luck, she'll screw up and do something we can use against her."

"Let's hope that it's soon. I'm dead in her sights now. There's no telling what she'll do."

Daisy wiped tears from her eyes as she turned away to stare out at the storm. Jimmy could feel her trembling beneath his arm. He hugged her closer as the thunder rolled above them. Slowly, Daisy turned to stare him in the eye. The surge of emotion was palpable.

"You're going to help me get through this, aren't you?"

Jimmy took Daisy by the shoulders and turned her to face him. "I'll be here as long as you need me."

Daisy leaned in and kissed him before he realized what was happening. When he did realize it, Jimmy committed with everything he had. Then, as their lips parted, Jimmy's awkwardness returned. He stared at Daisy confused. He felt fragile and invulnerable all at the same time.

"I'm sorry, Jimmy, I....Geez, are you OK?"

Jimmy's smile beamed like a beacon. He leaned in and kissed Daisy again. "I just wasn't expecting that to happen."

"It's what you wanted to happen, though. Isn't it?"

Jimmy's face reddened. "Since the first time I saw you. I just never for a second thought you'd have anything to do with me."

"Quit it." Daisy rested her hands on Jimmy's chest. "Don't doubt yourself. You're an attractive man, Jimmy. I feel safe with you. I'd have never come here if I didn't. This is a surprise for me too, you know. So let's say we don't analyze the hell out of it and just enjoy ourselves, okay?"

Jimmy grinned pulling Daisy closer. "Deal."

CHAPTER 26

Carol didn't bother to knock on Jerry's apartment door before turning the knob and storming along inside. There she found Jerry sprawled out on the couch essentially naked as the short red kimono he was draped in fell wide open around him. Across the coffee table from him, a dirty-dishwater blonde in her early twenties sat topless on the floor chopping up a mirror full of cocaine. Both jumped to their feet as Carol burst in. The girl fled to the bedroom with a boob in each hand.

"What the fuck, Carol? You can't just barge in here."

"Shut the fuck up, Jerry and close your goddamned robe. You know if you're going to lounge around in the nude soaking up an ounce of coke you should at least have sense enough to lock the fucking door."

Jerry's face went slack as he stared at Carol. "I thought I did."

He was bleached completely out of his mind. Seeing it only aggravated Carol more. She rolled her eyes as she walked back over to the door and snapped the deadbolt.

"Your little friend in there was probably planning on having her pimp come in and rob you while you had your dick stuck in her face. It's the oldest trick in the damn book. Christ, Jerry. Are you a complete moron?"

Jerry sat back down on the couch after wrapping the robe tightly around him. "She's not a prostitute, Carol. She's the singer for a new band I'm managing."

Carol huffed in derision, "Well, isn't that tidy? Jesus, you Neanderthal, is that what a girl has to do to get a break in the business with you? You should be ashamed of yourself."

The pained look on Jerry's face didn't give Carol any satisfaction. She knew full well berating him wouldn't do any good either. He was a small little man used to using his power to get laid. He had to. At his age, his lack of looks and brains weren't going to get him anywhere.

"Why are you here, Carol?"

Carol held up a finger before turning on her heel to march back into the bedroom. There, Jerry's coked-up chanteuse had gotten dressed and was busy strapping on a ridiculous pair of skull-studded platform boots. The girl looked up at Carol with a mix of awe and fear swimming in her watery blue eyes. "I'm sorry, Ms. Merrick, I didn't mean to..."

"Can it, kid. I don't give a rat's ass who Jerry's screwing. But if you're only doing him for the free coke and a shot at stardom you're fucking up, badly. Jerry's a dumbass. He's not going to get you anywhere. The only thing that's going to get you on top is a lot of hard work. There aren't any shortcuts. You have to earn it. Kerry used to have a saying; 'The stage is where the tale is told. If you can't go up there every night, whether you're pissed off, tired, hungry, or just flat burned out and slay the crowd, night after night, show after show, then you don't have any business being up there.' You might want to think about that."

The girl stared at Carol with stoned reverence as if she'd just been imparted holy wisdom. She stood up and smiled towering over Carol in her jacked-up boots. "Thank you, Ms. Merrick, I don't know what to say."

Carol frowned. She glowered at the girl. "Don't say anything. Just carry your narrow ass out of that door and run. I have business to discuss with that old pervert in there." Carol followed the girl out as she slipped past Jerry without a word and made for the door. Jerry watched the girl go, wide-eyed, as Carol leaned against the side of the arch leading to the hallway.

"What the hell did you say to her?"

Carol raised an eyebrow taking umbrage with his tone. "None of your business, you old letch, suffice it to say that you're going to have to find a new place to poke your pecker from now on."

"Goddamn it, Carol, what the fuck is your problem?"

"Right now, you are." Carol glared as a flop sweat broke out on Jerry's forehead. "You're supposed to be out finding Daisy. We need to get her internet shit shut down. Donna Day just made me look like a complete asshole on live TV with information that little bitch has been supplying. And what the fuck are you doing? You're here all coked up schtupping college girls! I mean goddamn, Jerry. That girl's barely twenty."

"Does that make you feel like a big man? Filling these little girls full of coke so you can unleash that tiny pecker of yours on them, you worthless piece of shit. I don't what in the hell possessed me to ever think that you'd be a suitable partner. You're as dumb as a fucking rock."

"Hey fuck you, bitch." Jerry jumped off of the couch. The rush of blood to his face was amplified by the cocaine in his system. "You've got a lot of fucking nerve after everything I've done..."

Jerry's voice cut out as a strange expression dawned on his face. He staggered back against the couch.

"Quit being so melodramatic," Carol said. "You know you really should lay off that shit. You're getting too fucking old to be a party boy."

The color drained from Jerry's face as he dropped on the couch. Fear burned in his eyes as he pulled his left arm tight against him. "Call an ambulance. I think I'm having a heart attack."

Carol frowned, watching as Jerry slid back on the couch clutching at his chest. It figured he'd have to freak out now just when she actually needed him. But, really, she guessed it was just as good a time as any for him to go out. It would save her the trouble later.

"Carol, please..."

Carol lifted an eyebrow picking up the straw from the mirror and filling it from the pile the girl had cut up on the mirror. She packed it tight against her fingertip then moved to stand over Jerry as he quivered on the couch. Jerry's dull gaze widened. His eyes bulged as he realized what Carol was going to do.

"My God..."

Carol smiled pushing his head back and staring into his eyes. She brought the straw to his nostril slipping her finger back to dump the powder directly into his nostrils. Jerry tried to turn his head but Carol tightened her grip. She leaned over to blow a quick blast of air through the straw to distribute it even further up into his sinuses.

A single tear fell from Jerry's eye as his pupils constricted to pinpricks. His convulsions slowly fell away as he stared out into the empty space above her.

"Good-bye, Jerry," Carol said, kissing him on the forehead. She stood over him watching as his body quivered for a few seconds, then, finally, fell slack. "Tell Kerry I said hello."

CHAPTER 27

Cori paused at the front door to the family mansion to take a deep cleansing breath before pushing it open to step inside. Even though Harry considered the house to be his personal domicile, it actually, in deed, belonged to the entire family. Cori hadn't been here in decades. Harry's Spartan lifestyle had always been a bit more than she'd been able to bear. At this time of the afternoon, though, she hoped the war college would be in recess and she'd catch Harry alone.

The house itself, which had been owned and abandoned by a who's who list of celebrities and old-world money, had been in their possession for the last fifty years or so. Harry had spent a great deal of time, effort and money restoring it to its original 1920's art-deco glory.

Cori wasn't enamored with the Jazz Age décor but as she wandered around searching for Harry she had to admit that it accurately reflected the flair of the period. There were some stunning pieces of lacquered furniture scattered about that she hadn't seen before and an authentic Tamara de Lempicka painting of a naked blonde woman holding a dove hanging in the drawing-room. It seemed that Harry was sparing no expense tinkering with the look.

After all of the strife their family had endured over the centuries Cori understood why this particular time period made Harry feel comfortable. The 1920s had afforded them an opportunity to relax and catch their breath as they made a new start in America. Harry had worked diligently to create a place for them here. His business acumen kept them all afloat when the world, once again, turned to shit a few short years later. But his heavy-handedness as head of the family had slowly driven them apart.

"Have we decided that knocking on the door was too much trouble, Terpsichore?"

Cori jumped when her sister Polly called down from the top of the stairway. "I have a lot more invested in this place than you do, my dear," Cori said, "so I'll stroll in whenever the hell I feel like it. Where's Harry?"

Polly scowled as she made her way down the steps. Cori rolled her eyes as the youngest of her sisters pulled her white terry cloth robe shut over the barely-there black bikini she was wearing. Unlike Harry, Polly reveled in a libertine lifestyle. She beguiled men with her beauty for both fun and profit. She hadn't committed a hard day's work in the entirety of her existence. "Last time I saw him he was out in the lanai talking on the phone."

Cori turned without comment and headed for the back of the house. Polly rushed to stay beside her.

"So just exactly what is it that Calliope has gotten herself into this time, Cori? Harry's been most grumpy these past few days. He's been watching that stupid television like he was consulting an oracle."

Cori didn't break stride as she moved through the kitchen and out toward the grounds. "Don't worry about it. Calliope knows what she's doing."

Polly giggled. "Oh, I'm sure she does. Just like every other time she's gotten involved with a mortal. And you all act like I'm the slutty one."

Cori stopped, turning to face her. "Well, that's only because you are, Polyhymnia. You don't care about anyone but yourself. Calliope, on the other hand, has the terrible habit of falling in love with these people. She is moved by their talent. And say what you will about that but she has a great sensitivity to it."

Polly smirked, "Still ushering souls into the in-between, still trying to restore the balance. That time has passed, Terpsichore. She needs to get a grip."

Cori sighed, running her hands through her hair as she glared at Polly. "Has it passed? Or have we all become so jaded that we just don't care anymore?"

Polly's eyes narrowed to slits. "Harry says that it was an Olympian tactic to keep us distracted from their agenda."

Cori scoffed. "Yeah and Harry's always right, isn't he?"

Polly sneered before storming away, her auburn hair flowing behind her. Cori shook her head then continued out into the courtyard.

The grounds behind the house were the part of the property Cori missed the most. The gardens that flanked the swimming pool were breathtaking when in full bloom. She stopped to admire the striking purple of the Sea Lavender and Lilies-of-the-Nile. Whoever Harry had taking care of the grounds was doing a fantastic job in her absence. She missed tending to it herself.

As Cori toured the rest of the garden she found Harry at the far end of the pool sitting in meditation in the shadow at the back of the lanai. Cori paused to gaze at his serene angular visage. It had been a very long time since she had seen him at ease, at peace within himself. He was, and had always been, a beautiful man. It wasn't until he opened his mouth that things went south. But she would always be grateful to him for keeping her and her sisters alive, even if she could only bear his personality in small doses.

"Terpsichore, what a great surprise, I wasn't expecting to see you again so soon."

"I told you I'd find out what I could about Calliope."

Harry opened his eyes and rested them upon her as he stretched his legs out from the lotus position. "Yes, but I didn't think you would come to visit. I expected a phone call."

Cori sat down on one of the long low couches that encircled the room and shrugged. "Yeah, well, I hadn't been here in a while and I figured I should come and check on my investment."

A small lopsided grin appeared on Harry's face. "You know you always have a place here. Besides, I could make good use of your skills. Keeping track of all our enterprises is more than I care to take on some days."

Cori smiled, taken with his compliment, "If you need help all you had to do is ask. I have no problem pitching in. I'm just surprised. Is Polly not pulling her weight around here?"

Harry laughed, loudly, as he leaned back into the couch. "That girl can't even take a phone message without making a mistake. There's no way I'd have her track investments. We'd all be living in the street."

Cori laughed, struck by how relaxed Harry was. He was actually pleasant to be around. She didn't know when he had taken up meditation but he needed to stick with it. It suited him.

"So what have you learned about Calliope?"

Cori hesitated not wanting to kill the mood. "I'm sure you've heard by now that they're headed for Denver. It's been all over the news. But I think I've figured out what she's up to."

Cori could see Harry's good humor recede from the tiny change of expression on his face. "And?"

"Well, there's new evidence that casts doubt on Kerry Vance's death being a suicide. If that's the case you know what she's going to do."

Harry frowned. "She's going to help him cross over."

"Exactly."

Harry stood and paced across the room. "Well, if he didn't kill himself he's certainly entitled. He was a talented man."

The statement took Cori by surprise. "You know his work?"

"I've made myself familiar. I wanted to understand what Calliope saw in him."

That Harry had gone to all the trouble told the tale of how much he still cared for Calliope. Cori could see it in his eyes.

"So you're saying we should just stay out of her way and let this play out?" she asked.

Harry resumed pacing. Evidently, the meditation had yet to overcome his innate restlessness.

"No. She has drawn too much attention to herself. We've worked too hard for far too long to go back into hiding. We have to find a way to shield her from scrutiny."

"I'm not sure that's even possible at this point," Cori said. "You've seen what's happening in the media? What can we do?"

Harry stopped to wipe sweat from his brow. "I don't know. I know if I interfere I will only drive her further away. But we can't afford not to do anything."

"Well, maybe we can help sway things from behind the scenes," Cori said, "Then when the time is right we get her the hell out of there."

Harry's brow furrowed. "It won't be an easy challenge. We'll have to be subtle. Calliope is no one's fool."

"You know better than anyone."

Harry face twisted into a smirk. "And it's a lesson I only needed to learn once."

Cori smiled. She was in love with the idea of Harry and Calliope being together again. If they could settle their differences it might go a long way in healing some other old wounds. Her family had been divided too long.

"So do you think the three of us can handle it?" Cori asked.

Harry frowned. "Three? You're not seriously considering bringing Polyhymnia along?"

"She has her uses. And I for one would like to see her do something constructive for a change."

Harry nodded, considering. "That's not a bad idea. She's just been taking up space around here lately anyway. OK, so what do you have in mind?"

Cori smiled. "We have a party to plan."

CHAPTER 28

The tap on the driver's side window startled everyone inside of the Temple awake and into full-blown panic mode. Calliope snapped forward in the driver seat, her short sword concealed along the back of her forearm.

Clyde looked around the seat and caught its cold steel reflecting sunlight. "Jesus Christ, girlie, be careful with that fuckin' thing. That's not a cop, is it?"

Calliope glared at Clyde via the rear-view mirror then shook her head. "No, it's just a boy. I'll handle it."

Her expression gave Avery pause.

There had been more than a few times when Calliope genuinely scared the hell out of him. There was a lot more going on with her than she'd been willing to disclose. He was more than ready to get to Denver and be done with her. Calliope slid the sword around to her left hand as she turned in her seat to roll down the window. If their visitor stuck their head inside the van Calliope had them dead to rights.

Clyde glanced over at Avery wide-eyed. "We need to keep a closer eye on her," he whispered. "That chick's a little off in the head."

Avery rubbed his eyes as the sudden rush of adrenaline knotted up in the pit of his empty stomach. He frowned, leaning closer to Clyde, "Yeah. No shit."

Outside a tall skinny wisp of a boy in his late teens took a slow step away from the door, no doubt taken aback by the sudden motion and the fire in

Calliope's eyes. Avery could only see a slim reflection of him in the side mirror but he looked harmless enough.

"Is everything okay, ma'am?"

Calliope smiled a big alluring smile and all of sudden she was back to her sweet and loving self. Avery watched the transformation closely. There was something heavy buried deep in that girl's psyche. He wasn't convinced she had it under control.

"Not entirely I'm afraid," Calliope said. "We were run off of the highway last night and one of our tires was damaged in the process. It was so late we decided to wait until daylight to fix it."

The boy looked out toward the road where a newer blue Ford pick-up pulled across the lane in front of them. "They got run off the highway, Dad. They have a flat tire."

The boy's father hopped out of the pick-up and headed toward them. He was tall, way over six feet, with longish salt and pepper hair tucked behind his ears. To Avery's surprise, he was wearing a black Motley Crue T-shirt over top of a ripped-up pair of blue jeans. He was far from the American gothic stereotype Avery expected in the wilds of Kansas.

"Okay, this guy looks hip," Jill said. "Maybe we'll be alright."

Calliope turned in her seat to look at Avery and Clyde. "I think we better all get out just in case. Let them see they're outnumbered. Just make sure you shut the door. The last thing we need is them peeking in and seeing Kerry."

"Yes dear." Clyde said as he opened the side door, "Let's just not try to slice anyone up, okay?"

Calliope arched an eyebrow. "Only as a last resort," she said.

The Motley Crue Dad seemed affable enough. If he was suspicious of them, he hid it. He seemed at ease as they all piled out of the van. Avery wondered if he hadn't already placed a call to the local police. If this was their property it would have been a prudent move.

"So you had a bit of trouble out on the highway, huh? It always gets crazy out there toward the end of summer."

"Yeah, some idiot in a black Mustang locked up the breaks and stopped sideways in the middle of the damned road dead in front of us. It was all I could do to keep from plowing into him. We took a rough path over onto the exit ramp. The back passenger tire is wasted."

The man watched Clyde carefully as he spoke. "I wonder if it had anything to do with the checkpoint the state police had set up."

Calliope glanced at Avery raising an eyebrow. Could the Mustang have actually helped them out?

Clyde never flinched. "A checkpoint, huh? Maybe that's why that asshole locked 'em up. He passed us like a bat out of hell just a few miles before that."

While Clyde was talking the man took a look at the van and then set appraising glances on both Calliope and Jill. Avery wondered if there was a Mrs. Motley Crue at home.

"You'll never be able to change that tire here. The ground's too soft. The jack will sink. I'll go get a tractor and we'll haul it down to my barnyard. It'll be a lot easier."

Calliope, Clyde, Jill, and Avery exchanged looks. None of them were sure it was a good idea to accept the offer.

"We don't want to be a bother to you," Calliope said. "We can just call someone to come out and fix it."

"Yeah, you could. There's a town called Wilson on the other side of the highway there a couple of miles. But then you'd run the risk of someone else figuring out who you are."

The Motley Crue Dad smiled as they all stared at him. "Hey, you guys have been all over the news for days, man. A blind guy could pick you out of a line-up."

Avery grinned but the truth of the remark didn't sit well.

"So you're not going to turn us in?" Calliope asked.

She sounded relieved but Avery still worried about the sword hidden inside the scarf at her waist. If this guy was up to something he couldn't be sure how Calliope would react.

The guy smiled then shook his head. "Hell no, we're big fans of Kerry Vance, Jake and me. We'd be happy to help. My name's Dan, by the way, Dan Lyle."

Avery saw a smile break out on the boy's face. Avery let out a sigh of relief. Maybe they were in good company.

Calliope smiled as she shook Dan's hand but still looked wary. "Well, we'd certainly appreciate it. We need to get back on the road as quickly as possible. We should have been in Denver long before now."

Dan nodded as he walked around the van to check out the tire. "Well, it sounds to me like your pit stop here may have been fortuitous. I don't know for sure but I suspect that checkpoint was put up specifically to look for you. They never put DUI checkpoints up on the highway. The last time I'd seen one out there was when a couple of cons escaped from Leavenworth a few years back."

Avery leaned back against the door only half listening as Calliope and Clyde continued their conversation with Dan. Jill sauntered up beside him and leaned in close.

"Are you OK, Avery? You look pale."

"I'm fine," he said. "I'm just ready for this to all be over."

"You need a drink, don't you?" Jill's amber eyes stared sharply into his.

Avery held her gaze as embarrassment returned color to his face. "I sure as hell wouldn't turn one down."

Jill shook her head turning to watch as the others examined the van. "You know you can't keep going like this. You'll hit the wall eventually."

Avery raised his arms up above his head to stretch. The muscles in his shoulders and upper back screamed from the motion. It wouldn't be long before his fever turned into a full-blown DT.

"I'm about to hit it now." He said. "Hopefully I can keep it together until we get out of here."

Jill leaned against the van next to him gazing out across the tall grass swaying in the breeze. Avery memorized every facet of her face as the soft morning light illuminated her. Avery wanted to tell her how he felt but couldn't summon the courage.

"Have you ever thought about quitting? I mean seriously, Avery. Haven't you ever wanted to just stop?"

Avery wanted to say something glib to break the mood, to defer attention, but he couldn't. He had to speak the truth. Something about her demanded it.

"Sure, I've thought about it. But, hell, it's just me now. There isn't much point."

Jill turned to look him in the eye. Her gaze was heavy. Its weight gave him pause.

"You know that's bullshit, right?"

Avery looked away. He couldn't match her intensity. "Yeah, probably, but fuck Jill, I don't know what to do. I mean ever since I lost Zoe....I can't just kill what's in my head, you know."

"Hey, you two lovebirds got a second?" Clyde's raspy baritone interrupted Jill's reply.

She touched Avery's hand as she walked past. "We'll talk later."

Jill and Avery joined the group at the back of the van. Avery didn't know a lot about automobiles but he was pretty sure that standing around and staring at it wasn't going to help much. But he'd been wrong before.

"So what's the problem?" he asked.

Clyde glanced up at him and shook his head. "The rim on this fucker is bent. We need a new one. We don't have a spare. I guess they took it out when they customized the van."

"Ah," Avery said. "So this is going to take longer than we thought."

Avery could see the tension on Calliope's face. He worried another setback might set her off.

"So what do we do?" Jill asked.

"The first thing we need to do is haul it out of here and stash it in my barn," Dan said. "Then I'll call a friend of mine over at the salvage yard and see if he has one. If he does, we can stop and get a tire on the way. My buddy will pop it on the rim for us. It shouldn't take more than an hour or two."

Calliope nodded. "One of us will have to go with you."

Dan's expression mirrored Avery's concern.

"Are you sure that's a good idea, Calliope?" Avery asked. "As he said, we're all over the news."

Calliope raised an eyebrow. She didn't like having her judgment questioned but, at this point, Avery didn't care. He wasn't going to allow her capriciousness to get them all busted.

"I'm not crazy about it," Calliope said, "but I think it's prudent."

Dan nodded. "What's the matter? You don't trust me?"

Clyde glanced over at Avery. It made sense. Calliope was being cautious. They needed to protect themselves.

"I'd like to," Calliope said. "But I don't have the luxury of time. So I think it best if Clyde goes along with you. We'll keep Jake here with us. I'm sorry it has to be this way."

Jake looked from Calliope to his father as he grasped the subtle shift in interaction. Dan smiled but there was steel in his gaze. "Yeah, I get it. You can't be too careful."

In that instant, the paradigm changed. A threat had not been voiced but one was clearly understood. Avery feared it left them in a vulnerable place.

Avery watched Calliope closely as she glanced around the group. There was a glimmer of remorse apparent in her eyes. There was also an indomitable strength of will there too. Avery couldn't begin to guess at the life path that had forged such an intimidating person.

It appeared Dan sensed something of this in her, as well. He held her gaze for a long few seconds before turning to Jake with a wink. "Well, I guess we better get started then. Jake, I want you to go grab the four-way out of the truck and check the lug nuts on that tire. Try to loosen them a little and make sure they're not screwed up while Clyde and I go down and get the tractor."

Jake headed for the truck without a word. As soon as he was out of earshot Dan moved in closer to Calliope. "I don't know who you are, lady. But I sure as hell hope you know what you're doing."

Calliope's eyes flashed. Their intensity forced Dan to take a step back.

"Calliope! Chill the fuck out."

Avery's bellow caught Calliope off guard. She whipped her head around to face him. In that interval, the anger in her drained away. It transmuted into a deep sadness, a sudden heartbroken woe that took all of them by surprise. She turned away dropping her head to wipe tears from her eyes.

"Unfortunately, I do know what I'm doing," Calliope said. Her voice sounded hollow, haunted. "I lament how many times I've had to do this over the years. But Kerry... Kerry has been, by far, the hardest. He's the only one I ever really loved."

The group stood about staring at each other in confusion. Clyde and Avery exchanged weary glances. They needed to get to Denver as quickly as possible.

"What are you talking about, sweetie? We don't understand." Jill moved to wrap her arms around Calliope. When she did Calliope leaned her head over onto Jill's shoulder.

"I ... can't explain it," Calliope said. "Not yet."

Clyde scowled, spitting in the dirt as he walked around the back of the van toward Dan. "C'mon, man, let's get this show on the road. Jill can handle this. Bring the kid, too."

Dan nodded. His bewilderment was apparent as he looked from Calliope to Clyde. "Yeah, I think that's a good idea."

Avery watched as the three of them climbed into the cab of the truck and followed their path down the road to the farmhouse. He couldn't help but wonder if there wasn't an ice-cold beer down there somewhere inside Dan's refrigerator. He wanted to have at least one more drink before he got locked up. It'd be a goddamned miracle if they made it the rest of the way to Denver without getting caught.

CHAPTER 29

Tears rolled down Carol's face as she stared out into the fathomless blue beyond her tiny airline window. She loathed herself for allowing such weakness to overtake her. But as Kerry's voice issued unbidden from her MP3 player she found herself unable to fight them back. The song, an old Zephyr ballad, had been a favorite of hers before she'd even met Kerry. It was the only song of his that she'd been unable to purge from her devise. Now in the void, at thirty-thousand feet, it haunted her.

No more secrets-No more lies-Our truth exposed-Undisguised-And so I stare lost in your eyes and wonder...

After everything that had happened, it was time to abandon New York. It was a cruel joke. She was taking a pounding in the press now and a lot of people were asking a lot of questions about the circumstances surrounding Kerry's death. The police commissioner had gone as far as to contact the authorities in London to ask for information on their investigation. As soon as Jerry's body was found it was only going to get worse. But at least they wouldn't be able to pin that on her. It would be just another tragic overdose. And an easier death than that idiot deserved. Despite all of her careful planning, a shit storm had descended. All she could do now was plan her revenge.

Carol wiped her eyes as she sat up in her seat. The first thing she had to do was find a lawyer to contest the will. She didn't have enough money now to hire a good one but hopefully, she could find a shyster willing to gum up the works for a few months. Let all the bastards Kerry had placed above her to sweat it out for a while including that little bitch, Daisy.

She supposed though she had to take the long view over Daisy's betrayal. She had raised the girl to be strong. She could have never, for an instant, allowed Daisy to turn into a weak-willed victim like her mother. That Daisy's fortitude had ultimately served to bite her in the ass was an irony she supposed she'd have to live with.

In her desperation to cover her tracks after Kerry's death, she had failed to consider how much Daisy would mourn Kerry's passing. She underestimated how much Kerry meant to her. She had kept the girl at arm's length, purposely, to conceal her role. If that thrice-damned Jerry hadn't run his mouth it would have never been an issue. But it was her own short-sightedness that didn't allow her to foresee Daisy's reprisal and prepare for it.

Avery Clark, on the other hand, was another story entirely. He and his mystery woman, no doubt some graceless backstage fuck of Kerry's, were going to feel the full weight of her wrath. Their meddling was going to cost them dearly. Carol eased back into her seat and tried to relax as Kerry's song faded. Once she got to Denver, all hell was going to break loose.

CHAPTER 30

Being a guest in the Zapata household was always a lively experience. Jimmy's buddy, Luiz, along with his brothers, Miguel and Raul had pooled their resources a few years back to buy the huge brownstone building. It now housed several generations of their family. As Jimmy knocked on the door, he could hear a group of children running around screaming just on the other side. Whatever game they were playing it sounded completely out of control. Jimmy smiled as a tiny little wisp of a girl opened the door. Her coal-black eyes bore into him suspicious of his appearance.

"Is Luiz here?"

The little girl nodded solemnly then turned to scream over her shoulder. "Uncle Luiz, you have company."

Daisy grinned as the little girl abandoned them to rejoin her playmates. "She has a hell of a set of lungs for such a tiny thing."

"She'd have to, to be heard over this crowd."

Within a few seconds, Zap appeared at the door with a big beaming smile. "Jimmy, brother, come on in."

As they walked inside Jimmy saw a hint of trepidation pass across Zap's face as he regarded Daisy. "It's nice to see you again, Ms. Merrick. Welcome to my home."

Daisy smiled reaching out to shake Zap's hand. "Please, call me Daisy."

Zap's smile grew wider as he held on to her hand. "Daisy it is."

He led them on a zig-zagging path around the wilding crowd of children to make their way up the stairs. "Sorry about all of the noise. There's nothing like a rainy day around here when they're all stuck inside."

Jimmy smiled. "They certainly have a lot of energy."

"Oh man, you have no idea. They've been going like this since this morning. I'm about ready to send them all out into the rain."

Jimmy wasn't used to having children underfoot. He liked them he guessed. But, at this point in his life, he couldn't see having any of his own. Daisy seemed to genuinely enjoy watching them running around. Jimmy was taken by the expression on her face as her eyes followed them.

"So you're coming back to work Monday aren't you, Jimmy?" Zap led them into his apartment motioning for them to have a seat on the couch.

"That's the plan," Jimmy said.

"But you're still trying to work out this Avery Clark thing."

Jimmy shrugged. "Yeah, well, what can I do? I know Avery's going to end up doing a stretch after all of this is over. But if I can find a way to make things easier for him I have to do it. At least I know now that he's trying to help."

Zap raised an eyebrow as he dropped down into a recliner opposite of them. "I guess you can call it that."

Jimmy frowned sitting forward on the couch. "What would you call it?"

Zap held up his hands, "Hey man, I'm on your side. I'm just saying whatever happened in Cincinnati looked pretty rough."

"Who knows what went down. I wouldn't take everything that the club owner said as gospel. He looked like a real scumbag."

Zap laughed. "True enough. He probably saw an opportunity to gain some quick publicity. Just like everyone else around this thing. I hate working these media cases. Every move is second-guessed to the point of inertia. I was glad when the Feds stepped in."

"I was too," Zap's wife, Elena, said coming out of the kitchen. "I hadn't seen a trace of him for three days."

Jimmy stood as Zap ran over to take the tray of beverages she was carrying. He sat it gently on the coffee table as Elena sat down on the arm of his recliner.

"Elena, you remember Jimmy," Zap said. "This is Kerry Vance's niece, Daisy Merrick."

Elena's expression turned sympathetic as she leaned forward to shake Daisy's hand. "I'm sorry for your loss, Mija. I'm even sorrier for what's happened since."

"Thank you," Daisy said. "It's been a tough week but Jimmy's been a big help. I don't know what I would have done without him."

Jimmy noticed the same expression pass across Zap's face that he had downstairs when he first saw Daisy. Something about her bothered him. Jimmy wanted to know what it was.

Elena stood patting Zap on the leg as she did. "Dinner will be ready in about ten minutes. Get our guests set up with drinks."

"Is there anything I can do to help?" Daisy asked.

"No, Mija, you stay put. You're a guest in our home. Please, have a drink and relax."

Daisy grinned sliding a bit closer to Jimmy on the couch. "Thank you."

Zap caught Jimmy's gaze as he watched Daisy's movement. Zap raised an eyebrow but didn't say anything.

"So were you making any headway before the Feds took over?" Jimmy asked.

"Quite a bit, actually," Zap said. "I got to interview that hearse driver. He was a sweet old gentleman. He told me that Avery was very nice to him. They even dropped the old guy off at a hospital on their way out of town. He also said that Avery's partner frightened him. He didn't like her at all."

Jimmy glanced over at Daisy. "So did you find out who she was? We've talked to a lot of people and couldn't find out anything."

"That's where it got weird. We must have gotten calls from half the kooks in the city after the Cincinnati thing broke. But we noticed a pattern emerge. We had about ten people, from all over the city, tell us the same story. They all said that her name is Calliope and she is an immortal Greek Muse."

"Huh?"

Zap stared at Jimmy. "I'm not kidding. We started chasing it down."

"That's crazy," Daisy said.

"So what did you find out?" Jimmy asked.

"That they honestly believe it," Zap said, "Every single one of them. And the stories were all too similar to dismiss out of hand. Evidently, she lived in the city once but was forced to leave over the death of some musician up in

Harlem back in the '50s. I even had one old guy pull out newspaper clippings showing her all over the country in the past sixty years. Every one of them looked like the same woman. She matched our security cam footage to a T. It was uncanny. But without the last name we really couldn't do any digging into official records. The Feds took the case over before we got any further."

"You don't believe it, do you?"

Zap shook his head. "I don't know, man. I shouldn't. But after seeing all that stuff I can't make up my mind."

Jimmy frowned running his hand down his face. "C'mon, Zap. You can't buy that bullshit."

"I don't know, Jimmy. You didn't see it. You didn't hear their stories. There's something to it. I just don't know what it is.

Jimmy stared off into space trying to process what he heard. "Man, I really need to get ahold of Avery. I've got to get to the bottom of this. This whole thing is insane."

"Yeah, I'd kind of like to know myself," Zap said. "You haven't been able to get in touch with him?"

"Daisy has been trying to reach out to him through social media but we haven't heard anything."

"I don't know, man. I don't know what to tell you. It'd almost be worth going to Denver to check out." Zap said.

"It would be if Nolan wouldn't can my ass," Jimmy said. "I guess I'll just have to wait until they drag him back home."

Zap rose from his chair and nodded. "It would be better for you, all around. You guys hang loose. I'm going to go see if Elena's ready."

Jimmy turned to Daisy as Zap left the room. "What do think about all that?"

Daisy let out a long sigh. "I don't know. I can't even process it. The only thing that strikes me is something Kerry once told me. He said that there was a lot more going on in heaven and Earth than they ever tell you about in school. So, who knows? Maybe Zap's right. Maybe there is something to their story."

"I doubt it," Jimmy said. "It sounds like she's some kind of con artist to me. She's probably just scamming people behind a bunch of New Age bullshit. Whoever she is she was probably born into it. It'd be the perfect scam if she looked enough like her mother to pull it off."

Daisy shrugged. "Could be, but I don't see Avery or especially Kerry falling for it. It makes me wonder how they're connected."

"I don't know. As soon as we get a chance we need to try and get ahold of Avery again. I wonder if he really knows who he's dealing with."

"Yeah, but really, Jimmy, does that even matter? I mean, say she is a con artist. What's her end game? All she's done is help Avery ostensibly carry out Kerry's last wishes. I mean if she was a used car salesperson would she go through all this just to sell a car? I think there's a deeper connection, one that we're not seeing. I don't think it matters what she does."

"That's a wise insight," Zap said, dropping back into his chair. "But I still thought it was worth looking into to try and discover her real identity. I figured it might be easier to find her connection to them that way."

Jimmy shook his head. He rose off the couch to stare out of the window. "It's just so goddamned frustrating. How in the hell could this woman go her whole life and not be in some kind of database? Do you think she's in Witness Protection?"

Zap shook his head. "No. If she was, we'd have had the U.S. Marshalls sweating us. They'd have taken over the case before the F.B.I had a chance to tie their wingtips. As far as I can tell, she's a ghost."

"There is no such thing as ghosts," Jimmy said. He smiled as Elena came out to load the table with food. "There has to be some way to track this woman down. We just need to find it."

Zap grabbed Jimmy's elbow holding him back before he could follow Daisy to the table. Elena struck up a conversation as Daisy sat down allowing them a few seconds to talk.

"So what are you doing with that girl, Jimmy? Why are you dragging her around the city?"

Jimmy frowned. He turned to stare Zap dead in the eye. Zap released his elbow but held his gaze.

"Because I think she's in danger. You heard about the guy that accosted her outside of the precinct the other day, right?"

"Yeah, I also heard that Nolan wasn't really crazy about you being there on the scene."

"That's his problem," Jimmy said. "The reason I was down there was to see you. Anyway, Daisy told me that Jerry Jewell sent that guy to find her. She thinks he was trying to drag her back to a vehicle."

Zap looked over Jimmy's shoulder at the girl. "Did she tell them that?"

"No. She didn't think it would do any good. See, she overheard Jewell tell Carol Merrick that he killed Kerry Vance. She left the house afraid for her life. It was just blind damned luck that I was there. So I offered her a place to crash until the investigation played out."

Zap shook his head. "So she's the one that's been all over Kerry Vance's social media apparatus saying that Jewell and Carol Merrick killed Vance."

"Yeah, and people are starting to listen. I heard about the commissioner making a call over to Scotland Yard. Do you know anything about that?'

"Just that it's all being handled at 1P.P. There holding it pretty close to the vest, too."

"I doubt it will lead anywhere," Jimmy said. "They probably just did it to get the media off of their back. But until this all blows over; I think she's safer with me."

Zap raised an eyebrow. "Are you sure that's the only reason?"

Jimmy sighed. He turned to look past Zap out through the window. "No. But fuck it, Zap, I know it's not going to lead anywhere. It's just been nice having her around."

Zap smiled. "I guess I can't fault you for that. She is a stunner. I just hope you'll be okay when this circus finally shuts down."

Jimmy laughed. "No. I probably won't be but I'll just have to deal with it."

"So are you two going to talk shop all night or are we going to eat?" Elena's voice cut through the chatter.

Zap smiled nudging Jimmy forward. "We're coming dear."

Daisy beamed as Jimmy sat down beside her. Her smile cut to the core of him. He really would miss her once this all played out. But he knew their worlds were incompatible. He had to accept it.

"Elena was just telling me that you two went to the police academy together," Daisy said. "She promised to pull out the photo albums after dinner."

Zap laughed. "You're going to love those pictures. Jimmy was so skinny back then. The biggest thing on him was his ears."

Jimmy chuckled trying to hide his embarrassment. "Yeah, well, that's nothing compared to that porn star mustache you sported."

"Hey, that was Puerto Rican pride right there," Zap said.

"You look better without it," Elena said.

"As good as you can, anyway," Jimmy said.

Jimmy took a deep breath relaxing into the laughter around him. He reached over and clasped Daisy's hand under the table. It was the perfect end to a stressful week. With so much going on around him it was nice to just kick back and enjoy a meal. The evening was off to a fantastic start. He wanted to enjoy every second of it. But, somehow, he couldn't escape the feeling that the other shoe was about to drop.

CHAPTER 31

Sarah had to force herself not to run through the house and out into the street when she heard Anna's taxi pull up out front. She managed to throttle herself down to a brisk walk as she looked around to make sure everything in the house was in its place. She was still amazed that Anna had insisted on coming.

They had had so much fun on the phone catching up that Sarah would have been pleased just to be able to keep in contact with her. After Sarah confessed her worries about Melinda and the strain Kerry's death had caused, Anna booked herself on the next flight out.

Sarah pushed through the door just as the cab driver set Anna's bags on the curb. Anna turned hearing the clap of the screen door shutting with a big smile shining on her face.

"Anna!" Sarah gave into her instincts and ran down the porch steps just as she had as a child rushing into Anna's arms. Tears rolled down both women's cheeks as they embraced. To Sarah, it felt like coming home.

"Oh my God look at you, baby girl. You are beautiful." Anna held onto her hand as she stepped back to take a good long look. "You look just like your grandmother when she was your age."

Sarah smiled. Her grandmother had been a powerhouse. Sarah wished she had half of her energy.

"Look at you. You've hardly aged a day. Are they hiding the fountain of youth out there in Utah?"

Anna grinned shaking her head. "You, my dear, are too kind. You're also full of shit. Trust me, since I've strolled on into my sixties I've noticed more than a few things starting to slide downhill, let me tell you."

Sarah paid the cab driver then grabbed Anna's bags off of the sidewalk. "Yeah well, that's kind of what I'm afraid is happening to Mom."

A pensive expression dawned on Anna's face. "I'm sorry, honey. I guess that was a poor choice of words. Tell me what happened."

"Well, it was weird. I finally got Mom to come off of the story about Kerry like I was telling you the other day, and she seemed fine. But then when I mentioned that this Calliope person contacted me about Kerry's will and his funeral she got really pissed off. She said that Calliope was the reason Kerry refused to have anything to do with me and that I should avoid her. Then, when that crap in Cincinnati happened, she called me just raging about Calliope. She said something to the effect that Calliope hadn't aged and she knew something was messed up, just rambling, pissed off. I didn't know what to say to her."

Sarah led Anna through the house to settle into the big comfy leather couch in the family room. She had a pitcher of lemonade waiting on the coffee table. She poured them both a glass and took a long drink.

"So, anyway, after Mom hung up I hopped on the internet to check it out. Mom swears that's Calliope in the video but that chick's younger than I am. I doubt she's thirty. So it has to be this Calliope's daughter or something. Which is what I tried to tell Mom but she wasn't having it. Mom said she had been nose to nose with Calliope and that was her. That's when I started to worry."

Anna frowned, concentrating. "And this is the first time you've seen anything like this out of her?"

"Yeah, she's always been as sharp as a tack. I do have to admit that I'm not around that much. Mom and I have had a lot of issues over the years and we're really not that close. I mean, hell, you know how she is. Age hasn't softened her attitude one bit. I think it's gotten worse."

Anna chuckled. "Your mother's a piece of work that's for goddamned sure. And I don't know a thing about this Calliope person. Your mom never told me about any of that. I do think I know where they met though. It's something I heard from a mutual friend after I moved back to Arvada when you were little."

"Oh yeah? What's that?" Sarah tried her to appear casual but deep down she was dying to know. She clamored for any new piece to the puzzle.

"Apparently at some point not long after you were born, Melinda took you to see Kerry up in Oregon. After Mark died Kerry split town just like I did. His parents eventually had to hire a private detective to track him down. Once they found him the four of you made the trip up there. My friend said there was some kind of big blow-up between Kerry, Melinda, his parents and the woman Kerry was living with whom I'm assuming is this Calliope woman. I don't know what all happened but my friend said that Melinda came back home shattered. They said she was an absolute mess."

Sarah felt tears welling up in her eyes. "He didn't want me."

Anna reached over to hold Sarah's hand. "Well, if he didn't, he was a goddamned fool. But I don't know, baby girl, I suspect it was a whole lot more complicated than that. You have to understand that Kerry was pretty well broken himself then. He was just a twenty-year-old kid when he held his baby brother in his arms as he lay dying.

"Mark's death nearly destroyed me. I can't begin to imagine what Kerry went through. After all of these years, I still don't know how your mother found the strength to make it through all of that. There was just so much heartache."

Sarah nodded, solemn, as she took in Anna's words. "I'm beginning to understand why Mom kept all of this from me. Reliving it had to hurt like hell."

"And now Kerry's death has drudged it all up again," Anna said.

"Yeah and I think it's hit her a lot harder than she's willing to admit," Sarah said. "This thing with Calliope has her unhinged."

"I've seen that footage on the news. There's no way that chick on the TV is the same one Kerry was fooling around with back then."

"I just wish there was a way to convince Mom of that. She was adamant that was her."

Anna shrugged taking another quick swig of lemonade. "That whole thing is a damned circus. It won't be long before it runs right through the center of town."

"Yeah, I've been thinking about that," Sarah said. "I have a bad feeling Kerry's funeral is going to be one huge mess. I heard on the radio this morning that people are flying into town just to be a part of it. They were debating if Avery Clark was a hero for doing all of this. It's out of control."

"It seems to me there's more going on behind the scenes than anybody knows about. I wouldn't be surprised if Kerry hadn't planned this whole thing just to screw with everybody."

Sarah laughed. It felt so good having Anna there with her. It seemed like all of the fractured pieces of her life were finally starting to come together. It was just too bad that it had taken Kerry's death to make it happen. "You really think so?"

"Oh, hell yeah, he was always like that. He loved to shock people. You've seen his shows, his music videos. He rattled cages. It's what a great artist does. They hold up a great big shiny mirror back at the world to see if people can deal with their reflection in it. I was thinking about this when I was flying in.

"Kerry was planning on divorcing that supermodel chick for fooling around with his manager. If he was afraid something would happen to him I know for sure he wouldn't just sit still for it. I think he got ahold of Calliope and Avery Clark and told them that if anything happened to snatch him up and make sure he got back home. It'd sure be a way to grab headlines and put those that had done him wrong square in the spotlight."

Sarah's eyes widened. The thought hadn't occurred to her. "Well, if that's what he did it's sure as hell working."

"Right? But the other thing to consider is that Merrick chick probably isn't going sit idly by and let all that money slip through her fingers, either. So when this all finally settles down you're going to have to be prepared for some legal bullshit to go down around the will. If he cut her out completely she's going to fight it, tooth and nail."

"Oh, I'd say so. But really, Anna, I don't care about the money. If I did I'd have tried to get in touch with him a long time ago. It was never about that."

Anna patted Sarah's hand. "So why did you choose not to contact him? I always figured that you would seek him out at some point."

Sarah ran her fingers through her hair. She shook her head as she tried to put the words together. "A lot of it had to do with Mom. I didn't want her to feel betrayed. But, really, I was just plain scared. I didn't know for sure if Kerry even knew about me because Mom would never come off of it. I didn't want to create waves. And I sure as hell didn't want to be put in the public eye to be seen as some kind of gold-digger looking for a pay-off. So, I just let it go. And now that it's too late I really wished I hadn't."

"That's a lot of pressure to be under," Anna said. "And I can understand your reasoning. It's just a goddamned shame. He would have loved you."

Tears filled Sarah's eyes as the futility of the situation fell upon her again. "I guess we'll never know now. All I can do is deal with what's in front of me."

"And it looks like you have plenty of it too," Anna said. "But luckily for you, my dear, you've got me here to help. And I'm not going anywhere until we've got this all put to rest."

Sarah leaned over to hug Anna as tears poured from her eyes. It was the first time since Kerry's death that it felt like things just might turn out all right.

"Thank you, Anna. You don't know how much I appreciate this."

"Don't sweat it, baby girl," Anna pulled Sarah closer hugging her with all she had. "I'm just glad that I can help. It's been a long time coming."

CHAPTER 32

The midday sun fell heavy on Dan Lyle's barnyard as a warm wind stirred dust devils along its empty width. Calliope stood in the shade of one of the barns watching as Avery and Clyde fit the Temple with the new tire and rim.

Embarrassment still burned raw in her chest. She had failed to keep her emotions in check. She failed to maintain control. She could hear Harry's voice in her head, *A warrior's life rises or falls over their ability to exert precise control.* But, this time, control escaped her. The thought of Kerry's essence stirring loose in the wind was maddening. More so than any other perfected being she had ever helped cross over.

She loved Kerry deeply. That was the problem. She allowed her emotions to overtake the logic of the situation. Dan and his son were perfectly willing to help. She let her desperation to get Kerry home to overshadow her understanding.

Her failing in Cincinnati weighed heavy on her mind, as well. It was only a matter of time until that blew up in her face if it hadn't already. By allowing herself to be photographed she endangered the entire Oikogeneia. She just hoped she'd have an opportunity to rectify the situation before Harry decided to swoop in and save the day. She didn't need his help.

Calliope moved out of the shadow of the barn to soak in the sun. She walked around the side, away from everyone, to face the warm west wind. Her memory raced as she stared out across the fields. Images appeared from millennia past that somehow didn't seem real anymore. There was the face of her first great love, Apollo, and that of their dear lost Orpheus. She saw her sisters, Urania, Clio, Euterpe, and Melpomene who refused to abandon the Olympians and shared their unknown fate. There were so many anchors stretched out in time behind her, so many places, so many people. It was overwhelming.

She took a deep breath and forced the images from her mind. For the first time in a long time, she felt the full weight of her age pressing down on her. She needed rest. Once Kerry was safe in the In-Between she saw about a year's worth of sleep waiting for her.

"Tire's done."

Calliope turned to find Avery at her side. He looked pale. Like the sweat pouring from his forehead was draining him of color. The process of detoxifying from alcohol was a terrible experience. She had seen it before. That Avery suffered it in silence spoke to his strength. He was determined to carry out Kerry's last wish. The doubts she'd had about him, in the beginning, had faded. He had proven to be a good man. She understood now everything Kerry had seen in him.

"Look, Avery, I'm sorry. I know I went overboard earlier. I just..."

"Don't worry about it, Calliope, really. It's been a long trip. Everyone is tired. Clyde explained everything to Dan and he's cool with it. He knows you were just trying to protect us."

Calliope nodded but it didn't make her feel any better. "I'll just be glad when this is over. I've made such a mess of things. I don't think any of us will escape unscathed. We have a lot to answer for."

"Then we'll answer for it." Avery said. "We know we're doing the right thing. Sometimes that comes with a price. And, for Kerry's sake, it's one we're all willing to pay."

Calliope smiled reaching over to grasp Avery's hand. "Thanks for coming with me."

"It's been an honor," Avery said. "It's exhilarating meeting a woman who knows how to kick a little ass."

Calliope laughed. It felt good to do so. "Yeah, well, I do get carried away sometimes. I'm afraid I have very little patience."

"Yeah, me too," Avery said. "So when are you going to be ready to take off?"

"Whenever we can get everyone loaded up. If we leave soon we could be there by nightfall."

As the two of them started back toward the barnyard, Jill came running around the corner of the barn. "Hey, you guys need to come in and take a look at the TV. Things just got complicated."

Calliope shook her head glancing at Avery. "Oh good, I thought things were going too well."

"Yeah, I guess we couldn't expect this whole thing to be a cakewalk." Avery laughed.

Jill grinned moving to Avery's side. "Joke all you want but you're going to flip when you hear this."

Avery took Jill's hand as they turned into the shade of the barn. "Great."

"So how are you feeling?" Jill asked. "You're awfully pale."

"To be truthful with you, I feel like a turd that got caught in a taffy puller. But, I'll be fine. Sweating has helped a little."

"You should drink some ice water with a bit of salt and sugar stirred in it," Calliope said. "You're burning nutrients you can't afford to lose right now."

Avery smiled as the three of them strolled onto the porch. "Yes, ma'am. Actually, I could go for a big glass of ice water."

"You go on into the living room and I'll get you one." Jill said. "Dan rolled back the story on his DVR. I wanted to make sure you saw the whole thing."

The interior of Dan's house had a relaxed, comfortable, vibe. Calliope got a quick sense of Dan's history from the generations of pictures lining the walls. Apparently, his family had lived here for quite some time. The thought of that kind of permanence brought a smile to her face.

They found Dan, Clyde and Jake sitting on a big blue suede couch that bisected the huge living room. It created a cozy little home theater at one end. Dan stood as Calliope entered the room. Calliope smiled hoping it was good manners that compelled him to do so. She hated to think she'd set him that far on edge.

"What did you find?" Avery asked as he and Calliope walked around to a matching love seat sitting perpendicular to the couch.

"Well, Jill and I were sitting here talking while Jake was flipping through the channels. He paused on that YMZ show because they had some model on there doing a bikini shoot."

Jake grinned. His face reddened with embarrassment.

"Then, after that story went off, we saw this." Dan picked the remote up off of the couch and clicked the DVR. There on the screen, larger than life, stood Carol Merrick.

"YMZ captured video of Kerry Vance's widow, former supermodel Carol Merrick, boarding a flight bound for Denver early yesterday morning. Ms. Merrick's departure coincided with the discovery of Kerry Vance manager Jerry Jewell's body by an employee in his New York City apartment."

Avery and Calliope stared at each other aghast.

"Holy Shit!"

"Police have declined to comment on this development other than to say that the investigation into Jewell's death is ongoing. But it looks to us like the Kerry Vance case just got a whole lot stranger."

Avery jumped up from the couch to pace around the room. "That's fucked up."

Clyde's eyes followed Avery around the room. "You think Carol did it?"

"I'd say at this point she's capable of damn near anything. And, really, it does makes a twisted sort of sense. I bet she thinks she can still get her hands on that money."

"What money?" Jill asked. She walked into the room with a pitcher of ice water and glasses. "I thought Kerry cut her out of the will."

Avery looked at Calliope and shrugged. "We might as well tell them."

Calliope nodded. "Yeah, I guess we better. If Carol's in Denver, we need to rework our plan."

"What in the hell are you all talking about?" Clyde asked.

Calliope looked around at all of the faces gathered. She wasn't crazy about telling them about the money. But it needed to be done in case something happened.

"One of the people who helped set us up with the Temple discovered that someone had stashed about 200 grand in Kerry's coffin. Our best guess is that it was Jerry Jewell."

Calliope assessed the expression on Clyde and Jill's faces. They were both surprised, to be sure, but she waited for the reaction that would come just after, when the first thought inherent to their nature revealed itself.

"Good Lord," Jill said. "So why did you wait so long to tell us?"

"There was no need," Calliope said, keeping a close watch on Clyde. "We decided we were either going to turn it over to the estate because we figured it was money Jewell embezzled anyway, or give it to charity in Kerry's name, like music in the schools or something."

Clyde nodded. He seemed satisfied with the answer. "So you think Carol cut Jewell out of the picture and is looking to get her hands on the cash."

"It's a good guess." Avery said, retaking his seat. "She's could use it to contest the will, too and invest it in getting a shot at the big pay-off."

The thought hadn't occurred to Calliope. "Does she have a case?"

"No." Avery said. "And I figure she knows it, too. But if she has enough money she can keep it tied up in probate for months."

"Sounds just like her." Clyde said.

"So how does knowing all of this change your plans?" Dan asked.

"We just need to make sure that we stay a step ahead of her," Calliope said. "I have a feeling she's going to cause a big stink now that she's in Denver and try to rally people to her cause. There will be a lot of eyes on the lookout for us."

Clyde frowned. "I'd say that's already jumped off. Everyone knows where we're going. It's going to be pretty fucking hard to sneak in."

"We need some kind of diversion." Jill said.

"It'd have to be a damned big one." Avery said.

Calliope dropped her head onto her closed fists. The answer was staring her dead in the face. Harry. She really didn't want to go there, though. Not again. She needed to prove that she could stand on her own. She didn't want his help. As she looked around the room, she realized that it was about more than just her. Avery, Clyde, Jill, they had all put themselves in jeopardy to fulfill Kerry's dying wish. She couldn't let her pride lead them to a fall.

They were going to need help to pull this off.

Harry had a few thousand years' worth of experience bailing her out of trouble. He was going to need every second's worth of it to get her out of this one. The whole world was watching.

Avery set his hand on her shoulder. Calliope reached up to hold on to it.

"What are you thinking?"

"I think we're going to need some help." Calliope said. "Dan, is it okay if we hang around a bit longer? Avery and I need to reach out to some people. But, if everything goes right, I think I have a plan."

Dan grinned. "Why not? I'm dying to see how all this is going to turn out, anyway. I can't turn down a front-row seat."

"Thank you. I really appreciate it." Calliope said. "Now, Avery, you need to get a hold your friend back in New York and see what you can find out about Jerry Jewell and Carol."

Avery nodded. "Okay. So who are you going to call that can possibly help us with this mess?"

Calliope sighed. "As much as I hate to do it, I'm going to have to call my husband."

CHAPTER 33

The Buckaroo Boom-Boom Room was a dive bar to end all others. Its rundown cowboy chic had kitsch down to a fine science. Carol eyed the log cabin motif with suspicion as she made her way inside. She wasn't sure if the ambiance was genuine or the product of clever design. It was just a little too good to be believed.

Not that it mattered. All she cared about was that it was supposed to be the roughest bar in Denver. It was the clientele that interested her.

There was already a decent-sized crowd gathered. A good portion of them packed onto the dance floor scooting their boots around to the latest in country music.

Carol hated country music. It reminded her of Blacksville.

She'd have preferred to listen to Yoko Ono sing German opera rather than suffer through this plowboy rap crap for very long. But she was on a mission and would just have to do her best to put it out of her mind.

As soon as the locals caught site of her sidling up to the bar she caused quite a stir. She had disguised herself in a long flowing blonde wig with a new make-up scheme to match. Her low-cut aqua cocktail dress was skin-tight. It highlighted her assets perfectly. When she slid up on the barstool she crossed her legs with a flourish before spinning around toward the bar. She made a concerted effort not to grin as a slew of younger girls hovering around flashed a variety of disapproving stares.

That's right, bitches, you just got outshined.

"What can I get you, darlin'?" The bartender's western drawl brought a genuine smile to Carol's face. She watched him cop a quick eye-full of boob before flashing a crooked little thin-lipped grin. He wasn't bad looking but not enough to distract from her intended purpose.

"Bourbon," she said, "three cubes, three fingers."

The bartender raised an eyebrow, "Well, hell yeah. I love a whiskey-drinking woman."

Carol grinned shooting the bartender a wink, "Oh, I just bet you do."

"So you here by yourself or are you waiting on somebody?"

A sly smile crossed Carol's face as she held the bartender's gaze. "Actually, I'm looking for someone."

"Oh, yeah, what's their name? I pretty much know all of the regulars around here."

Carol watched the bartender pour her drink. He gave off the vibe of someone that had run afoul of the law at some point in his life. His scruffy beard, dirty blonde hair and arm's length tattoos were all brilliantly haphazard. He wasn't trying to cultivate a look like the brood of transparent hipsters that assailed the Village on weekends. He was the genuine article. If Carol had a superpower it was her ability to spot a bad boy. She decided to take a chance on him to get things rolling. If he didn't want to help she was willing to bet he knew someone who would.

"I can't remember his name, right off," she said, "but I was told he doesn't mind doing a bit of dirty work if the money's right."

The bartender nodded thoughtfully as he sat Carol's drink in front of her, "How dirty?"

Carol smiled. Her question didn't faze him. "I don't want to kill anybody or anything but I have an ex whose new girlfriend could use a good scare."

The bartender stared at her for a long second. Carol could see the wheels turning behind his shy brown eyes. "What's it worth to you?"

Carol took a slug of bourbon. She shot him her best smoldering gaze as she returned her glass gently to the bar. "A couple grand if my plan is properly executed."

The bartender's veiled smile told Carol she was on the right track.

"I wouldn't mind having a crack at it but I'm still on parole. I get enough shit from my P.O. for working here. I might know someone that could help you though. He'll probably be here before too long if you want to hang out."

Carol shrugged. "I'll stay for a drink or two."

"Well, you just make yourself comfortable, darlin'.' I'll check back here in a few."

Carol watched the bartender move on to another customer. She really didn't feel like hanging around listening to the high-country hoedown but if she could land her fall guy tonight it would help move things along especially before the news cycle fired up in New York. Avery and his mystery woman had a hell of a head start on her. They were probably already in town. She needed to get at Kerry's daughter soon. She didn't have a lot of time.

Across the bar, Carol spotted a youngish brunette staring at her. Carol raised an eyebrow before nabbing another long pull of her drink. The girl didn't avert her eyes. She just continued staring with a puzzled look. Carol got the uneasy feeling that the girl recognized her. But with her well thought out disguise, she didn't think it was possible.

After a few minutes, the girl dropped out of her seat to stagger through the crowd. Carol finished her drink then took a deep breath preparing for the encounter. With the crowd, the noise and the God-awful cacophony coming from the jukebox she was in no mood to deal with a drunk.

"Hey, don't I know you from somewhere? You look familiar."

Carol flashed her best fake smile. "I don't think so. I'm from out of town."

The girl frowned, swaying, unstable on her feet. She had a loud brash voice that cut through the noise in the room. "I know I've seen you. You been on T.V. or something?"

The comment raised hair on the back of Carol's neck. There was no way this bitch recognized her. "Well, kind of. Back in my twenties I used to do porn. You watch a lot of porn?"

Seated next to Carol an older weathered-looking gentleman in a black Stetson spit beer all down the front of his nice white Wrangler shirt and out across the width of the bar. He got up quickly and dashed for the restroom.

Confusion settled across the girl's slack face, then, after a second's contemplation became indignant. "I don't think that's any of your business."

Carol shrugged. "Hey girlie, you came down here bothering me. I'm just trying to help."

The girl's face reddened. She glared at Carol, wide-eyed, before turning a sloppy about-face to push her way back to her seat. Carol's devilish grin lingered as she spun back around to face the bar. The hot blonde bartender shook his head as he swamped up the beer the old man spewed.

"What in the hell did you say? You've got 'em running in both directions."

Carol shook her head, "I just had to run that nosey bitch off. She thought she knew me and was asking a bunch of dumb ass questions."

"You must have a hell of a technique. I never seen 'ol Earl spit out beer he paid good money for."

Carol chuckled reaching into her purse to pull out a twenty. "Well, here buy him a few more on me. I have a feeling he'll need them."

"Are you leaving?"

"Yeah, I can't hang around here all night," Carol said. "I have shit to do."

Disappointment shone on the bartender's face. It was apparent he wanted to do a lot more than help Carol hire muscle. "Stay and have another drink. My buddy will be here soon."

Carol looked him over again. Maybe with a bit of pressure applied in the right places, she could con him into doing what she needed done. It wouldn't kill her to get a bit of exercise, either.

"I tell you what, forget about your friend. I really should handle this myself. I don't want to get anyone into trouble. It's just that bitch pisses me off so much."

The bartender reached out and touched Carol's hand. "Don't worry about it. I get it. You'll find a way to get over on her eventually."

Carol held his hand between both of hers. She looked him dead in the eye and smiled. "So, listen, if you're not doing anything after work, why don't you come on over to my hotel. I could use a little... company. Maybe bring along a little bourbon? I'll make it worth your while."

Carol's smile widened as the implication left him awed. When the slow grin overtook his face she knew he was hooked.

"I can do that," he said, "Won't be until about 2:30 or so."

Carol squeezed his hand. "That's fine. It'll give me time to warm-up."

The bartender lifted an eyebrow, clearly intrigued, but too embarrassed to pursue the details. "Where are you staying?"

"The Crawford. Room 419."

Carol slid off of the barstool and walked away without another word. When she turned to glance back from the door, his eyes were glued to her. She blew him a kiss before walking out. *Is there any simpler creature to train than a horny man?*

Carol giggled all the way to the cabstand.

CHAPTER 34

The ride out to Arvada passed between Sarah and Anna in uncomfortable silence. Sarah spent the trip fretting over Melinda's condition. She hadn't been able to get in touch with her, again, after several calls, so a thousand terrible thoughts filled her head as they closed in on home. After their last conversation, Sarah worried about her mother's state of mental health. Even at her youngish age dementia was a credible possibility. It was also too heartbreaking to conceive. Her mother had always been so strong, so formidable, that the thought of it chilled Sarah to the bone.

She resolved to put all of her worries out of her head and focus on the here and now. She was going to need a clear head to gauge Melinda's state of mind. Panicking now would do both of them an injustice.

Beside her, Anna looked comfortable enough kicked back in the seat with her legs pulled up into a half-lotus. Sarah marveled out how lithe she was for her age. Sarah could still see Anna just as she had been when Sarah was a child wrapped in the flowing peasant skirts with the paisley handkerchief halter tops that caused the local church ladies to turn up their noses. If their open disdain ever bothered Anna she had never let on, at least in front of her.

Now, as an adult, Sarah wondered at the whole of Anna's life, the choices she'd made, the conversations that had passed between Anna and her mother that she wasn't privy to. She was a much a dynamo as was her mother and a hell of a lot easier to get along with. It seemed nothing rattled her.

The distance in Anna's eyes though, told the tale of her state of mind. There was a resignation there as well as a calm resolve. Anna was every bit as worried about Melinda as she was. Anna just had the experience to deal with it better. She understood Melinda better than Sarah probably ever would.

"Geez, would you look at this place?" Anna turned her gaze out of her window as Sarah exited the highway and turned toward the center of town. "Looks like yuppiedom took full effect here."

Sarah chuckled. "Yeah, it's grown by leaps and bounds since I was a little, even more since I left. Wait until you see everything that's grown up around Mom's."

"I'm surprised Melinda held on to that old place. That house is too damned big to rattle around in all by herself. It has to be rough on her keeping it up."

"You know how she is. There was no way in hell she would let it go after getting it from Ken in the divorce. We thought maybe when he died Mom would give it up but I guess by then it had been home for too long. She does have a lot of help, though. My husband and I pay for a housekeeper to come out twice a week. And she has a handyman down the street that she trusts. She keeps him fairly busy. Her next-door neighbor keeps a close eye on her, too, Mrs. Younger. She's who I call when Mom's in one of her moods."

Anna giggled. "It doesn't sound like she's changed a bit."

"No, not really." Sarah said.

Anna turned to look Sarah in the eye. "But you're still freaked out."

Sarah's face flushed. "Big time. I mean, I feel bad about being so far away from her but we wouldn't enjoy the level of peace we have now if we were around each other every day. She's just too damned difficult."

Anna raised an eyebrow. "And I suppose you're not?"

Sarah's laughter echoed through the vehicle. "Did I say that? I'm just saying we're a bad mix. I love her, Anna. I really do. But it's a whole lot calmer loving her from a distance."

Anna smirked. "Yeah, I guess I get that. But you better start thinking about the dynamic of your relationship changing. She's going to need you a lot more now especially if she is sick."

Sarah's expression dropped. It had already occurred to her. "Yeah, I know. Once we get through Kerry's funeral and all the other bullshit, I'll get her to the doctor to see what we're up against. I already made an appointment."

Anna reached over and patted Sarah on the arm. "I know it's not going to be easy, honey, but you're doing the right thing."

Silence fell inside the car again for the last few blocks to her mother's door. Sarah was relieved to see her mother's Tracker parked in front of the garage. Still, she had a great big knot twisting in her gut for what was waiting inside.

"Don't worry so much, baby girl," Anna said, squeezing her shoulder. "We'll get through this. I've got your back."

Sarah smiled. She gazed at Anna wishing all their lost years could be returned. Anna's strength was a comfort she should have never been without.

"Well, let's go see what she's up to," Sarah said. "I can't wait to see the expression on her face when she sees you."

The corners of Anna's mouth twisted into a wry smile. "Maybe you should leave the car running, in case we need to make a quick getaway."

Sarah laughed, popping open her seatbelt. "Might not be a bad idea, actually. The first one to get to the car drives."

"Deal."

Sarah took a deep breath as they stepped up onto the porch. She was as ready as she was going to get.

Melinda appeared at the door just as Sarah was about to open it. She looked past Sarah, scowling, then her brow furrowed as she recognized Anna behind her. "Ah, I see you brought reinforcements. Hello, Anna."

"Hello, Melinda."

Melinda pushed the screen door open allowing Sarah to slide past leaving the two women to stand face to face. "So what'd the kid here tell you? That I've lost my damned mind?"

"Actually, she said you were mellowing in your old age. I couldn't believe that shit so I had to come to see for myself."

Sarah was surprised to see a slow smile cross her mother's face.

"Still a bull shitter, I see," Melinda said. "Well, I guess you might as well come in, then. We'll see if I can prove her wrong."

Melinda stepped aside to let Anna in. It wasn't the warmest greeting Sarah had ever seen, but a least her mother hadn't started screaming. That was a good sign. Anna raised an eyebrow glancing over at Sarah. It looked like it had gone better than she'd expected, too.

"Wow, I like what you've done with the place," Anna said looking around. "It looks like you've invested a lot of time and money since the last time I was here."

"Yeah, mom did a complete remodel about ten years ago. It really opened up space in here." Sarah said.

Melinda frowned leaning against the doorway to the kitchen with her arms crossed across her chest watching the pair gawk around the room. "Cut the shit, you two. Why are you here?"

Anna turned toward Melinda and smiled. Sarah could see a hint of menace in Anna's eyes as she moved closer.

"Ah, damn it, Melinda. You know why we're here." Anna said. "This whole thing, me, you, Kerry, Sarah, it's all finally come full circle. Sarah's worried that this deal with Kerry's abduction has pushed you over the edge."

Melinda's eyes narrowed to slits. Sarah knew the expression and waited for the blow-up to occur. Instead, her mother nodded looking over Anna's shoulder at her. "Yeah, well, I'm not going to say it hasn't affected me. But, before you decide to have me committed, I think there are some things you need to see."

Melinda turned and went into the kitchen. Anna looked back at Sarah and shrugged before following along. Scattered across the kitchen table were a bunch of magazines, books, and newspapers, some of which looked fairly old. It looked like her mother had been researching something. She may have well decided to finally get a sense of Kerry's career, after spending so many years willfully avoiding it.

Melinda sat down at the head of the table and rested her hand atop one of the books. "When I told you the other day that the woman that abducted Kerry's body was the same one he lived within Oregon, Sarah, I wasn't kidding. I haven't lost my mind and I'm sure as hell not ready to be put out to pasture."

"I started to look for her because Kerry had told me, back then, that she had been some kind of Muse to a few bands back in the sixties. She'd run away to Oregon to get away from that life. Well, ladies, I found her, in places that you're not going to believe. It's all here. I know you've both seen her on the news. So, I want you to take a look for yourself and then you tell me."

Sarah looked at her mother nonplussed as she sat down opposite of Anna at the table. There were bookmarks placed all through the pages of the material in front of her. "Where did you find all of this stuff?"

"Libraries, used book stores, thrift stores, I've been all over the place the past couple of days. I wanted to be able to prove my assertion."

Anna looked over the stuff on the table but didn't open any of it. "Which is what?"

"That something about that woman is completely unnatural." Melinda said.

Anna cast a quick glance at Sarah, the look of concern on her face deepening. "What are you talking about?"

"Look at this," Melinda said. She snatched up the book that she had rested her hand upon. "This is a picture of The Beach Boys playing on a TV show back in the early sixties. Look at the chick sitting to Brian Wilson's left on the riser."

Anna took the book from Melinda. "Well, yeah, it does kind of look like the chick on news but, Jesus, that was like fifty years ago. We weren't even in high school yet."

"That's what I'm saying, Anna. There's no way that's possible but I'm telling you that is her."

Anna sat the book down and looked Melinda in the eye. "Honey..."

Melinda lifted a finger. "Don't! Don't say a word until you've looked through this stuff. I know how absolutely fucked up this sounds, Anna. But I also know that the chick I saw on the news is the same one I stood nose to nose with forty years ago in Oregon. It's not her daughter. It's not her goddamned cousin. It is Calliope. I've hated that bitch for taking Kerry away from me for decades. I know who she is."

Sarah stared at her mother in silence. She didn't know what to make of the situation. Melinda was adamant. But how could it be true? It was insane. In the interest of keeping the peace, she decided it best to hear Melinda out. "So what else do you have?"

Melinda glared at Sarah. "Do you really want to see it or are you just trying to humor me?"

"I want to understand just exactly what in the hell it is you're talking about," Sarah said, with more of an edge than she would have liked. "I want to know everything."

Melinda nodded, satisfied with the answer. "I know you do. But this thing just hit me out from out of the left field. I'm not surprised Kerry asked Calliope to pull off this little stunt. I imagine they stayed in touch over the years. I just wasn't prepared for the bitch to still look like she was thirty."

"Well, maybe it's all just a bunch of plastic surgery. They can do all kinds of crazy shit these days." Anna said.

"I thought of that," Melinda said, shuffling through the papers on the table. She picked up another book and flipped it open to the bookmark. "Check this out. This is from a newspaper in Cincinnati when the whole Mapplethorpe thing happened there in the nineties." Melinda sat it on the table next to the Beach Boys picture "There she is in the crowd the night the exhibit opened. Almost thirty years have passed between the two."

"Christ. That is the same woman. She hasn't changed a bit." Sarah leaned forward to get a closer look. "What the hell?"

"Okay, that's messed up," Anna said, taking a good long look. "How the hell did you scare all this up, Melinda?"

"It's all over the internet," Melinda said. "The NYPD has been looking for information on her since this whole thing started. There's all kind of wild speculation going on about her."

Sarah looked at her mother, impressed. "I didn't know you were an internet sleuth. That's new news."

Melinda smirked. "Well, I don't just use the damned thing to look up recipes. I wanted to find out what was going on especially after I saw her on the news."

Sarah and Anna started looking through the stuff Melinda had gathered. They found the exact same woman hovering around all sorts of artistic endeavors over a span of fifty years and always in the periphery. The one that stuck out for Sarah was the picture of her sitting behind Mama Cass at the Monterey Pop Festival. Whoever this Calliope was she was definitely a scene-maker.

"So what do you know about Calliope, Mom? What was the deal with her and Kerry back then?"

Melinda frowned. She turning away from Sarah. The expression on her face grew stoic as the memories surfaced. "I didn't know a whit about her until Kerry's parents took us up to a logging town called Gilchrist. Jim, Kerry's father, spent a lot of money he didn't have tracking Kerry down. Jim and Bonnie were both so heartbroken over losing Mark that Kerry's running away terrified them. They were afraid they'd lost him too. So we arrived in town with only an address written on the back of an envelope. It was the address given on Kerry's paycheck for the logging company. When we knocked on the door, we discovered that the apartment actually belonged to Calliope. Kerry had shacked up with her."

The hurt in Melinda's eyes brought tears to Sarah's. Even after all of these years it still was a fresh wound.

"She was a beautiful woman, absolutely striking. As soon as I looked into those coal-black eyes I was intimidated. I knew then that I had lost him."

Anna reached over and grasped Melinda's hand. "You were going to leave Ken and stay with him weren't you?"

Melinda wiped a tear from her eye. "That was the plan. Ken had been such a bastard when he found out I was pregnant I knew I couldn't stay with him. The only reason he'd kept me around at all was to keep up appearances. His family was the pillars of the community. How could they ever show their faces in the First Baptists' when their only son's wife had a child from an illicit affair with the town hellion? The scandal would be too much. And I didn't want to deal with any of it. I didn't want to stay here. So I had it built up in my mind that when we found Kerry I was going to go to him and it was all going to be happily ever after. I was a foolish little girl."

Melinda rose from her chair and went to the cupboard to pull out a bottle of brandy. She poured a healthy dose for both her and Anna and returned to the table. "So, anyway, we're all standing there at the door staring at each other when Kerry comes out of the back. When he saw us his face just dropped. He didn't look surprised. It looked more like he'd just been sentenced to hang or something. There was fear in his eyes."

"He wasn't ready for his past to catch up so quickly," Anna said.

"Exactly," Melinda said.

"What was he afraid of?" Sarah asked.

Melinda shook her head before taking a swig of brandy. "You. You scared the hell out of him. He was having a hard enough time with me being pregnant before Mark died. That's one of the reasons he had gotten so drunk the night of the accident. He was freaked out. When he saw you in my arms he didn't know what to do."

"Surely this had to have crossed your mind before you went out there, Melinda."

Melinda glared at Anna for the briefest of moments. "I did. But I figured once he saw her it would be different. I was wrong. He ran away from Sarah and me every bit as much as he ran away from what happened to Mark. It was all too much for him and instead of dealing with it, he split."

Anna dropped her gaze. The comment hit close to home.

Sarah realized that was her mother's intention, to get a shot in at Anna. It was cruel but not out of character for her. The onset of dementia was hard to characterize because it came and went in the early stages. But, if Sarah had to make a call, she'd have to figure that her mother was still pretty damned sharp.

"So what did Calliope do?" Sarah asked.

"Oh, she was nice as she could be, at first. She invited us all in and stayed out of the way while Jim and Bonnie tried to convince Kerry to come home. And, while all of that was going on, I watched her. I was so jealous. I could've spit fire. But I could tell that she was really in love with him, too. She looked at him the way I did when we were kids. She was completely enamored."

"So the thought of him leaving didn't sit well with her," Anna said.

"No. But she really didn't have much to worry about." Melinda said. "Kerry told his parents he wasn't coming back. He said it was time he made his own way and that he needed to make a clean break from everything."

Tears welled in Melinda's eyes at the thought of it. Sarah found herself holding back tears seeing how reliving it affected her.

"That's when I lost it. I stood upright there in front of all of them and called him a selfish bastard." Melinda wiped the tears from her eyes. "I told him, 'If you walk away from this baby now, you son of a bitch, you walk away forever. She'll never even know your goddamned name.'"

A cold chill ran up Sarah's spine as Melinda's words pierced her brain. The truth she'd worried over for so long made her blood run cold. Her worst fear had been answered. Kerry didn't want her. He never wanted her.

"Are you okay, baby girl? You're white as a ghost."

Sarah looked up at the sound of Anna's voice. She found both of them staring at her.

"I'm sorry, sweetie," Melinda said, reaching over to hold her hand. "But that's how it really went down. Now you know why I never wanted to burden you with this."

"It's okay," Sarah said, trying to regain her composure. "I needed the truth. I've always been fairly certain that I wasn't going to like it. It's just different when you know it as truth."

"Well like I said, it was his loss, baby girl," Anna said. "I'm proud of the woman you've become. I'm sure your mother is too."

Melinda nodded, a big smile crossing her face as she squeezed Sarah's hand, "Beyond words. You're the best thing that's ever happened to me."

Sarah grinned as she stared into her mother's eyes. It was a rare occasion that her mother made her feelings known. Sarah wanted to enjoy it as long as she could.

"Thanks, Mom."

"I know how much of a strain this has been. At least now I hope you can understand why I made the choices I did."

"It's starting to make a lot more sense," Sarah said. "So what happened when you called Kerry out?"

"That's when Calliope got in my face. She said some crazy shit like Kerry was too rare a being to be bogged down by such mundane considerations. I told her that the only thing Kerry was, was a chicken shit bastard too scared to claim his own child. It pretty much went downhill from there. Kerry's dad had to get between us."

"So, I gathered you up and stormed out. I waited in the car while Kerry said his good-byes to his parents. Kerry didn't even have the balls to come out and talk. He had totally bought into this bitch's bullshit." Melinda tapped on the face of the woman in the picture behind Mama Cass. "This bitch, right here. The same chick I just saw on the news."

Anna glanced across the table at Sarah and raised an eyebrow. "OK. So how do we prove it?"

Melinda looked from Anna to Sarah and sighed. "We go to the funeral. I want to get close enough to look her dead in the eye."

CHAPTER 35

Distant pulses of lightning shone in diffuse angles across the carpet as the remnants of the evening's storm echoed through the blinds. Jimmy sat staring at the TV watching the local news rehash the events surrounding Jerry Jewell's death. His demise had kicked the Kerry Vance media circus into high gear once again, while clueless pundits attempted to weave Jewell's place into the larger context.

As far as Jimmy was concerned he was a bully and murderer and nothing more. That he met his fate in a violent manner was no surprise. He grew dismayed as the reporters carefully avoided connecting Jewell directly to Carol Merrick even though the logic of the events clearly called for it.

Jimmy hit the button on the remote to turn off the TV then tossed it over on the couch. He couldn't watch anymore. He should have gone to bed when Daisy did but felt compelled to learn everything he could. Daisy wouldn't be truly safe until someone tossed Carol Merrick into a cell. If there was a way he could help speed up the process, he was all for it.

As Jimmy hauled himself up from his chair his cell phone rang. He snatched it off of the coffee table to silence it before it woke up Daisy. He didn't recognize the number but he went ahead and accepted the call. If it was bullshit, he figured he could vent a bit of frustration on whoever was calling.

"This better be good."

Laughter rang from the other end. "Oh, I think you're going to like it."

"Avery?"

"You got it, big Daddy. What's shaking?"

"Jesus fucking Christ, I've been trying to get ahold of you all week. Why'd you wait so long to call me?"

The pause on the other end was telling.

"Look, man, I didn't want to involve you. I didn't want to cause any trouble. When I saw that you were trying to get a hold of me I panicked. I didn't know how to explain this to you."

Jimmy sat back down in his chair. He could hear exhaustion, plain, in Avery's voice. He also heard something he didn't expect. Avery was stone-cold sober.

"So have you figured it out?"

"Yeah, actually I have. I've figured out a lot of things over the past few days. And, I'm sorry for the way things have gone down lately. I've let myself wallow in self-pity for so long I never stopped to consider how it affected everyone around me, how it affected you. I appreciate you standing by me, Jimmy. I appreciate everything you've ever done for me."

Jimmy sat back in his chair. Avery's statement took him by surprise. Tears burned at the edges of his eyes. He was happy Avery was safe.

"So just exactly what in the hell is going on? We have a lot of theories on this end and not a lot of facts."

Jimmy heard Avery take a deep breath.

"At some point during Kerry's last tour he discovered that Jerry Jewell and Carol were having an affair. They were embezzling money, too. Someone stuffed Kerry's coffin with two-hundred grand in cash. We're pretty sure that was Jewell. Anyway, before he died, Kerry prepared a package for Calliope and told her that if anything happened to him to take possession of his body and get it home to Denver. He didn't want Carol having anything to do with his funeral plans. She wasn't going to abide by his wishes."

Jimmy's ears perked up when he heard Calliope's name. It seemed Zap's information was correct, at least for the name.

"So do you know this Calliope? How'd she get involved?"

There was a long pause. Jimmy wondered if Avery was discussing it with her.

"She's a friend of Kerry's. What does it matter?"

Jimmy paused. He didn't want to alarm Avery. But he had to say something especially after all of the crazy stories he'd heard.

"Well, man, all cards on the table. That woman is a ghost. She's been run through every database on Earth and no one's found a thing. There's been a hell of a lot of rumors but that's about it. I just want to make sure you know who you're dealing with."

"I don't know about all that. But I know I trust Calliope with my life. What's the deal?"

"I'm just trying to put it all together. I'm trying to see if I can find a way to keep your ass out of trouble."

There was another long pause. This time Jimmy could definitely hear Avery talking to someone in the background.

"Yeah, well, I doubt you'll be able to pull that one off, old buddy. Denver's crawling with cops. But it's okay. I'm prepared for whatever comes. We're doing the right thing."

There was a confidence in Avery's voice that Jimmy hadn't heard in a long time. Whatever had happened out on the road had changed him. Whatever the reason it was a good thing. Jimmy hoped it stuck.

"Yeah, I'm starting to think you're right. After everything I've learned I can tell you I have a whole new respect for Kerry Vance. Daisy has helped me get a better sense of who he was as a person. I can see why you two got along so well."

"Daisy? God, how's she doing? I can't imagine what all of this has done to her."

"She's had a rough few days but I'll think she'll be fine. She's pretty tough."

"How'd you get hooked up with her?"

"I saved her from being kidnapped."

"You what?" Avery's voice raised an octave. "What happened?"

"Jerry Jewell sent some goon to snatch her up. She overheard him and Carol talking. They were both in on Kerry's murder. It freaked her out so bad she fled. Now we're trying to gather enough evidence to prove it."

Avery let out a long low whistle. "Christ. So she's with you?"

"Yeah, I let her crash here. It was the best way to keep her safe." Jimmy decided to keep the rest of the story to himself for now.

Avery wouldn't have believed it anyway.

"So what's the deal, now? The police can't think Jewell's death was an accident. Can they?"

"I don't know, Avery. I'm out of the loop on that one. They haven't released a cause of death, yet. They're not letting any information out. But there are rumors that the commissioner talked to Scotland Yard about Kerry's death. Daisy's been putting out a ton of stuff about Carol all over the internet. People are starting to catch on."

"Well, at least that's something." Avery said. "Somebody has to find a way to nail that bitch on something."

"We're still plugging away. Hopefully, we can find something we can use. Now that we know Carol's gone Daisy wants to go to the house and get the rest of her stuff. I'm planning on taking a thorough look around while I'm there."

"Good. Well, it sounds like you're up on things. Hopefully something breaks and soon. We're heading into Denver tomorrow. Keep an eye on the news. You're probably going to see me in cuffs."

"Wouldn't be the first time," Jimmy said, laughing.

"Well, it's sure as hell going to be the last. I'm too old for this shit."

"It's about time you figured that out."

"Yeah, I guess. I figured out a few things these past couple of days. Once this shit is over, a lot is going to change."

There was a weary determination in Avery's voice Jimmy found heartening.

"It sounds like you've had a lot of time to think."

"I have." Avery said. "Kerry's death has brought a lot of things into focus that I've been afraid to face. I guess it's time to grow up."

"I'm glad to hear you say that. You know I'm here for you."

Jimmy's phone beeped signaling an incoming text. All of a sudden he was popular. And, now, well past his bedtime.

"Thanks, man. Well, I'm going to hop off of here. You got the number. If you hear anything that'll help us contain Carol, give me a yell."

"I will." Jimmy said. "And, if it's any help, I hear the jails in Denver are pretty nice."

Avery's laughter roared through the phone. "Thanks, gives me something to look forward to. I'll get in touch when I can. See you."

"Later." Jimmy said.

Jimmy smiled thinking of Avery sitting somewhere under the stars hidden in the western night. He still had a rough time ahead. But it sounded like he was on a better path. He was happy to have his friend back the way he was before the world wore him down. As Jimmy clicked the phone off, he decided to go ahead and check the text. He so rarely received one he was curious to see who it was.

The message was only three short simple lines sent by Glenny Ewes. They shook Jimmy to the core.

I have a smoking gun. Carol's going down. How quick can you get here?

Jimmy toggled the phone as he dashed to the closet to grab his coat.

I'm on my way.

It looked like he wasn't going to sleep any time soon.

CHAPTER 36

The thin air was bracing on Carol's bare legs as she perched uncomfortably on the passenger side of the beat-up old Jeep Wrangler. She'd thought the leather mini-skirt a necessity to keep a handle on her new bartender dupe, Brad. That was before she'd seen the open cab of his mud-spattered ride.

After the half-hour drive out of the city her ass was just about completely numb. Not unlike the skull of her big blond chauffeur. She rubbed her legs briskly as she checked the number on the innocuous little ranch house that occupied a nondescript corner in one of the dozens of anonymous subdivisions littering the outskirts of Denver.

The place just had no soul.

It was tidy enough, she supposed, with its black-topped driveway and a two-car garage. The smallish yard was freshly mowed and had neat little flower beds lining the walkway up to the front door. That this was the house of the only child of one of the most famous frontmen in rock-n-roll history was really kind of sad. From all that Carol could gather Kerry's daughter, Sarah had been raised in modest means and here with her second husband out in the suburbs it seemed that trend continued. The girl wouldn't miss what she had never known. Carol was determined it stayed that way.

"Well, this is the place," Carol said as she took a quick peek around the neighborhood. "That's where the little tramp lives."

Brad glanced around nervously. "Now all you want me to do is scare her, right?

Carol dropped her gaze on him and frowned. "Yes, but I want you to make damn sure she is scared. Break a few windows, drag her out of her bed, I don't give a fuck. Just make sure you tell her to stay the hell away from Kerry and if you catch her meddling around in his business you'll be back. Do you think you can do that?"

Brad let out a deep breath then nodded. "So why do you care who your ex does anyway? Are you still hot for him or something?"

Carol leaned over resting her hand on the inside of Brad's thigh. She smiled as she moved her hand higher up his leg transmitting her best 'come hither' gaze. "I don't care who he's screwing but this little chickadee is trying to horn in on my money. I still own a part of his business and she's trying to push me out."

"Ah, OK, that makes sense," Brad said, grinning, as he pulled the Jeep away from the curb. "I guess I don't blame you there. Don't worry, I'll get it done. She won't even remember his name when I'm done."

Carol forced a smile as the wind, once again, assaulted her chapping legs. She hoped he was right. But, seeing as how Brad wasn't the sharpest knife in the drawer she thought it best to consider a plan B. Nothing was going to keep her from what was rightfully hers.

CHAPTER 37

The ringing of a telephone was a maddening noise. Harry was startled by it every single time. Even after more than a century he still wanted to reach for a weapon when one decried without warning. And, as if the peeling of tiny bells wasn't aggravating enough, the mortals had spent the past twenty years or so inventing a host of even more cacophonous tones to set his ears on edge.

He missed the simple days of the keryx.

The phone strapped to his side now was the latest and greatest state of the art model. It was, in this day and age, a necessary evil. As quickly as commerce moved in this new century he would be at a disadvantage without one. Still, he jumped when the rustling chimes issued from his belt.

"Harold Asteri. How can I help you?" Harry frowned as silence issued from the other end. It was another of the various things he detested about modern communication; butt dialing. And this from a number he had no prior contact. He reached for the button to disconnect when the person on the other end finally spoke up.

"Heracles, I need your help."

"Calliope?"

"Yeah, it's me."

Harry took a deep breath and quelled the urge to yell. No mean feat given that everything inside him was twisted into a quivering mass of rage over her latest escapade. No. He needed to remain calm. She had reached out to him. It was something she had never done before. He couldn't risk scaring her off now by indulging his sense of outrage. "Where are you?"

"In Kansas at the moment, a few hours' drive from Denver. I take it you're aware of the situation."

Harry scowled. "Yes, Calliope, I am fully cognizant of your latest crusade."

There was a long pause.

Calliope was the most maddening woman Harry had ever encountered. She was also the most intelligent and the most beautiful. The combination of qualities had kept him tied in knots for millennia.

"I need your help."

Harry raised an eyebrow. Calliope's back truly had to be against the wall to reach out to him this way. "What would you like me to do?"

"How quickly can you get to Denver?"

Harry shook his head, keeping a tight rein on his incredulity. "I am already in Denver along with Terpsichore and Polyhymnia."

"Ah, geez." Calliope's voice trailed off into a whisper. "So you were already set to bail me out."

Harry's temper flared but he kept it in check. An argument now would be counterproductive

"How could I not, Calliope? There's too much at stake. Information is too easy to exchange now. Your face has been seen around the world. How could you not consider this before you took on this campaign?"

"I considered it, believe me. But, I had to do this. What happened in Cincinnati couldn't be anticipated."

"The pettiness of mortals should always be anticipated. That said. You defended your charges brilliantly and without bloodshed. You've absorbed more of my teachings than I would've considered."

"Yeah, thanks," Calliope said without mirth. "But, sometimes I think your teachings cause more problems than it solves, especially in this day and age."

Harry smirked, pausing to run his fingers over his beard. "These mortals have come a long way, I admit. But, they're not there yet. The way of the warrior will always be a necessity in theory if not in practice. You would do well to remember that."

As soon as he had spoken, he knew Calliope had discounted his words. But the training was ingrained in her. The evidence was clear. It was a necessary evil.

"So what's your plan, Harry? You know what we're up against."

"My plan is to collect you before the police have a chance to detain you. You need to meet us well outside of Denver. The authorities have the roads locked down."

"That's not good enough. I have to help Kerry cross over. I need to be there when his body is interred. I've not come this far to abandon my charge. We have to get into the city. We need a diversion."

A surge of blood pulsed in Harry's temples. His grasp on his temper grew tenuous. Calliope was going to death of him. If it was at all possible, it would be because of her. Then, a thought occurred to him, something Terpsichore had said before they'd left Vegas. *We have a party to plan.*

Harry rose from his chair and crossed the room to look out of the window. He was aware of the sudden influx of people coming into town to observe Kerry Vance's funeral. The locals were gearing up to capitalize on their arrival. A diversion seemed to already be in the works.

It just needed to be exploited.

"Harry? Are you still there?"

"Yes. I'm sorry, I was distracted. But, actually, I do think I have a plan. Do you remember how we got you away from that lascivious Duke in Bratislava?"

"Good Lord, Harry, that's been centuries ago."

"But, you remember."

"Yes."

"Good. Because that's what we're going to do."

Harry waited, smiling, as the particulars reoccurred to her.

"Are you sure that will work, Harry? It damned near didn't the last time."

"You'll have to make it work. If you're determined to carry out your mercy mission this is your best chance."

There was another long pause as Calliope weighed her options.

"Yeah, I guess, you're right. How long will it take you to prepare?"

"I'll set Polyhymnia and Terpsichore to the task as soon as they return. Plan to arrive at first light."

"OK. Now, I have one more favor to ask."

Harry tugged his beard resisting the urge to start screaming. "Oh, and what else is it that I can do for you, my queen?"

Calliope's sigh was audible through the phone. "I know I'm asking a lot of you and I'm sorry but I need to make sure that Kerry's daughter makes it to the funeral safely. She's set to inherit quite a bit of money and I have a terrible feeling that Carol Merrick might try to harm her."

"The jilted wife?"

"Yes. We know that she's already in the city and I'd feel a lot better knowing the girl, Sarah, was under your protection."

"And how do you suppose I pull that off, just knock on her door and abscond with her?"

The sound of Calliope's laughter lifted Harry's spirit, a phenomenon which also vexed him greatly.

"Just have Terpsichore call me when she gets in. It'd probably be better if she handled it, anyway."

"I defer to your wisdom."

"Yeah, well if you did that a little more often we wouldn't have all the trouble we do. I will talk to you soon. And, Harry, thanks again."

Harry shook his head. He didn't know why he indulged her. His love for her hadn't been reciprocated in a very long time. But he still wasn't ready to give up, not just yet. There was still hope. Pandora's Box was never empty.

"I will see you soon, my dear."

"Good-bye."

Harry returned the phone to its plastic holster still gazing through the window. It was going to take quite a bit of maneuvering to execute the plan. It had a lot of moving parts. But once Calliope returned to him it would be worth the trouble. This time he'd just have to find a way to make her want to stay. That was a much larger challenge.

CHAPTER 38

For all of Glenny Ewes bullshit, flash and endless bluster, he lived in a really crappy neighborhood. Jimmy had worked the 28th precinct when he was a rookie. As bad as some of the neighborhoods were here a lot of the beat cops had been even worse.

Jimmy was fully aware back then how tough the job could be. A lot of his fellow officers there just plain didn't care. It was just a paycheck to them. He was relieved when they shipped him out. His wide-eyed enthusiasm was definitely not appreciated.

Jimmy assailed the stairs to the third floor of the walk-up. He had been here with Avery once to pick up Glenny for a meal but had never been inside his apartment. As garish as Glenny's fashion sense was Jimmy wondered what the décor inside his apartment was like.

Glenny opened the door slowly looking out past Jimmy to make sure he was alone. He pulled the door open wider and did another quick check down the hall to make sure no one was watching. Jimmy had never known Glenny to be paranoid so whatever information he was sitting on must have thrown him for a loop.

"Thanks for coming over, Jimmy. I hate to drag you out so late but I really think you need to hear this."

There in the living room in front of him, on a purple and white paisley couch no less, a dirty dishwater blonde in torn red leather pants sat next to Glenny's girlfriend. The girl's mascara had run down her face following the tracks of tears. She was clutching a pillow to her chest as Glenny's girlfriend consoled her.

Jimmy glanced over at Glenny. "Is she okay?"

"She's in better shape than when we found her," Glenny said. "Dara and I ran into her outside a club downtown a couple of hours ago. Her name's Aria Zane. She's the singer for a band we know. We brought her back here to sober her up and find out what was wrong. We got a little more than we bargained for."

Jimmy raised an eyebrow. "What's that have to do with Carol?"

"I think it'd be better if she told you herself," Glenny said.

Jimmy followed him into the room watching as Glenny sat down on the other side of her.

"Aria, honey, this is my friend Jimmy. He's a police officer. Will you tell him what happened at Jerry Jewell's place?"

The girl looked up at Jimmy as tears formed in her eyes. She nodded slowly clutching Dara's hand for support. She cast her gaze away from Jimmy down toward the floor trying to put the words together.

"Carol Merrick busted in on Jerry and I just before he died. We were both doing coke out in his living room. I never met her before but I knew who she was. So she comes in and she was all pissed off. She started yelling at Jerry. I got up and took off for the bedroom. I could still hear her screaming from inside Jerry's bedroom."

Jimmy stared at the girl startled by what he heard. "Then what happened?"

Whatever the girl was processing was a lot to bear. She kept her head down, shaking it against the memory.

"It's okay, Aria. You're among friends." Dara said. "Tell us what happened."

The girl turned to look at Dara wiping the tears from her eyes. "Carol came into the bedroom and started talking to me. She wasn't yelling but she was fucking scary. She told me if I wanted to be famous I had to work for it and not rely on Jerry. Then she told me to leave. She said she wanted to yell at Jerry some more."

"So you left?" Jimmy asked.

The girl looked up at Jimmy. Her eyes were big watery saucers. She nodded slowly. "I left the apartment but I didn't leave the building. I climbed the stairs halfway up to the next floor sat down and waited for Carol to leave."

"So then what happened?"

"I don't know. I couldn't hear them once I went out. But it wasn't very long before Carol left, only a few minutes. When I went back in Jerry was dead. He was lying back on the couch staring up at the ceiling. He wasn't breathing."

The girl started crying again falling against Dara. Dara wrapped her arms around her and held her close.

"You didn't call anybody? The cops? An ambulance?"

The girl didn't reply. She started crying louder.

"C'mon, Jimmy, give her a break. She was scared." Glenny said.

Jimmy ran his hand down his face, aggravated. "But not so much that you didn't split with the rest of the coke, huh?"

The girl buried her head against Dara's shoulder and sobbed. Glenny got up and led Jimmy out of the room.

"What the fuck, man? Why are you giving her a hard time? That's not why I called you down here."

"Yeah well, it's fucked up, Glenny. She should have stuck around."

Glenny nodded. Jimmy was right. "We can't do anything about that now. So what do we do?"

"Get her cleaned up and take her down to the 1st precinct tomorrow. Let her tell her story. She's looking at being charged with criminal negligence for not reporting Jewell's death and that's if she manages to spin her way out of knowing Jewell had cocaine in the house. It's not going to be easy."

Glenny shook his head looking back at the girl as Dara tried to calm her. "I just hate to see her get jammed up. She's a good kid, talented. She's got a real shot at making it."

"What is it with all these artists and substance abuse?" Jimmy asked. "I mean really, Glenny. Avery, Kerry, the girl in there. What is it that makes them so susceptible? I don't get it."

"It's their sensitivity to the world around them," Glenny said. "They feel things more strongly than most people. They don't learn to block it out. Which, in a way, would also block their ability to channel it into their art, it moves them to create. But it can also get to be too much at times. So the drugs become a coping mechanism. I mean look at Avery. Especially, after

Zoe died. It nearly destroyed him. It's been over a year and he's still devastated. He'll get better eventually, at least I hope so. But I still worry about him."

Jimmy thought about how Avery sounded on the phone. He sounded better than he had in a long while. But it could have very well been a brave face, a façade. He couldn't be sure until Avery was home where he could keep an eye on him. Jimmy decided to keep their conversation a secret. In case things went badly.

"So what about you, Glenny? You're an artist. What's kept you from it?"

Glenny smiled. "I stand firmly by the grand poetic tradition and drink like a fish. I didn't like the way the other stuff made me feel. I swore it all off a very long time ago."

Jimmy laughed. "Well, that's good, I guess. Maybe not healthy but I guess everyone has their vices."

"Yeah, and what's yours, Sergeant?"

"The meatballs at Delmonico's," Jimmy said.

A big beaming smile crossed Glenny's face. "That's probably not healthy either."

"All things in moderation, I guess," Jimmy said. "Seriously get her to down to the precinct as early as you can. If I can find a way to help, I will. I just have to be careful."

"Anything you can do is appreciated. Thanks for coming over, Jimmy. Maybe this will give you a new direction to look in yourself."

"Yeah, maybe, but you didn't hear that from me."

Glenny took another quick peek out of the door before opening it fully. "You're secret's safe with me."

"Thanks," Jimmy said. "I'll talk to you soon."

Jimmy had no clue what was going to happen. But he knew for sure tomorrow was going to be a very interesting day. He had to be ready for it.

CHAPTER 39

Midnight came and went in a slow mad blur as Cori sat vigil outside Kerry Vance's daughter's house. She spent a good deal of the time pondering how Calliope had managed to drag her into another misadventure but now she was getting tired.

Of all her sisters, Calliope had always been the most impetuous. She never understood the boundary that divided her kind from the mortals or why it even existed. Her curiosity had led them all into peril more times than Cori dared count.

It was Calliope's fault they'd entered mortal mythology in the first place. She could never keep from venturing out to see a musical performance or a play and, after seeing how much fun she had among them, it wasn't long until Calliope had all of her sisters following her into Athens to rub elbows with the cultural elite.

To say they caused a stir was a gross understatement.

After the war between the Olympians and their bastard offspring their world changed. The whole world changed. The constant warfare, the Persians, the Romans and, later on, the Christians created a society where they were forced into hiding. It was a miracle that Harry and Kydon had kept them all alive. The fall into barbarity across Europe made it easier to remain anonymous but the conditions then made it even harder just to survive. Keeping Calliope reined in quickly became a task beset on all of them.

Through it all, Calliope remained the purest of heart. Even after all of the hell Harry had put her through to toughen her up and train her as a warrior. He never broke her spirit. Even after all of the centuries cast behind them Calliope's heart was still pure. Cori loved her for that, more than words could ever express.

Now, here she was cramped up in a rented automobile on her fifth cup of coffee waiting on the off chance someone might harm her charge's daughter. There were more important things she could be doing.

She had taken well to the task, though. She found an empty house for sale close enough to observe most of the woman's property. She watched the daughter, Sarah, come home with two older women and a little red-headed girl who were then joined later by a comely gentleman in a blue service van. It seemed a scene of domestic bliss. Though, in Cori's experience, that was, more than likely, an illusion.

Cori loved the idea of having a family again, in theory. In practice, she had never been able to make it work even before they'd been forced to run. Her time with Achelous had been a nightmare and after she lost Parthenope she'd wanted nothing more than to leave it behind. It was much too late to seriously consider now but the thought remained.

As she poured herself another cup of coffee Cori noticed a beat-up old Jeep cruising slowly along the adjoining street. It was worthy of note because there had been absolutely no traffic after about eleven. The neighborhood was a quiet place. The Jeep turned down the street where Cori sat and passed slowly. It wound its way around the cul-de-sac then started back toward the main street. When it passed again it was barely moving, pulling gently into the grass of the empty lot that separated the house where Cori was and Sarah's property.

She opened the car door slowly pushing the button to prevent the interior lights from activating. She dropped down behind the cover of a hedge pushing the door shut without engaging the latch. As she worked her away around the hedge she heard the driver of the Jeep drop to the ground from the open cab. There were a host of reasons why he could have been there. From the way he took position on the passenger side of the Jeep he could have well just stopped to answer nature's call. But, all things being equal, the odds were short. It wouldn't take much to subdue him.

Cori's urge to engage surprised her. It had been well over a hundred years since she'd last been in combat. It gave her pause to consider how eager she was to fight. Harry's training came to the fore, unbidden.

Cori pushed between the rows of hedges to see the man step away from the Jeep. He took a quick look around before dropping into a slow jog toward Sarah's house. Cori took a deep breath as she pushed through the hedges and onto the grass. She was fully prepared to do what she had to but she hoped it wouldn't go that far. She couldn't let Harry's thirst for violence mar her too.

Cori found a shadowed path across the lot paralleling her prey over his right shoulder. She kept low, spider-crawling over the grass silently. She moved into the darkness behind the family's shed and ran around attempting to cut her prey off at the steps leading to the back of the house. She brought herself to an abrupt stop when she saw her prey had stopped well short of the stairs and was talking to himself.

"You should have never let that bitch talk you into this."

Cori smiled stepping out of the shadows. "Ah, the things a moron will do for a shot at a shag."

Instead of running, as Cori wished, the tall blonde kid just stood stiff staring in shock.

"Um, this is the part where you run away?" Cori said, motioning for him to shew.

"I can't do that."

Cori smiled again only this time it was feral.

"It's really your best option." Cori said taking a few steps closer, "Because, if you take another step toward that house, I'll kill you."

The blonde kid took a small step back. Then set a hard stare on Cori.

"I don't see any gun, honey. And, short of that, I don't think you're going to do shit."

Cori crossed the space between them in an instant carrying the momentum into a strike to the side of the blond kid's neck.

He dropped with a dull thud at her feet. Cori reached down quickly to remove him. Their voices had to have caused a stir inside.

"I take it your Calliope?"

Cori snapped up to see one of the elderly ladies that had accompanied Sarah. "No. I'm her sister, Cori. Sarah's spoken of her?"

"Oh, she's been quite the topic of conversation around here, let me tell you." The woman furrowed her brow.

Cori stared at the woman envious of her wizened features. "I guess she's made her presence known rather vividly."

"In more ways than one," the woman said. "Sarah's mother swears she hasn't aged a day in well over fifty years."

Cori's heart skipped a beat but she kept her composure. "What do you think?"

"I don't give a shit, really. But, after seeing how you handled little boy blue there, I'm thinking there might be something to the story."

Cori smiled. This woman was sharp. "It's really not as interesting as it sounds, believe me. Just trust me when I say Calliope has Sarah's very best interest at heart."

"Well that'd certainly be a switch, but okay."

Cori stared at the old woman. "I'm afraid I don't understand."

"Calliope has been tangled up in Sarah's life since she was born. She was the one who convinced Kerry to walk away from her."

Cori turned away to stare out into the darkness. Calliope had never mentioned a word of it. If it was true it was troubling. "I had no idea."

The woman stared at her. "Yeah, well, there's been a lot of secrets coming to light around here recently. I think there's a lot of closure that needs to go around too. I'm starting to believe that this whole hootenanny was Kerry's way of making sure it happened."

"Well, now this whole episode is finally starting to make some sense," Cori said. "I really don't know anything about Calliope's history with Kerry Vance. But I figured it had to have been pretty deep to have led to all this."

The woman turned toward the stairs and held her arm out. "Well come on in for a cup of coffee and I'll tell you all about it."

Cori motioned toward the blonde kid lying at her feet. "What about him?"

The old woman smiled. "Ah hell, leave him where he is. If he has the brains God gave a head of cabbage he'll get the hell out of here when he wakes up. He can go back and tell Carol Merrick that he fucked up. If not, I guess you can always knock him out again."

Cori laughed following the woman up the steps. "Let's hope it doesn't come to that."

CHAPTER 40

The ride inside the Colorado border passed quickly with Suicide Clyde and his lead foot piloting. Avery relaxed into the passenger seat staring at the number punched into his cellphone.

"Are you going to call them or what? We'll be there in less than an hour." Clyde said.

Jill leaned forward between the seats. "Twenty minutes the way you drive."

Clyde grinned. "We're on a schedule. I don't want to be late."

Avery hit the send button and sat back in his seat. "Hello. I'm told this is the studio line for KOQZ. It is? Great, look this Avery Clark and I'd like to get on air with your morning show if I could."

Jill raised an eyebrow watching as Avery readjusted the phone at his ear. They were never going to believe it was him.

"Yeah, it's really me. We're close to town and we want to invite everyone to join us at the cemetery." Avery frowned. "Seriously? What do you need to know? I'm from New York. I'm a Gemini and my last book sucked. I don't know what in the hell else you want me to tell you."

Jill and Clyde both chuckled. Avery smiled putting his hand over the phone. "I think they're buying it."

"Let's hope so," Jill said. "We need as many people on the street as we can get if we're going to pull this off."

"Still going to be a longshot," Clyde said.

"Oh, hush. Calliope has this worked out." Jill said.

Clyde shook his head. His eyes level on the road. "If you say so but I want to be prepared in case something goes wrong."

"I'm going on air? Great." Avery grinned clutching the phone to his ear. "Ten seconds."

Jill smiled giving him the thumbs up.

"Give 'em hell, chief," Clyde said jockeying them past a line of slower traffic

"This is the Z-man, here on KOQZ, and we're not sure if this is a hoax or not but my producer is telling me we have Avery Clark on the line? Avery, are you there?"

Avery grinned staring into Jill's eyes. "Yes sir, it's really me. No hoax here."

"Wow, OK, well you've really been causing quite a stir this week, my man. I'm sure our listeners are well aware of the story. It's been on every media outlet from here to the South Pole. So why are calling in? What do you want our listeners to know?"

"I want to extend an invitation to all of your listeners to join us at the Fairmount later this morning for Kerry's interment. Kerry loved this city. He wanted all of his fans to be a part of it. We didn't go through all the trouble of getting here to keep it to ourselves. We'd like to get everyone involved."

"Wow. Thanks for that, Avery. I'm pretty sure our listeners already had the thought in mind. I'm not sure if you're aware but we've had a flood of celebrities descend on the city already this week preparing to do just that. It's been a who's who at Denver International for the past few days. From what we gather, they were invited by Kerry himself, after his death."

Avery frowned wondering if Calliope knew about this or if it was something Kerry had set up on his own. It shouldn't come as a surprise, either way. Kerry had decided that he was going out with a bang. He was doing exactly that.

Jill wondered at the confused look on Avery's face. She wished she could hear both sides of the conversation. "What is it?"

"Ah, I wasn't aware," Avery said. "That's fantastic. Well for everyone listening in, we're closing in on the city now. We hope to see you in about an hour."

"Be careful out there, Avery. The mayor's office and local police have decided not to interfere with the funeral as long as it doesn't get out of

control. But, apparently, the Feds aren't being as accommodating, so watch your back."

"Thanks. We're all prepared for what's coming next or we wouldn't be in this. The most important thing is that we lay Kerry to rest here at home. Thanks for your time."

Avery shut the phone off and sighed. "Hopefully our message went out to everyone that needed to hear it. We're playing this pretty close to the bone."

Clyde grinned. "Everything else has come off without a hitch so far."

Avery laughed and delighted in Jill's laughter as well. No matter what happened to them after the funeral he was happing knowing that his future was moving toward a different path, one where Jill could by his side. Taking this journey had pulled him back from the brink. He would be forever in Kerry's debt for pushing him into taking it.

He hoped that somewhere he and Zoe were smiling down on him.

CHAPTER 41

Carol sneered stalking around the room. That idiot, Brad, should have been back hours ago. Either he had screwed up and gotten arrested or wimped out and ran away. Either way, the little bastard had already gotten what he wanted. There wasn't a whole hell of a lot she could do about it now.

If he had been arrested, Carol knew, without a doubt, he would tell everything he knew. He was already jammed up in the system and would do whatever was necessary to cover his ass. Thankfully the little fucker didn't know anything. Once she checked out of the room, all traces of 'Carol Aaron' would be gone and poor little dumbass Brad wouldn't have a conspiracy to sell. That meant getting her shit together and ready to split. She didn't want to be anywhere around if the cops did decide to roll in.

She grabbed the remote off of the nightstand turning on the TV as she applied her blonde-haired disguise. She needed the noise. Kerry had been running through her mind all too often. Hopefully, when this whole funeral mess was over, she'd finally be able to put it behind her.

"There's a carnival-like atmosphere on the street here outside of Fairmount cemetery this morning. Fans of the late Kerry Vance are turning out in droves for his funeral later today."

Carol jumped nearly spilling a bottle of foundation in her lap. She grabbed the remote and bumped up the volume.

"We've seen a host of celebrities waving to the crowd as they entered the cemetery grounds as they were escorted to the mausoleum where Vance will be interred."

Carol set the make-up down on the table and turned her full attention on the TV. Kerry had planned this! The son of a bitch had this in mind the whole time. Carol had to stop and take a deep breath. She felt a full-fledged panic attack coming on. If Kerry had been able to coordinate this he had to have known what she was planning. Or he had planned on doing something to himself. It would be just like him to wait for her to have it done so he could wrack her ass for it. Did he really know what she had planned?

"Federal authorities are assisting with crowd control and security due to the sheer size of the turnout but a spokesman for the local FBI office insists that Avery Clark and his accomplices will be taken into custody at the conclusion of the ceremony."

Carol scowled at the mention of Avery's name. He had been in on this with Kerry. He probably thought he had found a way to lay this whole mess at her feet, too, along with that traitorous Daisy. She had been a little too cool along all of this as well. They had probably read her into the plan so she could take to the internet and turn opinion against her.

It was clear now. They all had set out to destroy her.

All she wanted to do was secure Kerry's legacy. He had to go out on top. There was no other way.

Carol got up, seething, as she tossed aside the make-up and the wig. She quickly jumped into a pair of jeans and a T-shirt, pulling her hair into a ponytail and through the back of a ball cap Brad had left behind. She slid a case out from beneath the bed and removed the gun she'd bought. It belonged to Carol Aaron, too. There was nothing to trace to her.

She pulled a hoodie over her T-shirt and placed the gun gently in the pocket. She needed to hurry. She had a funeral to go to. And as soon as she got close enough to Avery Clark, she was going to create the need for another one.

He wasn't walking away from this. She would see to that.

CHAPTER 42

Daisy packed the last of her belongings into a big cardboard box and taped the lid closed. She looked around at the empty sky blue walls remembering the day she'd first seen it. Kerry, not Carol, had hired a decorator to put it together for her. And she could remember feeling overwhelmed by how beautiful it was.

It had been a tough few months before they brought her here to stay.

The death of her mother hadn't been the all-consuming tragedy that one would expect. Daisy was old enough to know all about her mother's habits, the booze, the drugs, the dirty old men that would leer at her (or worse) as they used her mother for sex, or for a place to shoot up and daze.

At the age of six, Daisy had no illusions about the person her mother was. She could remember being hungry, having to fend for herself when her mother ran off with some new guy. She remembered having to go to school in cheap clothes bought at the Salvation Army and being made fun of by kids that had little more going for them than her.

She could remember coming home to no electricity or running water, moving from shitty apartment to shitty apartment as her mother lied her way into place after place. Always with promises to her about all the things that they were going to do, all the great things that were waiting in store for them, all illusions in her mother's hampered mind.

The morning Daisy found her mother dead in her bed she'd not been alone. Alongside her, just as dead, lay her mother's latest and greatest love,

Greg. To be painfully honest she was almost more upset about losing Greg. She hadn't known him for very long but he had always been nice to her. He'd never touched her. He had even bought her new clothes over her mother's objections. He insisted on taking them both out for brunch every Sunday morning. "A good breakfast to start a good week," he would say.

When Daisy spoke to him he really listened to her and was interested in what she had to say. He always took the time to compliment her on her school work and her art awards. Daisy had hoped more than anything that Greg would stick around and they could be a real family. But all of her hoping ended that Sunday morning there in her mother's bed.

For the next few months, it was all a blur, hospitals, funerals, court appearances, and the orphanage. She remembered talk of being sent to her grandparents in West Virginia and how scared she was at the thought of being shipped off to people she'd never even known.

But not long after Kerry and Carol came to claim her. She was never so happy to have seen their faces waiting for her at the bottom of the stairs at the orphanage. She had never spent a great deal of time around them while she was growing up, her mother and Carol could never see eye to eye for more than a few hours, but Daisy cherished the time she was able to spend in their home.

Kerry, when he was home, was like a big kid himself. He would sit right down on the floor and play with her, drawing pictures or playing with dolls, he was more than happy to jump right in and join in any game she was playing. He was always fun to be around. Daisy knew now that he had been shielding her from all of the heavy shit that went on in the next room between Carol and her mother.

She had found out later, in one of Carol's numerous dressing downs, that her mother had only ever brought her there when she was hitting her and Kerry up for money. Her mother used her to extort what she needed. Whatever else there was to say about Carol, she had been there for her when she needed her the most. Daisy felt a little better knowing that it all hadn't been at Kerry's urging.

"Are you all right? You look like you're a million miles away."

Daisy jumped then turned to smile at Jimmy. "Shit, you scared the hell out of me."

Jimmy grimaced reaching out to touch her arm. "Sorry, didn't mean to. I just didn't hear any noise up here. I wanted to make sure you were okay."

Daisy's smiled widened. Jimmy was a good man. He was warm and gentle. He was also devastatingly handsome with his square jaw and deep dark eyes. Daisy knew he was concerned about their age difference. She had a feeling he was afraid that he was a dirty old man for even wanting to be near her.

She didn't care. A good man is a good man. They were all too rare. "Yeah, I've just been reminiscing. I was just kind of struck by the realization that I'll never see this place again. I've had a lot of good memories here."

Jimmy looked around the room. Daisy could see he felt uncomfortable because it was painfully obvious that this was a little girl's room.

"But it is time to move on," Daisy said gazing at Jimmy with a sidelong look. "I'm not a little girl anymore. This place will always be in my memory. Carol was right. It's time I make my own way."

Jimmy nodded picking up one of the boxes off of the bed. "A bit of wisdom that would hold more meaning if she wasn't just trying to protect herself."

"True," Daisy said. "But, really, that's what she and my mother had been forced to do from a very early age, protect themselves. And I think now that it was so ingrained in them that they were both never really able to trust anyone else fully."

"Perhaps, but there's a lot of real estate between protecting yourself and purposely overdosing a dying man to capitalize on his legacy," Jimmy said. "However Carol started out in life she had a choice in how she wished to continue and with much better opportunities than most. Look, Daisy, I know you love her and I can't begin to understand how all of this is affecting you but she chose her own path."

Daisy sighed, "I know," as the knots retied in her stomach. She would always be grateful for what Carol had done for her. Her strength was the direct result of Carol's example. That was the memory of Carol that Daisy would hold on to. "So did you find anything downstairs that could help?"

"No. I did find a letter for you from a lawyer in Denver but that's about it."

"Ah," Daisy said picking up her suitcases off from the bed. "It's probably about Kerry's will. I'm not even going to worry about that right now. I figure

Carol went out there to contest it anyway. It could be years before that's settled."

"It's a reasonable assumption," Jimmy said. "Well, let's get out of here. As soon as we get your stuff dropped off, I'll buy you some lunch. Anywhere you want to go?"

"The Lowell Hotel is just down the street," Daisy said with a grin.

Jimmy raised an eyebrow then laughed. "Okay, maybe not anywhere. Maybe somewhere a poor beat cop can afford. Someplace uptown?"

Daisy giggled as they headed down the steps. "I'm just messing with you. All I need is a good Cobb salad."

"I know just the place."

As they arrived at the foot of the stairs there was a loud knock on the front door. Jimmy looked at Daisy and frowned. "Sounds like a cop knock to me."

"Shit. What do we do?"

Jimmy shrugged. "We answer it. You're here to collect your belongings. We're not doing anything wrong."

Jimmy sat the box he was carrying down before opening the door. Instead of the patrolman he expected, he was surprised to find Captain Nolan and Detective Barlow waiting out on the stoop. He was pretty damned sure it wasn't a coincidence.

"Well, this is certainly a surprise. Good morning, gentlemen."

Barlow grinned like he was expecting a free meal. Nolan didn't look nearly as enthused. Something was definitely up.

"Is it okay if we come in?" Barlow asked.

"Sure, c'mon in," Jimmy turned to look at Daisy. He stared at her, wide-eyed, warning her something was amiss. "Daisy, it seems you have company."

Barlow watched Daisy set her bags at the foot of the steps. "Taking a trip somewhere?"

Daisy smiled taking a quick glance at Jimmy before answering. "Moving out, actually, Carol's made it quite clear that I'm not welcome here anymore. I waited until I knew she was out of town before I came back to get the rest of my things. I didn't want any drama."

Barlow nodded. The fat on his neck wrinkled like an accordion. "A wise choice, given the situation."

Jimmy glanced at Nolan to find him staring back. Something was definitely on his mind.

"I understand you've kept yourself pretty busy during your leave, Jimmy. Anything you want to share?"

Jimmy grinned. There was no point in hiding anything. Nolan hadn't attained his position by being a fool. Jimmy just wondered how much he actually knew.

"God's honest truth? I don't have squat. I have a lot of theories, a whole lot of bullshit and conjecture but not a damn thing I can prove."

Barlow smiled crossing the foyer to stand next to Nolan. "I told you I liked this kid. He's smart. He thinks like a detective."

Jimmy furrowed his brow. "Uh, thanks? Am I missing something?"

Nolan smirked at Barlow then motioned toward Jimmy. "Go ahead, tell him."

Daisy moved to Jimmy's side brushing his shoulder. She wanted to convey they were in this together.

"Well, son, truth told, twelve hours ago, we were in the same boat as you. We looked at Vance's death from every angle. The Commissioner even managed to talk Scotland Yard into sending us their findings but it all came out blank. We couldn't find any evidence of wrongdoing, much less a conspiracy between Ms. Merrick and Jerry Jewell. You were the one who managed to get the ball rolling. It was a good thing you convinced that girl to come in and talk to us. After we spoke to her we were finally able to put it all together."

"How's that?" Jimmy asked.

"The coroner found that Jewell died of a heart attack due to a lethal combination of cocaine and Viagra but something stuck out to her that she couldn't explain. There was undissolved cocaine inside Jewell's nasal passage. She said it appeared as if he'd still been snorting coke after he was dead."

Daisy and Jimmy exchanged glances. It was a hell of a thing to hear.

"After talking to your witness we went back and tested the straw that was found at the scene and found Carol Merrick's DNA on it. Evidently, she blew more cocaine up his snout as he lay dying. Then, knowing we had a murder on our hands, we started digging deeper into Jewell's affairs. It turns out he recorded some of his conversations with Carol Merrick including one while he was in London where she advised him to hurry up and make Kerry's death happen. She said that it would have a 'more epic impact' if he died overseas."

"Jewell made sure he had an insurance policy in case Carol tried to hang him out to dry," Jimmy said.

"Exactly," Nolan said. "He had the recorder locked away in a safety deposit box."

"My God," Daisy said. Tears formed in her eyes as she leaned against Jimmy for support. "How could she do this?"

Nolan walked over and placed his hand on Daisy's shoulder. "I'm sorry, ma'am. I know it's hard to fathom especially when it's someone you're close to. I'm afraid there never are any good answers."

Daisy looked up at Jimmy as tears streamed down her face. Jimmy pulled her close. "I'm sorry, Daisy. I wish there was something I could do."

"Just hold me," she said. "I can't think about this right now."

Jimmy held Daisy close while she sobbed. Nolan and Barlow both patted her on the back before wandering off to explore the house.

Daisy had been through a lot in her young life. Probably more than she would ever be willing to tell him. As he stood there holding her he knew, beyond a doubt, that he was willing to put everything he had into making the rest of her life better.

He loved her. Right now that was all that mattered. Everything else could wait.

CHAPTER 43

Calliope took a deep cleansing breath before pushing through the anteroom door into the chapel sanctuary. Inside Cori awaited her along with Kerry's daughter Sarah, her mother Melinda and a family friend, a woman Cori had apparently taken a keen liking to, named Anna.

Calliope's guilt hung heavy from her heart as she mustered the courage to face the girl and her mother. The course of their lives could have all been radically different if not for her lust and her pride. There was no way she could change that now. She could only face up to her transgressions and accept the consequences. It was the only way she would ever find peace.

The door closed behind her with a solid strike that resonated through the room. The others turned to watch her approach.

Sarah's face was obvious as she moved closer. She had Kerry's angular features and striking deep-set blue eyes. Her hair and complexion were darker, like her mother, creating a striking balance between parents. Cori took a step forward to greet her with a quick embrace. "Calliope, thank goodness, I was starting to worry about you."

"I'm fine. It just took a little more time to get here than I expected. It appears everyone in the city has taken to the streets."

"That was the plan." Cori said.

"It's working better than I would have imagined."

As they spoke Calliope could feel Melinda's eyes cast upon her. She looked past Cori to lock gazes.

"Melinda."

"Calliope."

Melinda kept her emotions in check as they held each other's gaze. Calliope could guess at the storm brewing below the surface. This day had been a long time coming.

She was pleased to see how gracefully Melinda had aged. She was in great shape. Her salt and pepper hair lent itself to a regal appearance. After all these years she still looked formidable.

Calliope envied her while, at the same time, mourned for her too. Mortal life passed so quickly she knew that the better part of Melinda's life had been affected by her own willfulness.

"I guess I'm not exactly what you expected to see."

Melinda moved closer. Her gaze still locked with Calliope's. "Your sister has helped me to understand what you are. How you came to be. What she couldn't explain is why you made the decision to interfere in our lives. She couldn't defend your lack of morals."

"Mother, please." Sarah stepped to Melinda's side. "That's not fair."

Calliope held Melinda's gaze. "No, your mother's right, Sarah, I made a grave error where you were concerned. I should have never interfered. But you have to understand that I loved Kerry with all my heart. I only wanted what was best for him. I wanted him to live up to his potential. I knew he could never come back here and raise a family especially in light of the situation with you, Melinda, and knowing everything he'd lost. So, I gave him an out. It wasn't my choice to make."

Melinda cast her eyes down. "You're right. It wasn't your choice. But, deep down, I've always known you were right. Kerry wasn't equipped to take on a family then. If he'd have come back here it would have been a disaster. I still can't help but think that if he did though, he'd at least had some kind of relationship with Sarah. That's what pains me the most. He never got to find out how great she is."

Tears welled up in Sarah's eyes. Melinda reached over and took her hand.

Calliope found tears in her own eyes as she gazed at Sarah. "I'm sorry Kerry never reached out to you. I always hoped he would. I think he was afraid he wasn't good enough."

"Or he was afraid Melinda would put a bullet in his ass," Anna said.

Melinda smiled turning to her friend. "You might not have been wrong there."

Cori laughed wrapping her arm around Anna. "You are too much, lady."

"Thanks." Anna said returning the hug. "I get that a lot."

"I can see why you like her, Cori. She's spunky." Calliope said.

Sarah laughed reaching out to touch Anna's shoulder. "Yeah, we can't take her anywhere."

Calliope smiled relieved the tension had lifted.

"So," Melinda said looking a little more at ease. "What was it that drew you to Kerry? Knowing what I know about you now. Why would you choose to get involved with him?"

Calliope took a quick glance at Cori before answering. "Well, initially, I wanted to cheer him up. He was always so sullen. The guys he worked with told me he rarely spoke. They said he was a great guy, a hard worker, but something haunted him. It took me a while to get it out of him. When I finally did, it broke my heart. He was so vulnerable I just wanted to protect him."

Melinda nodded. A hint of sadness grew in her eyes. "That was a hell of a time. It nearly destroyed all of us."

Melinda reached out to take Anna's hand. Calliope looked to her questioningly.

"I was Mark's girlfriend," Anna said. "Kerry's brother."

"Oh my word," Calliope said. "I am so sorry."

Anna tightened her grip on Melinda's hand. "She's right. It was the end of our innocence. Within the space of a few days, we lost them both. Everything changed then. Kerry ran away. I ran away. Neither of us had Melinda's strength."

Melinda shook her head. She stared over Calliope's shoulder into the echoes of her past. "There was nothing else I could do. I had to be strong. I had Sarah on the way. I had Ken to deal with." She looked at Calliope. "When I went to Oregon, I was at the end of my rope. I just wanted to escape all of the bullshit here."

"And I robbed you of that," Calliope said.

"I robbed myself of it," Melinda said. "I didn't have the faith in Kerry you did. I wanted to avail him of all the rock-n-roll bullshit. It was cool for a bunch of kids right out of high school but I never thought for a second he'd go on to achieve what he did. And, when he did, I hated him for it. It took me a long time to realize that it was who he was. It was who he was always meant to be. I couldn't see that then."

Calliope wrapped Melinda in a hug. "When you're really in love with someone you can be blind to their faults. I guess sometimes you can be blind to their strengths as well."

Melinda held on to Calliope tightly. "Especially when you're afraid of letting go."

Calliope felt her guilt fading away as she held Melinda in her arms. This moment had been a long time coming.

Anna smiled as Sarah sidled up next to her. "I'm glad I got to see this. This is exactly what your mom needed. Now maybe she won't be such a grouch."

"I heard that, Colvin," Melinda said

Anna stuck her tongue out behind Melinda's back sending Cori into a fit of giggles.

"Let's hope," Sarah said laughing as she wiped tears from her eyes. "I'm glad you're here, too, Anna. We all needed this."

"We did," Anna said. "I'm glad I've got you two back."

Sarah gave Anna a hug and a kiss on the cheek. "Hell, yes. You're stuck with us now. It's going to be all I can do to keep Tracy from trying to go home with you. She's in love with you, too."

Anna smiled. "She's a great kid. How could she not be? Look at the women in her life."

Calliope looked at the faces around her and felt a depth of joy she hadn't experienced in a very long time. For the first time in ages, she just felt good.

"So, what happens now?" Melinda asked. "How's all this going to play out?"

Calliope looked at Cori. "After the public service, my people have a ritual that we perform after a loved one is laid to rest to help them cross over into Elysium. The Summerland, we call it. Kerry wanted me to perform the ceremony for him."

"So he knew about you?" Sarah asked.

"Mostly," Calliope said. "He'd seen me do enough crazy things to understand that I wasn't entirely 'normal'. So, I had to tell him. And, of course, Kerry being Kerry, he was fascinated and wanted to know more."

Sarah's eyes rounded as an epiphany struck. 'She waits for me beyond space and time, there between madness and soft sublime,' 'Waiting at the Edge of Eternity'."

Calliope smiled and nodded while the other three looked befuddled.

"Say what?" Anna said.

"It's one of Kerry's songs. It's on his first solo album."

"He wrote a song about you?" Cori said.

"Yeah, I'm pretty sure that one's about me," Calliope said grinning. "And I'm almost positive that he wrote, 'A Face in the Crowd', about you, Sarah. That was how I always took it."

Sarah had a faraway look in her eye. "Yeah, I'd thought that, too. At least I hoped it was. It always makes me sad when I hear it."

Melinda wrapped her arm around Sarah and pulled her closer. "Is it all right if we stay for the ceremony, Calliope?"

"I hoped you would. There are going to be a few of Kerry's friends there as well. I'd love for you to meet them."

"I'd like that," Sarah said.

"Great," Calliope said. "The first thing you need to do is get ready for the funeral. There's going to be a lot of famous people in here very soon. I hope you get to talk to them, too. I want you to get a sense of the man your father was, Sarah. It's the only gift I have to give you."

"You're not staying for that?" Melinda asked.

Calliope shook her head. Her eyes flared like she found the thought terrifying. "No. Cori and I have things we need to prepare. We'll meet you in the mausoleum as soon as everyone's gone."

"Okay," Sarah said taking the opportunity to hug Calliope. "Thank you for this. I know you've taken an awful risk, taking this on."

Calliope smiled looking at Sarah, Melinda, and Anna in turn. "I couldn't be anywhere else. Your father was a great man, Sarah. I owe him the world."

The three of them watched silently as Calliope and Cori went out through the anteroom door. As soon as they were gone Kerry's casket was brought into the room. Sarah held her breath, tears coming to her eyes anew as she watched it placed at the front of the room. She walked up to it slowly, mourning every step as one she should have made while he was still alive. She placed her hand on top of the casket and remembered him not as a daughter but as a stranger watching from afar.

It was the loneliest feeling in the world.

As she dropped her head against her hand and wept she felt her mother's and Anna's hands both placed gently on her back. Sarah realized as the tears poured down her cheeks that she was Kerry's living legacy. She was the only living thing left of him now in the world. She had to find a way to make that count.

CHAPTER 44

"This is Angelique Dupree and I am live here on Quebec Street just outside of the Fairmount Cemetery.

The crowd here has swelled well into the thousands awaiting the arrival of Kerry Vance's body for his funeral later this morning.

As you know, this story has captured national attention after Vance's body was taken from JFK airport in New York shortly after it arrived from London. Federal officials have stated that charges are pending for Avery Clark and his accomplices but have declined to state what those charges might be.

Sources inside Vance's camp have said that the funeral here in Denver was Vance's wish and that Clark and his accomplices were carrying out his instructions. A legal battle over his estate is pending as Vance filed for divorce from his wife of twenty-three years, the formal supermodel Carol Merrick, shortly before his death.

An outpouring of support from around the world has arrived here in Denver to be a part of Vance's funeral.

I talked to one couple who flew all the way from New Zealand to be here today. They told me losing Kerry Vance was like losing a friend of the family.

Action Ten will stay with the story today bringing you updates and reactions from Vance's fans and friends from across the musical spectrum.

For Action Ten News, this is Angelique Dupree."

CHAPTER 45

"Bloody hell. Would you look at that crowd? Unbelievable." Clyde stared out through the window as their limousine wound its way through the city streets toward the cemetery.

"And we still have a block to go," Jill said consulting her phone.

Avery kicked back in his seat and shut his eyes for a few minutes before they arrived. He was exhausted. It had been a long ride from Dan's in Kansas. It had been a really long haul all the way from Manhattan. Avery just hoped Calliope's plan was going to work. It was simple but had a lot of layers.

She seemed supremely confident in it when they parted ways at Dan's saying, 'if it worked in Bratislava it should work in Denver'. Avery wasn't entirely sure where Bratislava was but when he got a chance he was going to look it up. He figured it to be a place where crazy brunettes must run amok. It was the only explanation that made any sense at the time.

There were still a lot of unanswered questions about Calliope. The whole political dissident thing seemed a bit of a stretch. She was skilled at keeping her secrets close to the vest. Avery figured there was a whole lot more to her story than she would ever tell.

There was a moment, as he stood beside Calliope while they placed Kerry's casket gently in Dan's box trailer, when he got the overpowering feeling that time itself had been stretched to the width of a thread. It was terrifying and thrilling all in the space of a few seconds. It was as if some unseen force emanated from her. Whoever she was it seemed the normal rules of reality didn't apply. A feeling of terrible finality came over him as she, Dan and Jake drove away.

Avery jerked awake as Jill draped her arm across his shoulders. "Are you okay?"

"Yeah, I'm fine, just worn out. Hopefully, my cellmates will let me get some sleep tonight."

Jill laughed pulling him closer and laying her head on his shoulder. "Let's hope so."

Avery grinned, warmed by her presence. As much as Calliope vexed him meeting Jill had made him happier than he had been in a very long time. Avery leaned his head against hers. "I'm just glad we're here together even if we will be in separate cells."

"I just hope the sons of bitches don't drag me back to Cincinnati," Jill said. "I don't care if I see that place ever again."

"Well, I guess whoever gets out of jail first buys dinner," Avery said. "We'll just have to figure out where we want to land."

"Denver's not bad," Jill said gazing out of the window. "It's far enough away from everything to make a new start."

Avery found the idea exciting leaving New York behind for the mountains, especially now, with Jill at his side. After everything that had happened the idea of going back to his apartment bothered him. Zoe's memory would always be in his head and in his heart. He'd made a mess of his life there trying to hold on to her. It was time to move on. "We'll have to go exploring once we get out of trouble."

Jill looked up into his eyes and smiled. "Deal."

"It is a pretty country," Clyde said looking out through the window. "But it's a cold motherfucker here in winter with snow ass deep every other Tuesday. You might want to keep that in mind."

"Noted." Avery laughed. "So what are you going to do after this is over?"

"Get stoned, drunk and howl at the moon," Clyde said. "Then I was thinking I'd go back home to Texas. I have a nephew down near Lubbock that's been trying to get me to visit. I think I might just go down there and overstay my welcome."

"How long has it been since you were there?" Jill took Avery's hand as they regarded him. The circles beneath Clyde's eyes seemed deeper now, hollow. His hawkish face was pale as he looked away from the question. The trip had taken a lot out of him.

"A very long goddamned time," Clyde said keeping his gaze peeled out the window. "Not since my mother died back in seventy-two. My dad had been gone a long time by then, the rotten son of a bitch, so I went back home to help my sister settle the estate, such as it was. After that, there wasn't anything to go back to."

Avery squeezed Jill's hand. "Well, you can always come to hang out with us. You know we're a good time."

Clyde snorted a laugh turning to look them. "Y'all are fuckin' nuts. But, yeah, we do have to keep in touch. We're family now, too. Kerry's family. And I do have to say that little fucker had good taste."

Jill laughed. "Hell yeah, he did."

Avery noticed Calliope's husband, Harry, staring back at them through the rear-view mirror. He hadn't said a word since they climbed in the limo. He hadn't exactly been over-friendly when they'd met, either. After having driven the Temple close to Denver as a decoy they had met him in a parking lot well outside of town to hand the van off to a younger, breath-taking redhead, while Harry drove them to the funeral in a limousine like the other VIPs. It was quite clear that he didn't want to be here. Whatever their relationship was Avery knew Calliope had been desperate not to involve him. He was only here as a last resort. Avery was sure he was well aware of the fact.

Seconds passed as they sized each other up via the mirror. Harry's dark eyes had a sharp piercing quality. They were unsettling like Calliope's when her ire was up.

"So how long have you known, Calliope?" Jill asked catching his gaze in the mirror as well. "She's a pretty intense chick."

A thin smile appeared on Harry's face. "That she is. Reckless, too, I'd say."

Avery grinned feeling a little better knowing the man wasn't completely mirthless. "Yeah, it didn't take long for this to turn into a fiasco. But, really, I guess it was part of the plan. Calliope's done a hell of a job pulling it off."

Harry smirked as he turned into the cemetery. "Well, Mr. Clark, it's not entirely pulled off, yet. We still have a few things to attend to. And, to answer your question, ma'am, I've known Calliope for more years than either of us would care to admit."

"Young lovers?" Jill asked.

Harry laughed as he pulled the limo into the queue behind those of the other guests. "Something like that."

Avery looked out through the window to see a contingent of FBI agents standing next to the door of the chapel in their aviator's and sexy black and yellow windbreakers. They were keeping a close eye on everyone entering. As they exited the vehicle, he caught glimpses of members of a tactical response unit lurking in the shadows around the perimeter of the chapel. It was a creepy feeling knowing that they were looking for him.

"I hope they don't bust me at the door."

Harry shook his head scanning the scene. "The funeral is to go off without intrusion. Mr. Vance's lawyer has seen it. They will take you into custody afterward."

"I hope you're right," Avery said. "Hopefully, I can hire Kerry's lawyer to get me out of this shit."

Jill grinned. "Maybe we can get a Groupon."

The three of them walked toward the front of the chapel at a nice easy pace settling into the line as quietly as they could. It didn't take long before all eyes in the line were cast in their direction, a distinct murmur rising among them.

"So much for being incognito," Avery said nodding at the guitar player from Night Wish.

"Yeah," Clyde laughed. "Like that was going to happen."

As they made their way forward a younger agent in a spiffy FBI ball cap walked over to the man Avery assumed to be in charge. He was a tall, thin, chap with a graying blond crew cut. As the kid leaned in to speak the older man's eyes followed the line until he met Avery's gaze.

"Looks like their main man," Avery said nodding at the agent as their eyes locked. "This should be fun."

The older agent nodded to the younger man who then returned to his post. The older agent looked at him and nodded. Avery returned it and did his best not to smile. He didn't want to appear smug. He was in enough shit as it was. He didn't want to piss off the guy in charge. He would have much preferred not to make his acquaintance.

"He seems friendly enough," Jill said.

Avery shrugged. "He's here to do a job."

As the line moved up the steps toward the chapel, the lead agent, along with a shorter, portly, agent with an unfortunate looking bullfrog face walked over.

"Mr. Clark, it's nice to finally meet you. I'm Special Agent Tom Carson. This is Agent Grieg."

"Ah, like the composer, nice," Avery said shaking both men's hands. "Sorry about the kerfuffle. It's been a hell of a week."

Carson smiled. "I'd say. It's been quite a spectacle here these past few days. I've never seen anything like it."

"Kerry wanted to go out with a bang," Avery said looking around at the crowd. "It seems he got his wish."

"It does at that," Carson said. "So where is your other cohort? I thought she'd be with you."

Avery stared Carson in the eye. He seemed an honorable man. He didn't want to lie but he had to stick to the plan. "She abandoned us. After this whole thing blew up in the media, she couldn't handle it. She left us while we were sleeping at a rest stop in Kansas."

Carson studied Avery's face looking for signs of deception. Avery did his best to sell it but couldn't be certain if Carson bought it. The man was clearly no fool.

"Kansas, huh? That's unfortunate. I was looking forward to meeting her. The stories I've heard have been quite amusing. The guys in New York have had a field day investigating her."

Calliope was a lot of things but Avery hadn't once thought of her as amusing, terrifying was much more like it. He looked at Carson, confused. "I'm afraid I don't understand."

"The stories about her have been wild," Grieg said. "Probably ninety-nine percent of them are pure bullshit. As far as pure hard facts go the woman is a ghost. Did you know her before this whole thing began?"

Avery balked at the question. He looked from Grieg to Carson nonplussed.

Carson looked at the other agent and shook his head. "They'll be plenty of time for that later. These people have a funeral to attend."

"Thank you," Avery said. "So how's this going to go?"

"After the funeral and interment are over, we'll be right here waiting. You come with us quietly and we'll head downtown to the Federal building. I don't want to cuff you and cause a big scene. So we'll just keep it nice and friendly and I'll just be your ride out."

Avery nodded. "There won't be any trouble. I was well aware of what was waiting for me when I arrived. Getting Kerry home was more important."

Carson regarded him. "I admire your loyalty, Mr. Clark. And, if it was up to me, I'd just let the whole damned thing go. A man's dying wish is to be honored. But they're not looking at it the same way back east. The field office and lawyers there are all astir."

Avery looked at Jill and grinned, "Another reason to get the hell out of that town."

Jill smiled taking Avery's hand. "Exactly."

Music issued from inside the chapel as the line they'd side-stepped dwindled. Carson offered his hand to Avery and Clyde. "I'll be right here when you're ready, my condolences to all of you."

"Thank you, Mr. Carson. We appreciate it." Avery said.

Avery took a deep breath as they stepped inside holding tightly onto Jill's hand. Their goal had finally been achieved. Kerry was home.

CHAPTER 46

Calliope watched the funeral service through a crack in the anteroom door. The chapel was filled to capacity with rock stars and actors, models and show business brass, most of them here only to make the scene. Kerry's bandmates were all seated together with their families, their somber expressions reminding her, as with the scores of people outside lining the streets, how many people were really genuinely affected by Kerry's death. It warmed her heart to know how many people really loved him.

Calliope kept a close eye on Sarah. She sat holding her mother's and Anna's hands as tears streamed down her face. It gave Calliope pause that the girl was forced to learn about her father only through the eyes of others. Calliope's guilt still hung in her throat unabsolved by Sarah's forgiveness. The look of loss on her face would stick with Calliope the rest of her life. It was a fitting sentence for the pain she'd caused. She only hoped she would be able to ease Sarah's pain when she helped Kerry cross over.

Calliope choked up again watching Clyde fight a losing battle against his own tears as he gave his eulogy. It was an awe-inspiring portrait of Kerry from a man who had been with him since the very beginning of his career. Calliope's heart broke every time Clyde's voice cracked.

"It's as if I've lost my own child," Clyde said. "There will never be another one like him."

Then as Clyde made his way back to his seat, all eyes in the room turned as Avery stood and made his way to the podium. A hushed murmur followed him rippling through the crowd. Avery's face was gaunt, his color still pale.

His blue eyes red-rimmed from tears, from exhaustion, from the excruciating strain of detoxifying from alcohol as he put the whole of his being into fulfilling his best friend's dying wish. He had put his life and career at risk to get Kerry home. Calliope was grateful she'd had the opportunity to get to know him. He represented what was best in the mortal soul, no matter his flaws.

"I stand here today to bear witness to the life of one of the greatest people I have ever known, my best friend, Kerry Vance."

Avery's voice flowed over the crowd, warm, calm, yet steeped heavy in emotion. Calliope found herself spellbound as he spoke.

"I had known Kerry for quite a few years when my late wife, Zoe, got sick. We hung around some of the same people, meeting up at parties and running wild. We got along famously, from the very beginning and before long he started coming to the house to hang out with us when he wasn't touring. We'd drink together and Zoe and I always had the best time when he was there. We had the most brilliant conversations, talking about books and movies, bands and composers, you name it. We talked about everything. He and Zoe were both so sharp, so witty. They floored me. I found myself having to do research just to try and keep up with them."

Calliope smiled wiping a tear from her eye as laughter rose from the crowd.

"So, later on, after Zoe got sick, I was staying at a friend's apartment close to Zoe's hospital. Kerry and a few friends stopped over and I went and hid in the guest room. I was a mess, completely at my wit's end and I didn't want Kerry to see me like that. I didn't want to be a downer, either. So I just kept to myself. At that point, Zoe had been going downhill for about three months. We had been through all of the treatments, tried all of the alternative healing practices. We had been through every option there was to explore and none of it was working. She was fading right in front of me. I knew she didn't have long to go and, God love her, she knew it, too."

Calliope hung her head as tears fell out of control. Avery's voice was so clear and true it was haunting.

"That last month they kept Zoe in the hospital. I stayed with her for the first two weeks barely leaving her side. I couldn't bear the thought of her being alone. I was so exhausted that Zoe finally called our friend Tabitha to ask if I could come there and crash."

Avery smiled looking out over the crowd as he wiped his eyes. "She was worried about me."

He fell into a long silence as the memory played out before him. "Zoe kicked me out of her room that night. She told me she didn't want to see me again until after I'd had gotten good and drunk and had a good night's sleep. I tried to talk her out of it but she shooed me away and told me Tabitha was expecting me. So I left and fretted over the decision all evening.

"That night as I hid in the room Kerry strolled right on in like he owned the place carrying two full bottles of some high dollar single malt Scotch. He didn't say anything. He just smiled and slouched down in a chair beside the bed and put his feet up on the desk. I didn't feel like talking but I wasn't about to try and kick him out. He was an imposing guy, you know? So I just sat back on the bed and stared off into space as Kerry started drinking the first bottle. We just sat there in silence for a really long time. Kerry would take a big slug out of one of the bottles on occasion and we both just sat there staring out of the window. Then, after he was about half-way through the bottle, he turns to me and says; 'You know what, Clark, sometimes life just really fucking sucks, man, especially when you know there's not a goddamned thing you can do to change it.' I just broke down right then and there and started bawling. I had been holding it back for too long. Kerry came over and hugged me while I cried. Then, after I'd calmed down a little, he handed me the other bottle.

"We ended up sitting there all night talking and drinking the Scotch. We poured our hearts out to each other, laughing and crying. We got so blitzed we ended up singing old doo-wop songs along with the radio. It was exactly what I needed just then. And I think it was exactly what Zoe had wanted for me."

Calliope looked out to see that there wasn't a dry eye in the house. Even the scene makers had been touched by his story. Jill had leaned over and was sobbing on Clyde's shoulder as he held his arm around her. Calliope hoped that she and Avery could find a future together. They both deserved it. They had both been through too much in their short lives.

"And that's not the half of it," Avery said smiling through his tears. "I found out later that Kerry missed his flight that night to a gig out west just so he could stay with me. They almost had to cancel the show."

"I went back to the hospital the next day with my batteries re-charged. With Kerry's help, I was able to set aside my grief so that I could be Zoe's joy. I kept a smile on her face until the morning she passed. We were watching the sunrise from her hospital window. She had her head on my shoulder as I told her about an idea I had for a new book. And just as the sun broke out over the rooftops Zoe nestled into my shoulder and I heard her sigh with contentment and then... nothing. She was gone. I just sat there holding her and crying until one of the nurses came in. I'm only just now starting to recover from it. I will love that woman until the day I die."

The room was silent. All eyes stared at up Avery as tears flowed. Avery's soul opened in a way they'd never expected. It was a powerful moment.

"Kerry canceled part of the European leg of his tour that year so he could be at Zoe's funeral. He did everything he could to keep me on my feet and moving forward. Sadly though, I think I let him down. I was too hurt. My whole life was broken. I spiraled out of control there for a good while."

Avery looked down at Jill and smiled, "For too long. But through it all, Kerry was there for me. He was always only a phone call away, no matter where he was in the world. He helped talk me down more than once and I will always be grateful. Kerry was a great man, beyond the music, beyond the genius. He had a pure soul. If you were his friend that was it, he was there for you, come hell or high tide. He never turned his back on a friend. So there was no way in hell that I wouldn't be here for him now. There was no way that I wouldn't do everything in my power to honor his last wish. Kerry wanted to come home to rest beside his parents and his brother, Mark. I regret absolutely nothing about helping to make that happen. He was my best friend and I loved him. Thank you all for coming here today to help me say good-bye."

In all of Calliope's considerable years, she had never seen a crowd rise to their feet to applaud a eulogy. But, somehow, it was happening now. It just seemed fitting.

CHAPTER 47

Avery returned to his place at Jill's side surprised as a wave of people came forward to pat him on the back or shake his hand. He shook his head, embarrassed by the display, holding on to Jill's hand like he was about to come unmoored. The litany of faces passed in a blur for several minutes as he was regaled by more tales of Kerry's help and generosity. It warmed his heart to hear them all but by the end, he was starting to tire.

He, Jill and Clyde had one more duty to perform before it was all over. The interment ceremony Calliope wished to perform intrigued him. If he could identify it, it would be a clue into discovering something about Calliope's past. Though, truthfully, he wondered why it mattered to him. Calliope was at heart a great person.

She was intimidating and definitely a badass with that big damned dagger she hustled around in her girdle. He wondered why he felt compelled or entitled, for that matter, to know more. He was better off not knowing especially now when he was about to be interrogated about her. Perhaps it was better if he just held on to his memories and hope she was able to get away. Perhaps it was better if her mystery remained intact.

As the well-wishers dwindled around him, a slender dark-haired woman approached wiping tears from her eyes. As soon as Avery got a good look he realized that she had to be Kerry's daughter. She looked too much like him not to be.

"Mr. Clark, can I talk to you for a second?"

Avery smiled as Jill turned to regard her a look of surprise registering on her face. "Oh my God, are you Sarah?"

Sarah grinned nodding her head. "Sure am."

"It's so nice to meet you. I'm Jill." Jill extended her hand. "Avery and I weren't sure you would come."

Sarah smiled shaking Jill's hand. "I had to. I couldn't go the rest of my life not knowing what I had missed. It's been a tough few day trying to process all of this."

"As I would well expect," Avery said. "It's been difficult for all of us to process."

Sarah nodded. Her solemn expression looked so much like Kerry that Avery just wanted to hug her.

"I wanted to tell you how much I enjoyed your eulogy, Mr. Clark, truly. I know so little about my Dad, it was nice to hear."

"Ah, honey," Jill reached out and gave her a hug. "I'm so sorry. I know this must be difficult. If there's anything you want to know about Kerry don't be afraid to ask."

"Thanks."

Clyde strolled up after ending a booming conversation with another rough-looking old road dog. "My God, is this Sarah?"

Jill grinned. "Sure is."

Clyde took Sarah's hand and looked her dead in the eye. Sarah was taken aback by the sudden gesture but didn't try to break it.

"I want you to know that there wasn't a day that went by that your father didn't think about you. It was a damnable situation and one I always hoped he'd try to fix. But don't ever, for a second, think that he didn't care. He just didn't think that he could ever make it right."

Sarah stared up at Clyde as another tear dropped from her eye. "Thank you, Mr. McGee. That means a lot to me."

"Ah, hell, honey, call me Clyde. We're practically family."

Sarah laughed as she held on to his hand. "Clyde it is. I really liked your eulogy as well. I have a much better sense of how my father was with his friends. How much he meant to you. Hopefully I inherited some of his traits."

"I'm sure you did," Avery said. "I'd say just as sure as you have his eyes."

Just then, two older women came to Sarah's side. Avery guessed the taller one to be Sarah's mother. They shared a lot of the same features as well.

"This is my mother, Melinda, and our dear friend, Anna." Sarah said.

"Are you ready, Sarah? I think Calliope and Cori are ready for us."

"You're going to the internment ceremony too?" Avery said. "That's great."

Melinda smiled though it didn't bear much by way of warmth. "We've had a hell of a road in front of us getting here, too, Mr. Clark. It's time for all of us to make our peace."

"Well said, ma'am." Clyde said.

Melinda looked up at Clyde. This time her smile was warmer. "Thank you for taking care of him, Mr. McGee. I'm thankful Kerry had friends as good as you."

"Thank you, ma'am," Clyde said trying hard not to tear up again. "I loved that boy with all my heart."

"I know you did," Melinda said reaching out to touch his arm, "He was damned lucky to have you. All of you."

Melinda took Sarah's hand as they made their way across the chapel toward the anteroom door. Avery looked into Jill's eyes and smiled taking her hand. They walked through the door together anxious to see what Calliope had waiting for them.

CHAPTER 48

Carol waded into the mob gathered outside the cemetery looking for a way in. The cops had the entrances guarded and weren't allowing anyone to pass. Undeterred, she shoved her way through the mass of sweaty humanity until she was up against the fence near the gate. From there she was able to see the line of town cars and limousines parked outside the chapel.

Carol stared at them calculating just exactly how it was that she came to be here on the outside looking in at her own husband's funeral. She should have been inside. Once again it seemed Kerry had gotten the best of her. If she'd believed in an afterlife, she could easily see him laughing his ass off, taunting her. Carol, the little Blacksville Barbie, so obsessed with money and status that she would tear down everything real they'd created in a desperate attempt to acquire more.

In the end, he had seen her as a joke. For as long as she had known Kerry she never understood him. Fame meant nothing to him, money even less. All he'd ever wanted to do was perform and party. That was great when you were a twenty-something kid out on the road for the first time. But when you're in your sixties, it's just ridiculous.

All of that hard work, all of the interviews, the touring, having a camera stuck in your face twenty-four/seven, what was it all for? What was the point? If it wasn't for her the man would have had nothing. She and Jerry had built his empire. It was by sheer force of will that she put them in a position where they could have lived comfortably for the rest of their lives.

Kerry didn't need to tour anymore even before he got sick. Carol was convinced the only reason he'd done that last album and tour was as an excuse to stay away from her.

He would have rather died out on the road. So she'd made his wish come true. Kerry Vance was now a legend. His place in the rock-n-roll pantheon was secure. It had cost Carol everything. So, if she was going out it sure as hell wasn't going to be alone.

Carol glowered at the motley crowd trying to figure out a way to get inside when a unique opportunity presented itself. A few steps up closer toward the gate she noticed an exchange between a creepy-looking older guy and a youngish hard-rock bimbo with too much ass stuffed into a pair of black yoga pants. Evidently, the creepy looking guy had been paying too much attention to the bleach-blonde bimbo's boom-boom booty when she told him to fuck off and quit staring at her. Carol grinned slipping through the crowd to place herself between the creepy guy and the blonde. Carol gained the big man's attention bestowing her sweetest smile on him and beckoning him closer.

The guy was definitely creepy. He had a tall, freakish, Frankenstein's monster kind of vibe with long stringy black hair and pale skin. His greasy T-shirt looked like it hadn't been washed in ages. When the guy smiled back at her Carol found it entirely disquieting. She got the distinct impression that he may well have had someone tied up in his basement. As soon as the big man was close enough Carol reached out and ran her middle finger, two full knuckles deep, straight up the blonde's big ass.

"What the fuck?!"

Carol spun the opposite way from the blonde as she whirled around to see the creepy guy left standing there with a big dumb look on his face.

The blonde charged him swinging her purse like a set of nunchucks. "You pervert motherfucker I told you to stay the hell away from me."

Carol slid up next to the gate watching as the big guy did his best to shield himself from the blonde's assault. It only took a few seconds before the guards were forced to intervene. As soon as they moved, Carol, along with a few others, scrambled through the gate. As the others made a beeline for the chapel, Carol dropped down and made her way along the ground behind a row of larger tombstones towards a vault that was out of sight of the FBI team. She took a quick peek around the corner to see the Feds swooping in to intercept the others but no one appeared to be heading her way. She sat down on the grass and took a deep breath as she leaned back against the vault. She smiled, at peace with her purpose, as she reached into her jacket pocket to rest her hand on the pistol inside.

As soon as Avery Clark stuck his head outside of that chapel she aimed to put a bullet in it.

Carol stayed low to the ground as she moved around to the far side of the vault. From there she could see people starting to come out of the chapel. But then, something else caught her eye. Out of the back of the chapel, she saw a group of people, Avery among them, following Kerry's pallbearers over to the mausoleum. Along with Clark, she saw Clyde McGee and a dark-haired girl holding the hand of an older woman. Carol assumed this to be Kerry's daughter. She favored him, especially around the eyes.

Carol took a look around watching as the Feds kept a close eye on the crowd as they returned to their limousines and town cars. It was the perfect opportunity to sneak over to the mausoleum and join her extended family. With a little luck, she just might be able to kill a few birds and still get out with her skin intact. Then she could just disappear.

CHAPTER 49

The late morning sun fell warm through the stain glass windows lining the walls to wash the room with a warm crimson glow. Sarah enjoyed the sunlight on her skin as the cool air inside was bracing. The mausoleum looked a lot smaller than she remembered. The place had stuck in her memory for so long it took her by surprise. The hallways were narrower and the rows of vaults and columbarium didn't stretch to the sky like they did in her dreams. In her memory the room was cavernous.

Sarah held her mother's hand as the group followed Kerry's casket to its final resting place. Ahead of them Calliope, Cori and another sister, Sarah couldn't remember her name, stood wrapped in pure white hooded robes their eyes closed and their hands held up before them in prayer. The sisters were beautiful. Each was a variation on a powerful genetic theme.

That there were immortal beings among them was a difficult thing to ponder. But here, now, seeing them together, Sarah could feel a warp in gravity around them, a gravitas made whole by grace. There was no doubt in Sarah's mind that they were who they said they were. To be in their presence was a heady experience.

The group came to a stop as Kerry's casket was placed on a low brass frame in front of his vault. Sarah looked up at the wall to see that Kerry would be placed to Mark's right below their parents, Jim and Bonnie.

Sarah wished she knew more about each of them. She resolved to ask her mother and Anna to tell her more about them. The story of her family was still only half-known. She needed to change that.

As soon as the casket was placed, Calliope and her sisters started chanting in breathtaking harmony. Sarah didn't recognize the language but, really, she didn't need to. The spirit of their voices was stirring.

Sarah looked around, to her mother, to Anna, to Avery, Jill, and Clyde, all of them staring off into their own space, enrapt as the sisters stirred their souls with a song. There wasn't a dry eye among them as each individual's memories of Kerry played out in the air before them.

Then a shot rang out. It echoed through the hall with a terrible rip. Everyone whipped around to see Carol Merrick standing with a pistol held above her head.

"Having a party without me?" she said.

Out of the corner of her eye Sarah saw Calliope take a step forward. She turned to see an expression of outright rage emanating from her. Sarah found it more terrifying than the woman with the gun.

"How dare you defile this holy place," Calliope said. "Kerry wanted nothing more than to be rid of you."

Carol smirked leveling the gun on Calliope. The expression on her face was calm but in her eyes was a terrible resolve. She was completely off balance.

"Oh, I am well aware," Carol said waving the pistol to pass across the whole group. "The thing is, I don't give a fuck. That son of a bitch thought he was going to leave me penniless, too. But I'm here to tell you that shit ain't happening."

Sarah felt her stomach drop, grateful she'd made the decision not to bring Tracy along. Carol was out to eliminate anyone standing between her and Kerry's money which put her right at the top of the list. The fact Carol thought it a viable plan told Sarah all she needed to know about her state of mental health. The chick had lost it.

"What the fuck is wrong with you, Carol? You really think this stupid shit is going to work? There's like fifty fucking FBI agents wandering around outside. What the hell do you think you're going to get away with?"

Clyde's baritone echoed through the hall. He looked like he was about to go over and smack the pistol out of her hand. He clenched his fists when Carol pointed the gun his way.

"I'm not worried about getting away," Carol said. "I'm getting even. All of you, every damned one of you, had a hand in taking Kerry from me. All I wanted was for us to be together. I wanted him to retire, to stay home with me, not out running around the damned planet fucking any woman that would have him. He was supposed to take care of me and you all fucked it up."

"You're the one that fucked it up," Avery said.

Avery's voice cut through the room resonating like cold steel cast against the walls. Sarah jumped at the sound of it then took a step back as Carol moved forward to point the gun straight at Avery's face.

"Ah, this from the mastermind of fucking up my shit," Carol said. "Give me one good reason why I shouldn't blow your head off right now."

Avery took a step forward, the muzzle of the gun pressing into the skin of his forehead.

"Do it, bitch. Pull the trigger. It doesn't matter what happens now. You lost. And you'll just have to deal with that for however long you have left in the world."

Carol's armed stiffened as she pressed the gun further into Avery's head. Sarah's heart leaped into her throat. She was close to hyperventilating. She reached out and squeezed her mother's hand trying to catch her breath. Carol stared into Avery's eyes. She tilted her head like she was trying to see inside it.

"Well, I'll tell you, Clark, it's not going to be that long for either of us."

Just then behind Carol's back, at the far end of the hall, a large, well-muscled, specimen of a man slid the door open slowly. Sarah did her best not to react. Beside her, she saw Calliope brace herself with the slightest of grins sliding across her face. Everyone in the room prepared to move as Harry slipped the door shut behind him.

"Hey!"

Within the space of the thousandth of a second it took for Carol to turn her head, Calliope and Cori moved past Sarah with a speed she never imagined was possible. Before she could blink Cori had taken Avery to the ground, shielding him, while Calliope hit Carol Merrick with the force of a train.

As soon as they collided Carol flew backward off of her feet to slam into the floor, head first. The gun flew from her hand to slide across the floor.

Calliope snatched Carol from the floor pulling her up face to face. Carol was stunned. Her eyes rolled in her head as she stared at Calliope, fear evident on her face as blood dripped from her ears from the force of impact. The expression on Calliope's face burned with hatred as she held Carol in thrall her feet barely scraping the ground.

"You're damned lucky I didn't kill just then. I could've broken your neck and you would have fallen dead where you stood. You're a parasite. The only thing you ever loved about Kerry was his money. That was the only thing he had that ever mattered to you."

Carol's eyes were wet with tears. She stared at Calliope horrified. All of the defiance had gone out of her. "I did love him, once. He made it impossible."

Calliope glowered at her. Her eyes were feral. Sarah was afraid she was going to finish the job when Harry pulled Carol from her grasp.

"This isn't you, Calliope. It's time we let this end."

Calliope stared at Harry as her anger slowly subsided. She reached up and touched Harry's face staring deep into his eyes. "I'm sorry for all of this, Harry. After all this time I just couldn't let him go."

Sarah understood now just how much Kerry had meant to her. It was sad knowing why she had to leave him behind.

Sarah wrapped her mother up in a hug. "Are you okay?"

Melinda nodded watching Calliope. "I'm fine. I think I feel better seeing how much Kerry really meant to her."

"Good," Anna said leaning in close to join them. "I guess it was a good thing you got to see this."

Melinda turned to glare at Anna. "No. This is a fucked-up mess. It figures you'd get me right in the middle of this, Anna Colvin."

Anna smiled wider as Melinda grinned, too. She wrapped Melinda in a great big hug, years of resentment slowly washing away. "What else were you going to do today, kill a bottle of sherry?"

"I'm sure ready for one now," Melinda said.

Across the room, Jill and Cori helped Avery to his feet. He looked a bit disheveled but none the worse for wear. He looked at Calliope as he pulled himself together. "Jesus bloody Christ, Calliope. What the hell was that?"

Calliope grinned walking over to dust him off. "Well, there might be a few things about me that I haven't told you about. It's kind of a long story."

Avery smirked. "Really? Well, as soon as there's time, I think we should get into it."

Clyde moved toward Harry frowning as he held Carol at arms-length. She looked around the room in a daze as trauma from the impact kept her docile. "What are you going to do with her?"

Harry shrugged. "I suppose the proper thing to do is to get this poor dumb creature medical attention. Which may take a while as the scene outside has turned rowdy. My charge here managed to start a riot as a means of diversion to get inside. The authorities are pretty busy at the moment."

"That's why they didn't respond to the shot," Jill said.

"Exactly," Harry said. "I was lucky to have heard it with everything else going on out there."

Calliope glanced over at Harry. "So we should use that to our advantage."

Harry nodded. "Yes. And do not fail in your duties. You have a ceremony to perform. I will keep things held down until you're ready."

Calliope rose on her tiptoes to kiss Harry on the cheek. "Thank You."

Everyone stood together watching as Harry escorted Carol from the room. It was a miracle they all came through unscathed. As soon as they were gone Calliope went to Kerry's coffin. She rested her hand on it as the others gathered around. She turned to look each of them in the eye, her solemn expression bringing them all to silence.

"I want to thank you all for being a part of this journey. I know it's not been an easy one for any of us. I know now though how much Kerry loved each and every one of you."

Sarah dropped her head regret burning raw in her chest. Calliope reached out and set her hand on Sarah's shoulder.

"Sarah honey, I know you feel cheated. You can't begin to understand how sorry I am for having a hand in that. I know Kerry loved you, too, even if he was afraid to face you. He thought about you a lot near the end. I hope, above all things, that you can forgive him this weakness."

Tears came to Sarah's eyes. She knew, deep down, it was a weakness they shared. "Thanks, Calliope. Kerry wasn't alone in that. I was afraid to reach out to him, too. Evidently, we were a lot alike."

Melinda and Anna wrapped their arms around Sarah and held her close.

"Kerry would have been proud of you," Anna said.

Calliope's face lit up with a smile as she turned to regard the others.

"Avery, Jill, Clyde, I want you to know, too, how much I appreciate everything you've done to help get us here today. It was a hell of a run. And I can see now how much this trip has affected each of you. In your case, Avery, I think it was Kerry had planned all along. He wanted to rattle your cage and I think, just maybe, it had the intended effect."

Avery smiled wiping tears from his eyes as he held Jill close. "I sure as hell hope so. I'd hate to let the big guy down."

"I want you to know I think of you all as family now," Calliope said turning to look each of them in the eye. "We've been through too much together not to be. So please remember that if I don't ever see any of you again, don't think that I don't carry each and every one of you in my heart. I will remember you always."

Calliope placed the hood of her robe back over her head. She followed Cori and Polly around the casket to the circle of candles placed on the floor. She smiled as they took their places and held her arms out wide.

"It's time to put Kerry to rest."

CHAPTER 50

Reality, Avery knew, was a subjective experience. It was a marriage of inner knowledge and external stimuli. That anything existed beyond those boundaries had always been a stretch for him. For all of his knowledge, for all of his wild imagination, the answer to what lay beyond the mortal coil didn't satisfy him in any of its varied theories, until now.

As Calliope, Cori, and Polly started the ceremony for Kerry the logic of reality slowly slipped away around him. Somehow the confines of the mausoleum seemed to have been pushed back beyond a pale horizon. Avery found himself standing in a void of limitless light. It was as if they were still in the room but not constrained by its physical limits. The echoes of the trio's song reverberated through him anchoring him in the infinite.

He felt Jill squeeze his hand. He looked over to see the phenomenon reflected in her eyes. The whole group gazed around them with a stunned wonder but somehow, guided by the women's voices, they all relaxed peacefully into that wonder.

"We stand in joy at the bridge between worlds and ask for our beloved passage."

Calliope's voice took on a life of its own as it encompassed the space around them. Cori and Polly's chanting rose in intensity, its accompaniment merged with Calliope's voice to raise the energy in the room. Beyond them, out in empty space, a tiny pinpoint of light appeared. It grew in intensity as it grew larger. Avery watched it, mesmerized, wondering why he wasn't pissing in his pants at the sight of it. Next to him, Sarah reached over and took his other hand, her eyes growing wider as everything they knew was gently pushed away.

"Oh, great guardians of the in-between grant our fallen peace within your realm."

Then, in a flash, the light opened up into a great bright passageway bridging our infinite to the next. Avery stared in awe as a shadow shape moved past them to step into the light. Standing before them, illuminated by its brilliance, Kerry stood in all his glory, smiling.

Gasps rang out among them. Sarah started trembling, tears falling in torrents as her father waved to them in farewell.

Calliope turned to face him holding her hand over her heart as the other reached out in salute. "Go with our love, Kerry Vance, until we meet again. Let our blessings light your way home."

As Kerry turned to step into the light Avery could see a crowd gathered just inside waiting to greet him.

"Oh my God, there's Mark." Anna's voice broke the silence as Kerry's brother gathered him in a hug. Mark looked out at the sound of Anna's voice smiling as he pulled Kerry close to him. Beyond them Avery could see, Elvis and Jim Morrison standing with Buddy Holly, Darrell and Vinnie Abbott, Lemmy Kilmeister, David Bowie, Neil Peart, Tom Petty among dozens of others, all waiting to gather Kerry into their fold. Avery started trembling too, a great overwhelming joy washing over him when through the crowd he saw his Zoe.

She stood aglow looking just as she had the day they'd met. Her smile melted his heart as she looked out at him. Zoe pointed at Jill, who raised her hand over her mouth and sobbed as she looked on. Avery couldn't hear Zoe speak but he was certain he understood what she said.

Love her like you loved me.

Avery cried as he never had before as Zoe returned to Kerry and wrapped her arms around him. Then, slowly, the group turned to walk into the light, a great conversation roaring among them all as the tunnel followed them on. Then....they were gone.

Avery was near collapse as the space around them slowly returned to the way it was. He stood staring at the point in space where the light disappeared. He felt shattered and rejuvenated all at once. His mind raced as the experience burned into memory. There was a realm beyond them and Zoe and now Kerry were both safe inside.

The realization left him with a depth of comfort he had never known before. Around him, the room remained silent. Everyone stood lost in their own amazement. After a few seconds, Avery realized he was still holding on to both Jill's and Sarah's hands as they all stood together gazing into emptiness. Then he realized that Calliope, Cori, and Polly were gone. Everyone slowly broke from their reverie, confusion apparent on their faces. It took a long few moments before anyone could gather their voice to speak.

"Where did the girls go?"

Clyde's voice startled Avery as he looked around. Beyond Kerry's coffin, there was no trace of them. The candles and laurels defining their sacred space were gone. It was as if they'd never been there.

"How long have we been standing around?" Anna looked from Sarah to the rest of the group. "There's no way they could have gotten out of here so quickly."

"They hypnotized us," Clyde said. "Maybe none of this was real."

Avery frowned. He didn't agree with Clyde's analysis. It had to have been real.

He needed it to be real.

"It was real," Avery said.

He looked at Jill. She nodded rapidly. "It was real. We were just so wrapped up in what we saw that they had time to leave."

"It happened," Melinda said, a wistful look appearing in her eyes as she gazed toward the spot where the light tunnel manifested. "Mark looked just the way he did the night he died. Didn't he Anna?"

Anna nodded slowly. She looked over at Melinda the evidence of tears appeared in her eyes. "He hadn't aged a day."

"Zoe was here," Avery said. He looked at Clyde to make plain his point. "She told me to love Jill as much as I love her."

Jill's eyes lit up. "That was Zoe? Oh my God. I could have sworn she told me to take care of you. She was looking right at me."

Avery smiled pulling Jill into a hug. "Well, however it went down, I think we have her blessing."

Clyde shook his head. "I don't know man. I've seen a lot of weird shit over the years but this one tops them all. I knew something was off about

Calliope but I'd never guessed this. I don't know what to make of it. It sure as hell seemed real but how the fuck did they pull it off?"

"They're immortal," Sarah said. She hadn't spoken until now. Everyone turned to look at her. "They're the last of an ancient race. Cori told me that Calliope was the only one of them left that still took her duty to protect us seriously. The others that are left are just trying to survive. They've lost faith in us."

"Immortal?" The word hung in the air as it left Avery's lips. "She told you this?"

"It took some convincing, trust me," Anna said. "But after the shit I saw her do. I wasn't going to take any swamp gas explanation."

Avery, Clyde, and Jill stared at each other. Avery started thundering with laughter. "Immortal. Well, hell, I guess that'd explain some of the crazy shit we saw Calliope do. But it's still a lot to ponder."

"It is," Melinda said. "But I know it's true. Calliope looked the same today as she did back in Nineteen seventy-four, right after Sarah was born. That was when she first met Kerry."

Surprise registered on Avery's face. "That's why she felt guilty over Sarah. Oh my God! She's the one Kerry was broken up over when he first met you, Clyde."

Clyde ran his hand down his beard. "Damn. That's crazy. So he called on her to do this thing because he knew this whole mess needed to be cleaned up. He wanted to get all of you together to hash this out."

"Exactly," Melinda said. "He was a crafty son of a bitch."

The group hung together reminiscing as the workers from the cemetery came in to place Kerry's casket in its vault. None of them wanted to be the first to leave as the experience of what they'd seen had bound them together.

Calliope's words rang true. They were family now.

Avery noticed Agent Carson waiting outside the door as the workers left mausoleum. Jill followed his gaze then nodded. It was time to pay the piper.

"Well, as much as I hate to leave good company, folks. I guess we better get this over. Jill and I have another debt we have to pay."

They hugged everyone, in turn, promising to meet again once they were out of stir. Anna looked up at Clyde as they all started toward the door. "So what about you Clyde, what are you going to do?"

"I don't know about tonight but I'm thinking about moving on to Texas. I have a nephew that lives down there."

Anna smiled. "Well don't get in too big a hurry. I think Melinda here could use a bit of company."

Sarah laughed loudly struck by the look of surprise on her mother's face.

"Anna!" Melinda hissed, embarrassment turning her face a bright shade of red "Leave the poor man alone."

Anna grinned taking Clyde by the arm. "What? Look how skinny he is. He could use a home-cooked meal."

Melinda gave a sigh of relief. "Oh, okay, that I can do."

"Right?" Anna said. "Then, after you get his strength up, you can jump his bones."

Clyde and Melinda both turned blood red with embarrassment. Avery laughed so hard he thought he would bust. He wished he could stay with them all a while longer. It was nice just being there with them. The group was still laughing together as they stepped outside. Avery nodded to Agent Carson as he and Jill stopped beside him. Anna, Melinda, and Sarah ushered Clyde quickly away waving and grinning as they made their way back toward the chapel.

"Well, I guess we're ready," Avery said.

Carson nodded watching as the others walked away. He looked at Jill and grinned. "You can go on and join your friends, honey. I don't have a warrant for you."

Jill glanced from Avery to Carson, nonplussed, "But what about that shit in Cincinnati? I figured they'd have a fugitive warrant after all this."

Carson shook his head. "No. I looked into it. It's an appearance ticket for a misdemeanor. That's a local matter. My suggestion is you go back pay your fine and forget about it. Calliope's the one they really want."

Avery smiled. "Well hot damn. There you go. Go on and catch up to the others. I'll get ahold of you as soon as I know what's going on."

Jill leaned in and kissed Avery. It had enough heat to cause Carson to look away. "Let me know as soon as you know something."

Avery and Carson watched as Jill caught up to the others. They all turned to look back again as Jill told them about what had happened.

Avery smiled waving at them again. "I tell you what, man. It's been a hell of a week."

Carson grinned. He took Avery by the arm and led him around the side of the mausoleum where his car was waiting. "I can imagine. I know no one around here is going to forget about it for a while."

"Fitting," Avery said. Smiling as the entire arch of the week passed through his brain. "Kerry liked to do things big. I suppose his funeral couldn't be any other way."

Carson opened the back door of the sedan for Avery grinning as he slid inside, "A good way to sneak people in and out, too."

Avery couldn't help but grin. Carson was sharp. He was really starting to like the guy.

"It didn't work very well for Carol."

Carson held Avery's gaze. "True, but it worked out just fine for Calliope."

"Yeah, well, if you ask me, Agent Carson I think they both got what they deserved."

CHAPTER 51

Denver winters proved to be the exact pain in the ass that Clyde had warned him about. It had taken Avery and Jill over an hour to make their way into town from the airport and another twenty minutes to assail the few blocks between them and the lawyer's office. Neither of them really needed to be here. They didn't have a stake in hearing Kerry's will.

Jill had done well with the money Kerry had left her the previous summer and now the two of them were the proud proprietors of a rock-n-roll bar and grill outside of Reno. They both liked the heat a hell of a lot better than they did the cold. Jill ran the day to day at the bar leaving Avery time to work at his writing. His article for the New York Times on Kerry's passing and the events that followed had earned him a few awards and helped reestablish his career. The only reason they made the trek up from Nevada was as an excuse to hang out with their new family and catch up with everyone.

The last six months had been a watershed period for all of them. All of the charges against Avery had been dismissed at trial. The spotlight on his case cast too much light for the DA's office. They didn't want to start a riot in the streets by convicting a folk hero. So they let him go.

Now he sat with a big wicked grin on his face watching as Jimmy and Daisy stood talking with Clyde and Melinda. He and Jill had been overjoyed to learn that each had found each other. It seemed they were all puzzle pieces no one would have ever thought to put together. Through Kerry, a wealth of change had come into all of their lives. That was what made it special.

Avery sat up in his chair as Kerry's lawyer, one Mr. Everett Meyer-Esquire, entered the room. He was followed by a sweaty younger man in a pale puke green sweater vest pushing a flat-screen TV on a cart with a laptop below it on a shelf. Kerry had decided to video-record his new will. With everything that had gone down, it was a wise choice. There was no room for anyone to contest what he had set forth. It was all about to come straight from his mouth. It was another reason he and Jill wanted to come down. It would be nice to see Kerry again.

Meyer stopped in front of his desk as his assistant struggled to rig the video feed.

The guy looked amiable enough. He was short and stocky, lingering just on the shy side of obesity with a round jovial face. He was dressed in what looked to be an off the rack gray suit from a department store which meant he was probably loaded. In his experience, the lawyers with the most money were usually the ones that wore their shoes until they had holes in them. They were way too tight to spend money frivolously. Kerry probably hired him for that very reason, that, or he just trusted his big jovial face.

"I'd like to thank you all for coming today for the execution of Mr. Vance's last will and testament. While I am aware of the complications leading up to you all being here today I've been assured by Ms. Merrick's new attorney that this document will not be contested."

Not now that she's doing twenty to life in Bedford Hills, Avery thought.

The lawyer glanced over at his assistant to see if he was ready. The sweaty guy in the sweater vest nodded. Avery looked over to see Jimmy grinning at him. He smiled shooting a wink back. Avery owed him a lot. He didn't think he'd ever be able to repay him fully.

"Without further ado, we will now hear from Mr. Vance in his own words. This video was filmed here in my office just over nine months ago and will address fully all of his wishes."

Avery reached over and took Jill's hand squeezing it as the lights went down. As the video started Avery was surprised to see how thin Kerry looked. The transcendental light was still there, still fully present in his big blue eyes. But he looked frail. The gray in his wavy dark hair seemed more prominent. It had only been a couple of months since Avery had seen him before this and here he looked like he'd aged a decade. All of the stress over Carol and the damnable cruelty of cancer had taken quite a toll on him.

It was sad to see. Avery couldn't help smiling though as Kerry had decided to film his last will and testament in a well-worn Captain America T-shirt and blue leather pants. The man was one of a kind.

Well, I guess if you're all here watching this then I'm dead. That or somebody's discovered the secret to immortality and we're all partying together and having a good laugh.

Avery suppressed a giggle as tears formed in his eyes. He'd have much preferred the latter.

Anyway, if I am dead, then I know that a chosen few of you have had a hell of a few days getting me out of Carol's clutches. I'm sorry for that but, as I thought about the quandary I found myself in, I decided that I could use the situation to try and do some good for those of you I'm closest too. I hope I haven't failed.

Avery could see the sadness in Kerry's eyes for the briefest of moments, the great unnamable woe that underscored his entire being seeped out just then in the tiniest of increments. Then, just as quickly, Kerry smiled and leaned forward in his chair. The sadness, once again, contained.

Avery Clark, you sexy son of a bitch, you damn well better be sitting right there in the front row if you know what's good for you. I know I've asked a lot of you, my brother, but I hope you were able to make it through. You're a brilliant man and the world needs you. It needs your insight and humor. This is an insane time and we all need people like you lampooning the absurdity that the world sometimes heaps upon us. Avery, I sent you on this journey because you needed to get the hell out of New York. You needed a change. I know how much you miss Zoe. But my friend, you can't live the rest of your life in mourning and Zoe would be the first to tell you that. Do you remember when you had the book release party for "Inner Light"? How Zoe walked around all night clutching her copy like someone was going to steal it from her? She was so proud of you. She knew you were destined for great things. And goddamn it, Clark, you better not let that little girl down.

Tears formed in Kerry's eyes as he spoke. Avery wiped at his own eyes trying hard to keep from breaking down.

So, what you're going to do to get your writing skills back on point is you're going to write my biography. And I don't want any of this staid academic bullshit, either. I'm giving you full access to all of my archives, the family photos, the interviews over the years, all of it. I want you to create something that's worthy of both of us, OK? I want something wild. Then you take that money and doing something good with it. Help some people out. Put yourself out there and write, man, make the rest of your life into something great. Because if you don't I swear I'll come back as a ghost and kick you square in the balls, you got me?

Everyone in the room snickered as Kerry ran his fingers through his hair and slid back into the chair.

"You got it," Avery said.

Now, on to Daisy... Daisy, Daisy, Daisy, ma petit fleur, you know I love you, girl, a whole lot more than you'll ever know. You've had a hell of a life so far, kiddo, with all the shit with your mother and your crazy fucking aunt. But I hope, above all things, that I made you feel loved and welcome in my home.

Avery turned to see Daisy leaning on Jimmy's shoulder sobbing. She was a hell of a woman. It took a lot of wherewithal and bravery to hold Carol's feet to the fire over all of this. Of all of them, this had to have been the hardest on her. Avery was glad Jimmy had been there for her. She could have done a lot worse.

So for you, my dear, I leave you the sum of two point five million dollars. Now, don't you dare get lazy on me. If you really want to be a singer this will help get you where you want to be without having to struggle. And, when you get your first album is recorded, I want you to come back and leave a copy for me, okay? I can't wait to hear it.

"I will, Uncle Kerry. I promise."

Daisy's voice was hoarse from crying but Avery could hear its strength. He didn't know why he never noticed it before. He was eager to hear what she came up with, too. He had to make it a point to tell her.

Now for the shakiest part of our little adventure, Sarah, baby, I sure hope that you're sitting there with everyone today. I know it's a longshot. But, hopefully, Avery and Calliope were able to convince you to come.

Avery glanced over at Sarah. If Kerry only knew how that all went down he would have laughed his ass off.

Darlin', I don't have the right words in me to explain just exactly how I feel about you. I also don't know exactly how to tell you how badly I feel, either. I never should have run away from you all those years ago. I should have fought to be a part of your life. At the time, though, all I could think about was the scandal it would have created and what it would do to your mom and her family. And, most of all, I was afraid to face Ken. I betrayed him and I was ashamed. So I took the easy way out. The truth of it was, honey, I was a scared little boy and I ran away. I can't defend it but that's what happened.

Now I do want you to know that I have stalked you here and there over the years. I had to know who you were even if I was too chicken shit to knock on the door and say hello. But, I just couldn't face you. I did see your daughter outside once playing in the yard. She is absolutely beautiful! I don't know if she told you or not but she saw me walking down the sidewalk that day and we exchanged smiles. If you've ever wondered where the wavy red hair came from on that girl, it's because she's the spitting image of my mother, Bonnie. I couldn't believe it when I saw her and I can't tell you how happy it made me. That girl definitely has the Donnelly fire flowing in her veins. But I bet you've already noticed that, huh?

Sarah wiped at her eyes as she smiled. "It's hard to miss."

So, Sarah, for you and your daughter I leave you the rest of my holdings. That includes all of my papers and belongings, the rights and royalties to all of my work, the house in Florida and all of the investments and insurance, all told about eighty million dollars give or take and probably more if there's the upswing in sales that usually happens when one of us kicks the bucket.

Avery watched Sarah's eyes widen when she heard the sum. Beside her, Melinda looked like she had just swallowed her tongue.

My lawyer has a shit ton of paperwork for you to fill out. I'm sure he can help you set up a trust fund for your daughter, too, if you want. He can help you can sell the house in Florida, too. It was just a party house where the band and I used to go to unwind after a tour. You can ask Avery there about it. We had some wild times there. But it costs a lot for upkeep and I don't want to burden you with it in case you thought there was some sentimental attachment. It was just a place where I could go to get away. I've been there a lot here lately.

The lost look in Kerry's eyes broke Avery's heart. Tears returned in desperate waves as he watched Kerry struggle with the reality of his own death. It was almost too much too bear but then again, the flash of pain and regret was gone and Kerry smiled into the camera.

So, I guess that's it. Everyone else I wanted to reach out to have already received what I wanted them to have. I doubt that Calliope is there with you but if you are honey, I hope it wasn't too hard on you pulling all of this off. I can't tell you how much it means to me. Meeting you was one of the greatest experiences of my life. I hope you find some measure of peace along your path. I know it can't be easy. I love you, Calliope. I always have. And I love you too, Sarah and you Daisy and even you Avery, you little bastard. I wish you all a long and loving life. Don't ever take it for granted. It can all be over in a flash. And, whatever you do, don't any of you waste a second of your time worrying about me. If there's any justice at all in the Universe I'll be sitting under a tree somewhere playing my guitar. Take that image with you... Goodbye.

And with that, the screen went dark. One of the greatest frontmen to ever take to the stage was gone.

It was the end of an era.

Avery sat quietly for a moment resting his head on Jill's shoulder as he wiped the tears from his eyes. With Kerry, almost as much as with Zoe, a piece of him had died as well. This time he'd found the strength to pull himself together and move on. He had a clear vision of what he wanted to do with his life and who he wanted to share it with. He wasn't going to take a second of it for granted.

"You okay, man?"

Jimmy stood behind him resting his hands on both shoulders. Avery could see that he'd teared up a bit, too.

"Yeah, I'm fine," Avery said. "It just hit me harder than I expected to see him there on the screen like that."

Jimmy walked around the row of chairs to sit beside him as Daisy and Sarah discussed the details of their inheritance with Mr. Meyer.

"That's completely understandable. I realize now how great a man Kerry was. You had a hell of a friend there."

Avery smiled. The whole of his time with Kerry raced through his mind. It left him with a kinetic feeling that he didn't want to lose. "He really was, Jimmy. He was a beautiful man."

Jimmy shot him a wry smile. "But you know, I still don't like the music."

Avery laughed, loudly, reaching over to push Jimmy's shoulder. "Well, you've always had terrible taste, anyway. Look at who your friends are."

"You're definitely a pain in the ass," Jimmy said.

The comment drew a roar of laughter out of Jill.

Avery leaned back in his chair and grinned. "Screw you both."

"So how do you like Reno?" Jimmy asked. "Sounds like you've pretty much settled in there."

"It's been great. We have the club up and running now. Jill's become the surrogate mother to about a half a dozen bands there. We have local showcases during the week. We just had our first fundraiser for music in the schools. Clyde's helping us pull in the bigger bands. It's been pretty cool."

Jimmy was impressed. "And you're still not drinking?"

Avery shot him a sly smile, "Real subtle there, Werner. No man, I haven't had a drink in six months. That's been the cool thing. I go to our bar nearly every night and I'm not even tempted. Jill keeps the coffee pot going and I'm good to go."

Jimmy smiled. "I'm glad to hear it, Avery, truly. That's awesome."

"It's like Kerry was saying, I needed to get out of New York. I was stagnating there. It was the same with Jill. We both needed a new start. It's been great."

"I haven't wanted to kill him yet," Jill said smiling.

"That's great," Jimmy said. "Daisy and I will have to come out and visit."

"Hell yeah, she needs to bring her band out and play, too," Jill said. "I have an open booking whenever she wants."

"I know she'll like that," Jimmy said. "They're really starting to garner some notice. She's a hell of a performer."

"We've been watching some of the videos," Avery said. "She's great."

"Yeah, she is," Clyde said. "Hell, look who raised her."

Avery smiled as Clyde and Melinda joined them. "Right? You can definitely hear Kerry's influence. She's got that growl down cold."

Clyde grinned, "Gives me goosebumps every damned time."

Avery looked at Clyde beaming. It was easy to see Melinda's influence in his wardrobe. He was dressed in a clean pair of jeans and a button-up shirt. His goatee was neatly trimmed and the red-dye was gone. He'd been domesticated. Avery decided it suited him. He would always be a legend.

"So you're all coming to the house for dinner, right?" Melinda said. "Sarah and I have been cooking all morning."

"Wouldn't miss it," Avery said. "When Sarah told me she was making me an apple pie, I clicked right over and booked the airline tickets."

Melinda grinned. "We missed you guys. Now that she's got control of Kerry's holdings she said you all were going to collaborate on Kerry's biography."

"That's the plan. I think it'll be cathartic for both of us. We're going to need your input too. We'll need your help putting his childhood together."

"I'm happy to help," Melinda said. "It'll be good for me too. I'm still trying to put it all into perspective."

Avery and Jill both nodded. There wasn't a day that had gone by when they hadn't thought about the phenomenon inside the mausoleum. It had left them with a great feeling of hope. It also left them with a lot of questions.

"A riddle of a lifetime, I'm afraid," Avery said. "It's hard to put into words."

"It is," Melinda said.

Daisy and Sarah finally sauntered over to the group chattering wildly after shaking hands and thanking Mr. Meyer. Avery hopped up out of his chair to gather them both into a great big hug. He couldn't have been happier for the girls if they were his own. Kerry's legacy lived on in them.

"I guess you ladies are in a whole new tax bracket now, huh?" Avery said.

Daisy laughed leaning her head against his. "Shit, I didn't even think about the damned taxes." She glanced over at Jimmy. "We can find a way to hide it, right?"

Jimmy's disturbed expression threw Avery into a fit of laughter. "I see you've learned how to push his buttons."

Daisy roared with laughter walking over to wrap her arms around Jimmy. "He's too easy."

"Is everyone ready to eat?" Sarah asked. "Mom and I have a ton of food at home."

"Lead on," Avery said. "We have a future to discuss."

Sarah smiled as she took Avery's arm opposite of Jill. "A future we owe to you."

Avery waved his hand dismissively. "I can't take credit for any it. Kerry's the man of the hour. Kerry and Calliope both are. I was just along for the ride."

"I wish Calliope would have stuck around to see how it all turned out," Jill said.

"Do you think we'll ever see her again?" Sarah asked.

Avery shook his head as they all made their way out into the cool brace of winter sun. "I don't know. I hope so. I never got a chance to tell her how much all of this meant to me."

Avery looked around as he slid his sunglasses down over his eyes.

I hope she knows.

THE END

ABOUT THE AUTHOR

Lawrence "Ace" Parlier is an author/poet/musician from Cincinnati, OH. His work has appeared in *The Writer's Bone, Murmurations Magazine, Heartbeat; A Literary Journal* and *The Best of Ohio Short Stories Vol. 2.* His first novel, *Sierra Court Blues*, was published in 2013.

When not working on writing, he can be found on stage playing lead guitar for the heavy metal band, *Chaos Ritual.*

NOTE FROM THE AUTHOR

Word-of-mouth is crucial for any author to succeed. If you enjoyed *The Frontman*, please leave a review online—anywhere you are able. Even if it's just a sentence or two. It would make all the difference and would be very much appreciated.

Thanks!
Lawrence

Thank you so much for reading one of our **Urban Fantasy** novels.
If you enjoyed our book, please check out our recommended
for your next great read!

The Graveyard Girl and the Boneyard Boy by Martin Matthews

"... a compelling and eminently likable cast of characters."
–Authors Reading

View other Black Rose Writing titles at
www.blackrosewriting.com/books and use promo code
PRINT to receive a **20% discount** when purchasing.